THE
SILENT
BRIDE

ALSO BY SHALINI BOLAND

The Daughter-in-Law
A Perfect Stranger
The Family Holiday
The Couple Upstairs
My Little Girl
The Wife
One Of Us Is Lying
The Other Daughter
The Marriage Betrayal
The Girl From The Sea
The Best Friend
The Perfect Family
The Silent Sister
The Millionaire's Wife
The Child Next Door
The Secret Mother
Marchwood Vampire Series
Outside Series

THE SILENT BRIDE

SHALINI BOLAND

THOMAS & MERCER

Published by Thomas and Mercer, Seattle

www.apub.com

Amazon, the Amazon logo, and Thomas and Mercer are trademarks of Amazon.com, Inc., or its affiliates.

ISBN-13: 9781662507083
eISBN: 9781662507076

Cover design by Faceout Studio, Spencer Fuller
Cover image: © Evgenyrychko / Shutterstock; © ModernewWorld / Getty Images

Printed in the United States of America

For Pete – I'm glad it was you at the altar

Prologue

I shouldn't have come here today.

If I hadn't come, then it would never have happened. He wouldn't have seen the expression on my face. But when he turned to look at me, he froze for a second. His eyes widened and I could tell he knew. The knife in his fist was proof of that.

My chest went so tight it felt as though someone was sitting on it. Even now, I'm massaging the spot between my ribs to try to loosen it. To get my breathing under control instead of these rough gasps squeezing from my lungs. A sound I've never heard before.

There was no time to think. I just lifted the brass lamp and threw it as hard as I could.

She screamed, of course she did. But now she's as quiet as the grave.

And me?

Well . . . despite my jagged breathing and shaking fingers, all I feel right now is an overwhelming sense of relief.

Chapter One

Now, 10 June

This is it. *The moment.* After all the years of daydreaming, of failed dates and underwhelming relationships, and of finally finding the one, this, right here, right now, is the culmination of it all. The moment that I, Alice Porter, walk down the aisle to marry Seth Evans, man of my dreams.

Dad takes my arm. He's looking dapper in a charcoal suit and burgundy silk tie, a white rose in his buttonhole, same as all the groomsmen and, of course, the groom. I can tell by the softening of his gaze that Dad is happy. He's always been ambitious for me and my sister Elizabeth. Wanted us to have good careers and good husbands. My father is the VP of a large logistics company. Almost at retirement age, he jets across the world as though he's twenty years younger.

Seth, my husband-to-be, is a successful London doctor, an endocrinologist, who also happens to be the only child of wealthy parents. We met in a local pub just over a year ago when he was staying in his parents' New Forest holiday cottage with friends. I was supposed to be on a blind date that night, but got stood up. It was shaping up to be an awful evening until Seth came over and saved me from swearing off men for life. It's been a whirlwind romance ever since.

'Ready?' Dad asks.

I take a deep breath and gaze down at my simple bouquet of ferns and roses, at the beaded lace bodice and silk organza skirt of my wedding gown. At the tips of my satin shoes peeking out beneath layers of tulle. Of course I'm ready. From my manicured French-tipped nails to my gleaming dark curls, I'm more than ready. I swallow, trying to summon a reply for my father, but emotion has stopped up my throat. Instead, I nod and blink, glancing ahead to see my bridesmaids come to a graceful halt at the end of the aisle.

As the Wedding March begins to play, my heart lifts. All my hopes and ambitions are finally coming true. I'm marrying my handsome fiancé, we're moving into a beautiful home, even my career is heading in the right direction. Why am I thinking about work? Plenty of time to concentrate on that when we're back from our honeymoon. Right now I need to soak up every second of my wedding day because I don't plan on doing this more than once. I want this to be forever. The day that kick-starts the rest of my life.

Dad and I begin walking down the aisle, approaching familiar faces. Friends, colleagues, aunts, uncles, cousins. Everybody is here. Seth and I invited an almost equal number of guests, which is great as it balances out the church. The pews on both sides are full. Everyone is smiling, eyes filled with love, mouthing that I look beautiful.

A packed church means that it's more than a little warm in here. We're having a June heatwave at the moment and guests are using the order-of-service booklets as fans. But I'd rather have heat and sunshine than chilly rain. This beautiful weather is a good omen.

The clichés are true – my feet barely touch the ground. I feel as though I'm walking on air. I'm glowing, radiant, my eyes bright. As I glide down the aisle, my head feels light and my fingers and toes are tingling. I inhale, absorbing the joyful atmosphere, breathing in the scent of polished wood and fresh flowers. Wafts of perfume and cologne mingle with that faint dusty, damp odour that belongs to Ellingham's beautiful thirteenth-century church. The same church where my parents were married. Where Elizabeth and I were christened.

It's strange, but I don't even feel like myself right now. It's almost an out-of-body experience. I feel like a movie star walking the red carpet, or a model on the runway. Everyone is here for me and Seth, but all eyes are focused on *me*. Me and me alone. It's actually a little unnerving. I gaze ahead to the altar and to Seth, who's turning my way. My heart lifts as I prepare for my first glimpse of my groom on our wedding day.

Oh.

I freeze.

That's not Seth.

I blink and shift my gaze to the left and to the right of the man standing where I'm certain my groom should be. Where is he? Where is my fiancé?

'Alice,' Dad hisses in my ear.

We've come to a halt a third of the way down the aisle. My pulse is racing and sweat begins to prickle between my breasts and under my arms. A strong scent of vanilla hits me, catches in the back of my throat, sweet and thick.

'Alice.' Dad tugs on my arm, but I'm still frozen in place, unable to move or speak.

I throw another panicked glance up ahead at the groom, and the groomsmen standing next to him. Why is nobody saying anything? Am I dreaming? Is this some horribly realistic nightmare?

4

Or have I somehow got it wrong and Seth is standing in another spot? I look across to the other side of the aisle. But that's where my bridesmaids are gathered. I drag my gaze back to the right side. To the stranger who's looking back at me. He frowns. Maybe he doesn't recognise me either and this is just some terrible wedding mix-up.

'You okay?' he mouths, his eyes filled with sudden concern. With *love*. His gaze is intimate, as though he knows me.

My heart clatters against my ribcage and blood pounds in my ears. Why is no one saying anything? Where is Seth, and why is this stranger standing in his place?

What the hell is going on?

Chapter Two

THEN

I can barely get the front door open. I'm so excited to get inside and tell Daisy the news. She won't believe it. I can barely believe it.

Finally, my key slots into the lock. I turn it and push open the door to the apartment I've shared with my best friend for the past three-and-a-half years.

'Hello!' I call out, heaving my small case up and over the threshold before wheeling it across the hall and dumping it in my bedroom. I rub my hands together to warm them. It's dark and sleety out there. Most rainy Sunday nights would have me returning from London in a gloomy mood. Sad at the end of a weekend spent with my handsome boyfriend. Not tonight though. 'Daisy! You home?'

'In the lounge,' she calls back.

I head along the hall, unable to control the massive smile that's already making my cheeks hurt.

'Hey, good weekend?' she asks, glancing up from her phone. She's reclining on the sofa, feet up, her blonde hair piled on top of her head in a messy bun. 'Shall we have a cuppa?' she asks, stifling a yawn.

'No, I'm opening a bottle,' I reply.

'On a school night?' She frowns and then laughs. 'Oh, go on then.'

I grin and race off to the kitchen where I lift out a bottle of white that's been chilling in the fridge since Friday. I pluck two glasses from the cupboard and head back to the lounge. 'Surprised this is still unopened, to be honest,' I say, waving the bottle of Sauvignon Blanc.

'I've been over at Martin's most of the weekend helping him with his coursework.' She rolls her eyes. Last year, her financial consultant boyfriend of three years decided to retrain as a paramedic and Daisy has found his new student status a little challenging. She holds out her hand for a glass, so I pour hers first. 'I can't believe we've got another three years of this,' she says. 'And once he's qualified it's all going to be shift work, so we'll hardly get to see one another.'

'You do shift work too,' I reply.

'Exactly.' She takes a swig of wine. 'It'll be a miracle if we meet up more than twice a week. And he's not going to want us to buy a place together until he's finished training, so we'll be in limbo. Meanwhile house prices keep going up . . .' She throws her hands in the air, sloshing wine over herself. 'Shit, sorry. Don't mean to moan.' She rubs her sweatshirt ineffectually. 'Well, I do mean to moan, but, you know.'

With Daisy in this kind of mood, I'm not sure I want to tell her my news any more. It would feel like rubbing salt in the wound. I wonder if she'll be pleased for me.

'Oh my actual God, what's that on your finger?' Daisy's eyes widen as she points to my ring. She puts her wine glass down, gets to her feet and grabs my hand, staring hard at the beautiful emerald-cut diamond set into its platinum band. 'Is that what I think it is?'

I nod, hoping she'll be happy for me and Seth.

'He proposed?'

'Last night,' I reply, reliving the moment again in my head, unable to stop the smile returning.

'I can't believe it!' she cries. 'Congratulations, Alice. You have to tell me everything!'

She sits back down and I plop next to her, relieved that she's excited for me. I take a sip of the chilled wine, savouring the sharp, fruity taste on my tongue. I wonder if I've ever felt this happy before.

'So?' Daisy prompts.

I settle back into the sofa. 'Okay, so, yesterday Seth told me he'd arranged a fun evening out, which was great because I feel like we've been getting quite boring lately – staying in and watching TV, or going to the local pub. Nothing like our first couple of months together where we went out for dinner and theatre trips and mini breaks.'

'I'd kill for a mini break,' Daisy says, topping up her wine.

'Anyway, a posh car comes to pick us up late afternoon and drives us to this beautiful five-star hotel. We get in the elevator and go right to the top. So I think, cool, we're going for drinks and dinner with a view.'

Daisy's nodding along, eyes wide.

'But then we—'

'Wait!' Daisy cries. 'We need Loz here for this.'

'Oh. Okay.' I'm a little disappointed that I don't get to finish telling her what happened. But I guess she's right that I should tell Laurence too. The three of us have been best friends since school and we've always shared all our ups and downs with one another. His flat is only on the other side of our small market town, so he can be here in ten minutes.

'I'll text him to come over.' Daisy lunges forward for her phone.

'Okay, you do that, I'm going to have a quick shower and get into my pyjamas.' I neck my glass of wine and leave her to finish texting Laurence.

By the time I'm showered and changed into my pink-and-grey check pyjamas, Laurence is already ensconced on the living-room sofa. As I walk in, he brandishes a bottle of champagne. 'Congratulations, Porter. That was fast work!'

I look at Daisy. 'You told him?'

She claps a hand over her mouth. 'Oh, yeah, sorry. Hope that's okay?'

Bit late now, I think. But I guess she's just excited for me. It's a shame though, because I really wanted to be the one to share my news. Laurence comes over to give me a hug, his messy blond hair damp with rain. 'So happy for you both. But I'd be even happier if we could at least meet the guy.'

'I know, I know. Sorry. Seth's so busy at the hospital we hardly get time for just the two of us, let alone meeting up with friends. But the good news is that he'll be moving down here after the wedding. He's got a job at Southampton Hospital.'

'Pleased to hear it,' Laurence says. 'I can't believe you're getting married. When did we all get so grown up?'

Laurence Kennedy is a successful counsellor with his own practice. He studied psychology at uni which is where he met his girlfriend, Francesca. Although she decided that field wasn't for her – she found it too stressful – and ended up working in an animal shelter instead. Fran has become really close with me and Daisy, but there's a different vibe when it's the four of us. When she's around, Daisy and I are careful not to be over-friendly with Laurence or share jokes from our school days that might make her feel excluded.

'So anyway,' I say, shoving him along the sofa and accepting a glass of champagne. 'I was just in the middle of telling Daisy how Seth proposed.'

Laurence nods. 'She told me about the lift in the five-star hotel, so you can carry on from there. Sounds like he might be too classy for the likes of us.'

'Oh, definitely,' I reply with a grin.

'So, carry on,' he says.

'Oh, right, okay. So we get out at the top floor and it's this nonde-script corridor next to a fire exit.'

'Oh, I know!' Daisy interrupts excitedly. 'I bet it was one of those helicopter proposals, wasn't it?'

I experience an irrational burst of annoyance. First she cuts me off when I'm telling her about the proposal, then she tells Laurence my news without me present, and now she's ruined my story by guessing correctly. And, added to that, she's made his proposal sound run-of-the-mill, when I thought it was devastatingly romantic and unusual.

Daisy and I have had quite a competitive relationship since school. Nothing serious or mean, just a subtle rivalry over popularity, career, boyfriends etc. Up until I met Seth, Daisy was winning hands-down in the boyfriend department, but now that I have a fiancé who's also a doctor, well, it's unfortunately put her nose out of joint. It sounds petty and ridiculous, but I think it's a childish hangover from our school days. I guess we should have grown out of it by now, but I can sense her trying to stifle her jealousy. It's a habit I wish we could break.

I blink and try not to let my disappointment show at her attempt to minimise my news. 'It was incredible,' I reply. 'We took off from a helipad, the blades were whirring . . . I felt like I was in some kind of action movie. Then we flew across London just before sunset and we saw all the lights and the landmarks. He proposed while we were over the Thames.'

'Sounds amazing,' Laurence says. 'Let's cheers.' He holds his glass aloft. 'Congratulations, Porter. Wishing you all the happiness in the world.'

'Congrats, Alice,' Daisy adds.

We clink our glasses and take a sip.

The thing is, despite my excitement at Seth's proposal, there are still a few little niggles in my head that I need to deal with. Nothing is ever perfect though, is it? Relationships, like everything else, are all about compromise. But I won't think about that now. No. Tonight is all about celebrating, and that's what I'm determined to do.

Chapter Three

Now

I literally can't move. I don't dare catch anyone's eye. I'm partway down the aisle and I can feel Dad staring at me, holding my arm too tightly. He'll be irritated that I'm going off script. That I'm making a scene. Although he's not showing it. No. For the sake of everyone here – especially his business colleagues – he's being the model of concern.

Why am I even worrying about what Dad is thinking? That hardly matters when right this second I'm gazing at a stranger who's standing where my groom should be. I simply don't recognise him. This man is tall, dark-haired and handsome, same as Seth. But it isn't him. I close my eyes tight and snap them open again, vainly hoping that everything will have righted itself. But I still find myself staring at the same handsome stranger.

I wonder if we might have somehow shown up to the wrong wedding? No, everyone else is here. Mum, my sister and maid of honour Elizabeth and her husband Graham. My friends and family. I see them all. A whispered muttering starts up and guests begin to shift in their seats, uncomfortable that I've stopped my traditional walk down the aisle. Can't any of them see that it's not Seth? Is it going to be up to me to say something?

'Alice,' Dad says quietly. 'Are you feeling okay? Are you well?'

I open my mouth but I can't find my voice.

'You're not having second thoughts, are you?' he hisses in my ear.

I blink. Can he really not see what the problem is? I gulp down air and manage to croak out the words, 'Where's Seth?'

'What are you talking about? He's there.' Dad discreetly points to the stranger standing where my fiancé should be.

My stomach drops. So Dad thinks that man is Seth. I don't understand. Is this some kind of elaborate prank? If it is, it's not very funny. Not even a little bit. I feel Dad's annoyance. It's coming off him in waves. 'Come on, Alice, I thought you loved the man. Why are you having second thoughts now? Is it nerves?' Dad runs a hand through wavy grey hair thicker and more lustrous than that of most men half his age.

My heart is thumping and my brain feels so woolly; I wonder if I might be having some kind of a breakdown. Perhaps the stress of the wedding is catching up with me, manifesting itself in this weird way. Everyone is really staring now. The smiles have been replaced by confused frowns, whispers, a couple of stifled giggles. Alongside my confusion, I'm absolutely mortified. Should I go ahead with the ceremony to save face? Should I tell everyone what's really going on? What would they say if I told them I don't recognise my husband-to-be?

I open my mouth to try to explain, but nothing comes out. What could I even say? *See that man over there who you all seem to think is Seth . . . well, he's not. I've never seen him before in my life.* I can't say that. I can't say anything.

To my further dismay, tears begin to prick behind my eyes.

I vaguely notice someone coming up the aisle towards me.

'Alice, are you okay?' It's one of my bridesmaids, Miriam. She's a work colleague and a good friend. Her sleek, dark hair brushes my cheek as she puts an arm around me. I cling on to her like a drowning woman holds a lifebuoy.

I don't know what to say, but her kindness has given rise to the threatened tears. I feel them slide down my cheeks. Taste them on my lips. Miriam's concern has galvanised more guests to get to their feet. A few are asking Dad what's going on. It's all too much. I want to just sink into the floor and disappear.

'What's wrong?' asks an older woman on the groom's side.

'Nothing,' Dad replies gruffly. 'She'll be fine in a minute.'

'Does she need to sit down? Maybe some fresh air,' someone suggests.

'Has she changed her mind?' a woman asks.

'Alice.' A deep, commanding voice cuts through the growing hubbub.

I glance up to see the man who isn't Seth walking up the aisle towards me. Miriam squeezes my shoulder and steps back. The wayward guests part to let him through. The sight of him – tall, broad, handsome and real – is entirely unnerving. His eyes are hooded and his mouth hangs slightly open as though he's about to say something else. I stumble backwards, trying to get away, holding a hand out to ward him off, the other hand still gripping my bouquet. His close proximity makes it hard for me to breathe. I can't explain it, but I don't want him to speak or even look at me.

'Please . . . can you not come any closer?' I ask. I'm too embarrassed, too scared to say that I don't know him. That I've never seen him before in my life, when everyone else clearly believes he's the groom.

'Alice, what's going on?' He frowns and takes another step towards me.

'Dad!' I clutch my father's sleeve. 'Tell him to stay where he is.' Waves of unease flood my body at the sight of him. A primal feeling of danger.

'You'd better stay where you are, son,' my dad says reluctantly before turning back to me. 'Has something happened? Did he do something to you?'

'*What?*' the stranger cries, his whole body stiffening. 'I haven't done anything. What is this, Alice? Do you not want to get married?' His words hang in the air, loud and shocking.

Whispers fill the church as our guests realise there might not be a wedding today after all.

'I don't believe this,' the stranger mutters, shaking his head and pulling at his collar.

'Of course she wants to get married!' Dad replies.

Not-Seth glances from my father to me and back again, his expression growing darker by the second. 'I think I need to hear that from Alice,' he replies. 'She doesn't look certain.' I can't tell if he's upset or angry. Possibly both. 'Alice, talk to me,' he says softly, desperately. 'Are you okay? Is it nerves? Are you ill?'

I daren't catch his eye. Instead, I snatch glances to examine his features, trying to compare them with Seth's, to pinpoint what it is about him that's different. But I can't do it. My mind is fuzzy. I'm suddenly exhausted. I realise I haven't replied yet, but I don't know how to tell him that I've never seen him before in my life.

'Alice?' my father prompts, using his trying-to-be-patient voice. 'Seth wants to know if you still intend to marry him. I think he deserves an answer, don't you?'

In my head I'm screaming, *That's not Seth!* But I daren't voice my fears aloud. Not when it's clear I still seem to be the only one who doesn't recognise him. I glance wildly around the church for an ally. For someone who might say aloud what I'm thinking. But no one speaks out. No one is looking at him with suspicion. They're all looking at *me*.

Standing with the other bridesmaids, my younger sister Elizabeth tries to catch my eye. She's frowning and mouthing something, but I can't have a conversation with her across the crowded church, so I don't respond.

Mum is making her way nervously up the aisle towards me from the front pew where she's been sitting with Dad's brother, Uncle Matthew, and her younger sisters Aunty Amanda and Aunty Rachel, who are still seated, but are gazing my way with worried expressions.

'Are you all right, Alice?' Mum says quietly, coming alongside me. 'Maybe we should go outside and have a chat?'

'Yes please,' I whisper.

'She needs to speak to Seth first,' Dad interjects.

Mum bites her lip and nods.

I wish Mum wasn't so meek. I want her to tell my dad that he's wrong. That what I need now is to leave this crowded church and clear my head. Instead, she squeezes my arm and says nothing.

'Seth' is still waiting for an explanation along with everyone else, looking at me as though I've got two heads.

My hands are trembling so much that I drop my bouquet and clutch at my fingers, trying to still them. The beautiful arrangement falls to the floor. I spent hours selecting the perfect design, going back and forth on my decision, wanting something simple yet striking. My single friends were all so excited about lining up to catch the bouquet. I don't bother bending to retrieve it, and no one else attempts to rescue it. I don't suppose there's much point anyway. Not now I realise that I absolutely cannot marry this stranger.

'Are you going to tell me what's wrong, Alice?' the stranger asks. 'Have you changed your mind?'

Fear and anger mix in my gut. How dare this man talk to me as though he knows me. As though he's my fiancé.

'Alice,' my dad says, warningly. 'Can you answer him? He deserves an explanation. We all do.'

'I'm sorry,' I reply, 'but where's Seth? That's not him.'

15

My words are met with a moment's confused silence.

'Of course it is,' Dad replies. 'Alice, what's going on? Have you been drinking?'

'No. I've never seen this man before. How can you even think it's Seth? He doesn't look like him, he doesn't sound like him . . .' My voice is getting higher in pitch. 'Where's my fiancé? Why isn't he here?' My heart is pounding. Am I trapped inside some realistic nightmare? 'Where's my phone? I need to call him, find out where he is.'

'I think she's having some kind of anxiety attack,' my mum says. 'She's overwhelmed. Don't worry, Seth, she'll be fine in a minute. We'll go outside for some fresh air. Get this straightened out.'

'Let me take a look at her,' he replies, taking another step closer. 'Alice, it's okay, it's me, Seth, your fiancé. Remember, I'm also a doctor. Let's go somewhere private and sort this out.' He looks around. 'Maybe we can go into the vestry.'

'No!' I cringe away from him. I can't explain the panic I feel at the thought of this strange man coming anywhere near me. 'I don't know what you're doing here, but you need to tell us who you are and where Seth is.'

'Alice!' my parents cry in unison.

'Please,' I beg them. 'How can you not see it's not Seth? I don't know who this person is, but he's not my fiancé. I'm supposed to be getting married! Where is he? Mum, do you know where my phone is?'

She nods. 'I think it's in the back room. Do you want it?'

'Please.' A sliver of hope rushes through me. If I can just call Seth, then maybe this will all be straightened out.

'She's hysterical,' Dad says. 'Maybe she needs something to help her calm down. Seth, please just take a look at her, will you?'

He shakes his head. 'You heard her. She doesn't want me any-where near. I don't want to make things worse. I'll fetch my parents over, maybe she'll talk to Mum.'

Both Seth's parents are doctors. I wonder if it's actually them here today, or if they too will be strangers. I hope I recognise them and that they'll agree with me that this is not their son.

He finally does as I ask and backs away, turning and striding down the aisle where he's approached by a man and a woman who I don't recognise. My heart sinks. The way they're fussing over him makes me think they might be his parents. But they're not *my* Seth's parents. Are they in on it too? Whatever *it* is. Some weird conspiracy? A sick joke?

I breathe a little easier now he's moved away from me. Everyone else is pretending not to stare my way. It's mortifying. I wish Mum and Dad would just tell all our guests to leave instead of having them all here gawking.

How has the day of my dreams turned into such a fiasco? It was supposed to be the happiest day of my life. Instead, it's becoming the most unsettling, horrible, nightmarish experience I've ever had. And, unless I can find the real Seth, I'm pretty sure it's only going to get worse.

Chapter Four

I honestly don't believe it. This is beyond my wildest imaginings of what I thought might happen. As I watch her face – her confusion and speechlessness – I almost laugh out loud. But of course I can't do that. I have to show shock and distress like everyone else in the church. I have to turn and ask in a whisper what's going on. To seem concerned and confused.

It feels like I'm having an actual out-of-body experience. She's scared. Terrified. And the worse the situation gets, the more elated I become. Joy and relief bubble up inside me like a bath bomb in a water fountain. Flooding my body with endorphins. I love that word. It makes me think of dolphins leaping in the ocean, chirping and squeaking with big grins on their faces. I bite my lip to keep the grin off my own face.

I gaze down at the church floor and try to think of something sad. Something terrible that will show in my expression.

Once I have my emotions under control again, I look up, confident that the dismay I'm faking will be accepted as real. Yet, all the while, I'm laughing inside with actual glee.

The wedding is ruined and I'm ecstatic.

Chapter Five

Then

As I stride along the street to work, I hum a tune to myself, still enjoying yesterday's high. Even the freezing rain can't dampen my mood. I'm engaged to be married. I'm a fiancée! How mad is that? Even though it's tricky in this icy wind while trying to hold my umbrella, I extend my hand to admire my ring for the fiftieth time. It's so elegant and understated. I love it.

Daisy was subdued at breakfast this morning and I think it's partly down to my engagement. Maybe it's highlighted the problems with her own relationship. I'm a little sad that she can't set aside her feelings for one day to be pleased for me. I love her like a sister, but surely you're supposed to celebrate your friends' good news. Is it selfish of me to want her genuine best wishes? Maybe. I don't know.

I'd have thought, after my troubled dating history, that Daisy would want me to be happy with someone. My previous boyfriend, Damian, was emotionally abusive, and Daisy and Laurence both helped give me the courage to leave him. Since then, I've had a hard time trusting men, and I didn't have any serious relationships for five years. Until I finally met Seth.

During those years, my friends and family were constantly trying to set me up, but I just wasn't ready. I threw myself into work instead.

Seth helped me to trust again, with the added benefit of shutting everyone else up. I hadn't realised how wearing it was to constantly have my family ask: Have you met anyone yet? When are you getting married and having babies? Stop working so hard and pay more attention to your love life. Your sister has a career and a relationship, why can't you do the same? And on and on, ad infinitum. No. I don't miss that at all.

Faraday Accounting is situated halfway along the High Street above a busy bakery. The building is old and the decor desperately needs updating, but my boss Paul Faraday is good at what he does, and business is thriving.

I shake out my umbrella and climb the narrow flight of stairs to our offices. When I joined the practice as an accountant almost five years ago, Paul told me that if I worked hard and hit my targets, I'd have the opportunity to become a partner further down the line. Well, I'm now a chartered accountant, I've consistently hit my targets, and I've also brought in a ton of new clients, mainly those specialising in the equestrian world. Word of mouth has worked really well for me in an industry where everyone knows everyone, so I'm confident that Paul will soon make good his promise and offer me a partnership. I work my arse off, so I know I deserve it.

'Afternoon, Alice,' says our other accountant, Charlotte Emerson, looking up from her desk, her glossy dark-brown hair tied back in an elaborate chignon.

I'm only five minutes late and I'm in too good a mood to rise to her jibe. 'Morning, Charlotte. Want a coffee?'

'No thanks, I had one half an hour ago.' This is obviously her way of telling me she came into work early.

Miriam Patel, our office manager, gives me a look of solidarity over Charlotte's head.

Charlotte joined a couple of years after me. She's a hard worker, but she's also sneaky and very ambitious. I worry that she's also going after a partnership and will throw me under the bus to get there. My *saving grace is that she can be a bit snooty and abrupt with her clients. They don't necessarily like dealing with her and I've had to field more than a few complaints over the years, including requests for me to take over their accounts – which obviously hasn't gone down well with Charlotte. Consequently, she's not my biggest fan, which is a shame because we're a small team of four, and it's an open-plan office.*

'Morning, Alice.' Paul looks up from his desk and peers at me over the top of his wire-rimmed glasses. 'I'll take a coffee if you're making one.'

'No problem, Paul.'

'Good weekend?' Miriam asks.

'I had a great weekend, thanks,' I reply, hanging up my dripping coat on the peg.

'What's that smile for?' she asks, folding her arms across her chest.

'Nothing.'

Her dark eyes narrow and she walks over to where I'm standing. Charlotte's interest has also now been piqued and I feel them both staring. I was planning to keep the news on the down low until after talking to my family, but it's almost bursting out of me. I've already told Daisy and Laurence, so I guess it won't hurt. I do an elaborate twirling movement with my hand, before thrusting my ring finger under Miriam's nose.

'Is that what I think it is?' she asks. 'It's gorgeous!'

'Seth proposed on Saturday night,' I say with a skip in my heart.

Paul looks up at my news. 'You're getting married?'

'Congratulations, Alice!' Miriam gives me a hug. She's so tiny that her arms barely reach my shoulders. 'We should go out for lunch to celebrate.'

'Yes, congratulations, Alice,' Paul echoes. 'Isn't your boyfriend in London?' I can tell he's already wondering what this might mean for my work. He needn't worry; I love my job and won't let my personal

life interfere with it at all. It's part of the reason Seth loves me – he likes my independence and ambition.

'Is this the imaginary boyfriend that none of us has met yet?' Charlotte drawls.

'Very funny.' I give her my unamused look, but even Charlotte's bitchiness can't dampen my mood.

'So now he's graduated to your imaginary fiancé. Loving that for you.' She smirks before adding a reluctant, *'Congratulations.'*

'Thanks,' I reply before turning back to Paul. *'Seth's been offered a job at Southampton Hospital, so he'll be moving down here. He's been wanting to get out of London for a while.'*

'You'll probably want to leave to start a family soon.' He says it as a joke, but I can tell he's partly serious.

I ignore his inappropriate comment and head into the kitchen to make coffee. I need it. Why is my engagement provoking such selfish reactions? Laurence and Miriam are the only ones who seem genuinely happy for me.

This prompts me to wonder how my family are going to take the news . . .

Chapter Six

Now

I follow the vicar and the woman who says she's Seth's mother into a room off the back of the church. My parents come too, but I've asked if 'Seth' and the man who says he's his father can wait outside.

Seth's parents, Christine and Geoff Evans, are both doctors – GPs. We've only met a handful of times, but neither of these people are them. Perhaps they're in on this ruse as well.

'Please, take your time,' the vicar says with a sympathetic smile.

'Thank you,' my father says, shaking his hand like they're concluding a business meeting.

The vicar leaves the room, pulling the door closed behind him.

'I need my phone,' I cry.

'Here.' Mum passes me my white silk clutch and I open it with trembling fingers. I pull out my mobile and call Seth. My head starts to throb when the automated voicemail kicks in. I walk over to the corner of the room, my back to everyone, and hiss into the phone:

'Seth, where are you? I'm at the church . . . everyone's here. Have you changed your mind? Are you okay? There's a man who says he's you. I . . . I don't understand what's happening.' My voice breaks and I try to swallow down the rising hysteria. 'Please call me back and get here as soon as you can.'

I end the call and turn around to see my parents and the fake Christine looking at me. She appears calm, but my mum and dad are wearing expressions of shock and horror.

'Why don't you sit down, Alice,' the fake Christine says gently. She's a good-looking woman in her early sixties with dark wavy hair held back by a jade comb that matches her fitted green dress.

I hitch up my wedding gown and sit on one of the red leatherette chairs that faces a large mahogany desk. She sits next to me and opens a traditional brown leather doctor's bag that she must have fetched from her car. My parents hover awkwardly beside us.

'Would you prefer if it was just the two of us?' the woman asks.

My distress surges at the thought of being alone with her. 'No, I want them to stay.'

'Okay.' She nods and takes an iPad from her bag.

My hands twist in my lap. I don't want to be examined by this stranger, but I also don't want to cause any more of a scene than I already have, and perhaps there really is something wrong with me. Although, how do I know I can trust anything she says? If it weren't for Dad insisting, I wouldn't have come in here to talk to her.

'How do you feel?' she asks.

I pause and try to think. 'Terrible!' I finally blurt out. 'My head feels strange, I don't know what on earth's going on. I feel like I'm trapped in a nightmare. This was supposed to be my wedding day, and now everything is ruined. I don't know who that man is, but he's not my fiancé. And I don't think you're his parents either!' I'm panting after my outburst. I know I sound hysterical.

The woman hardly reacts, other than to give me a sympathetic smile. I try to discern if it's genuine or not, but now she's typing something into her tablet. She looks up after a moment. 'Are you currently taking any medications of any kind?'

'No,' I reply.

'You're sure? Whatever you tell me is confidential. I think it might be an idea if we had some privacy.' She gives my parents a pointed look.

My mum touches Dad's arm to lead him from the room.

'No. I want them to stay,' I insist. 'And I'm absolutely not on any medication.' I pull at the bodice of my wedding gown. It's so tight I can barely breathe. If I thought the main church was over-heated with all our guests crammed into it, this small room is like a sauna. None of the windows are open, for goodness' sake. Should I ask Dad to open a couple?

'Have you had any episodes like this before?' the doctor asks, interrupting my thoughts.

'*Episodes?*' I take offence at the word. 'This isn't an episode. I genuinely don't know who *you* or your son are. I don't understand why you think this is an episode. I should be asking *you* the questions. Who are you? Where's Seth? Are you really a doctor?'

'Just answer her, Alice,' Dad chimes in. 'Dr Evans is trying to help you.'

'It's fine,' Christine responds, holding out a hand to quiet him. She stays focused on me. 'So you've never had this . . . feeling before, where you don't recognise someone?'

I pause and swallow, my throat dry as dust. I see my parents give one another a look and I wonder if it means something or if I'm being paranoid. 'Never,' I snap. 'I don't recognise my fiancé, or you and your husband, but I know everyone else here. Which makes me think that you're the problem. Not me.'

'Okay,' she replies mildly, not batting an eyelid at my outburst. 'Have you taken any non-prescription drugs recently?'

I screw up my face. 'No.'

'Maybe something to calm you down before the ceremony? Something to stop those pre-wedding jitters?' She's staring at me hard. 'There's no judgement here. I just want to help us get to the bottom of this.'

'I haven't taken any drugs of any kind.' I roll my eyes. 'And I haven't had anything to drink either, in case that was your next question.' I know I'm being rude, but I don't care. I absolutely don't trust this woman and I won't be gaslighted into thinking *I'm* the one with the problem. I check my phone to see if Seth has replied, but there's nothing on the screen. I call voicemail.

'*You have no new messages.*'

Where the hell is he? I realise everyone is staring at me, but I don't care and I don't enlighten them as to what I was doing.

'Have you had any head injuries recently?' fake Christine asks, once I've moved the phone from my ear. 'Doesn't matter how minor. Any bumps or bruises?'

'No.'

'Any existing conditions I should know about? Diabetes, epilepsy, anything at all?'

'Nothing,' I reply, briefly panicking that perhaps I might be suffering with something serious. Something that's making me lose my memory. But why would I only have a problem recognising Seth and his parents? Surely if I had some kind of amnesia, I would have forgotten them completely. But I haven't. I still love my fiancé. I still want to get married. Don't I?

'I'm going to check your vitals – pulse, temperature etcetera.' She reaches into her bag again.

My chest constricts at the thought of this woman touching me. No matter how much she and my parents want me to get checked over, I don't think I can cope with it. I don't think I should sit here submissively letting this imposter control the situation. I lurch to my feet. Why am I allowing her to ask me all these personal questions? I'm not going to let her examine me too. No way.

'What are you doing, Alice?' Dad asks. 'Sit down and let Dr Evans check you over.'

'She's not Dr Evans!' I cry. 'And I'm not going to stay here and let her do God knows what to me!'

'Alice!' Dad's voice is stern. Angry.

'She needs some help,' says the woman to my parents. 'If she won't let me do it, then you need to get her checked over asap. It could be something physical, or maybe she needs a referral to mental-health services, but without checking her vitals it's difficult to rule anything out.'

'Mental health?' Dad scoffs. 'I don't think that can be right. Alice is as level-headed as they come.'

'It's not about being level-headed,' the woman says patiently.

I skirt around my parents and head towards the door, pulse racing, palms slippery with sweat.

'It's the stress of the wedding,' my mum interjects quietly.

'Come back here, Alice,' my father orders. 'You heard what the doctor said.'

I yank open the door and push past my startled fake groom and his supposed father who are waiting right outside. I wonder if they were listening in. To my dismay, the church is still quite full. Don't these people realise there isn't going to be any wedding today? Why are they all still here?

I glance around for a friendly face, for someone who might be able to calm me, but all I see is a blur of suits and summer dresses, shiny hair and flowers. I know I must look a sight – bewildered, sweaty and wild-eyed. But I'm too upset to care. My mind is racing. I'm desperate to lock myself away in my bedroom and close the curtains. Calm this whirl of dark and frightening thoughts.

'Alice.' A warm, familiar voice by my side catches my attention. It's Laurence. I almost didn't recognise him dressed up in his navy suit, his messy blond hair cut shorter than usual.

27

'What's happened?' he asks, concern on his face.

'Can you take me home?' I'm trying to keep it together, to not cry in front of all these people, but I'm right on the edge. I realise if I let go of my emotions now, it won't be pretty.

'*Home?* You mean, back to the flat?' he asks.

I was supposed to be moving out of the flat I shared with Daisy and moving in with Seth. But that's obviously not happening any more. Well, not unless I can figure out what's going on.

'Yes, the flat, please.'

'Let me quickly tell Fran,' he says, glancing through the crowded church to locate his girlfriend.

'Don't leave me.' I clutch his arm. 'Text her.'

'Okay.' He nods.

Francesca Davies is one of my bridesmaids. I spot her sitting in one of the pews, deep in conversation with Daisy and my younger sister Elizabeth. Elizabeth sees me and rises to her feet. She says something to the others and they instantly look my way, brows creased. I can tell they're about to come over.

I turn away, my heart pounding. 'Quick, let's go.' I gather up the skirts of my dress and drape them over my arm.

Laurence takes my other arm and guides me up the aisle and through the entryway. I ignore all the concerned looks and questions, feeling bad that I'm being so rude to friends and family who are obviously worried about me. But I can't face any of them. I'm profoundly grateful that Laurence hasn't asked me anything, passed any judgement or tried to talk me into staying. He's a true friend, just doing what I want and getting me out of here.

We finally exit the church through the stone arch, out into the warm afternoon. I had thought it would be Seth and me leaving this way, to cheers and showers of confetti. If I think about that image too much, I'll cry. I squint in the lemon-bright sunlight, relieved to be out of the oppressive heat and gloom of the church. Swallows flit overhead, calling to one another. A warm breeze rustles the leaves of the oaks and sycamores. It's the perfect backdrop to a summer wedding. But right now the birdsong sounds discordant, and the whispering of the trees feels sinister, setting my teeth on edge.

'Car park's this way.' Laurence leads me along the narrow path past mossy, age-spotted gravestones.

Despite my confusion and shock at what's just happened, now that I'm out of the church and away from all the stares and whispers, I feel as though I can breathe again. I know it's a temporary reprieve though. This thing, whatever it is, has to be resolved.

And above all else, I still need to find the real Seth.

I jump as my mobile pings in my bag. 'Wait!' I cry. 'This could be him. It could be Seth, calling back.'

Laurence stops and waits while I fumble for my phone. I inhale sharply as I see that I've received one new voice message. My palms sweat as I press play and hold the phone to my ear, my heart thumping.

'*Alice, it's me. I'm here in the church. I don't understand why you don't recognise me. Can we talk?*'

'Oh no,' I cry. My mobile slips out of my hand and lands on the stony path.

'What? What is it?' Laurence asks, stooping to retrieve my mobile. 'It's cracked,' he says, handing it back to me with a sympathetic look in his eyes.

I stare at my fractured phone, at the intricate cracks spiderwebbing across the screen. 'It's not him,' I say, trying to stifle the fear that's oozing from every pore of my body.

'Who's not him?' Laurence comes closer and tilts my face up so he can see me.

I stare at my friend without really seeing him, trying and failing to make sense of what's happening.

'Alice?' he prompts.

29

'Sorry, yeah, I called Seth's number, but it wasn't him who replied. It was that man in there . . . he has Seth's phone. I don't know what to do.'

Laurence stares at me in confusion as a growing terror squeezes its way through my veins. I feel as though I'm trapped in a nightmare, a horror movie, like my whole reality has been wrenched upside down. My hands are shaking and my vision blurs. This isn't how today was supposed to go. This can't be happening.

What has happened to Seth?

Where *is* he?

Chapter Seven

Then

I pull into the large gravel driveway of my parents' five-bedroom home on the outskirts of Ringwood. My sister's silver Peugeot 208 is already in the drive, so I brace myself for the full Porter family experience, although Elizabeth is a Porter-Charles now. She and Graham both hyphenated their names after they married last year.

Despite the grandeur of my parents' current home, I didn't have what you'd call an idyllic childhood. My parents struggled financially for years, and we moved from one rented apartment to another. I was never truly relaxed as a kid. I somehow felt like I was always in the spotlight – the poor kid, the odd kid, the one who was a bit different. I also felt pressure from my dad to do my best, to never disappoint, always worrying about doing the wrong thing. On the outside I was confident and feisty, but on the inside I was a crumbling bag of nerves. I suppose since then I've learned to fake it till I make it. But I still get the occasional flashback to that old insecure me. Especially when I come to this imposing house that's never really felt like home.

My father worked hard to get to where he is today. It was his insight and innovation twelve years ago that saved his boss's logistics firm from going under. They rewarded him with a huge bonus, a raise and a promotion, and he hasn't looked back since. Now, he and Mum have a nice house on the edge of the New Forest, two holidays a year, and a membership at the local golf club.

I get out of my little red Toyota Yaris and pick my way across the driveway, avoiding the shaded patches that are still covered in ice. I'm fairly certain my parents will be happy with my news, but with Dad you never really know. So, I'm excited but also apprehensive.

Mum opens the door before I'm even at the porch. She's flawless as ever in a pair of black trousers and a pale-pink cotton-knit top, her brown waves pinned off her face with a silver comb. 'Come in, darling. It's freezing out there.' We hug and she takes my coat and hangs it in the hall cupboard. I have an instant flashback to coming home after school and Mum telling us to hang up our coats and take off our shoes.

'Something smells nice,' I say, following her through to the kitchen where my brother-in-law, Graham, is turning the roast potatoes.

'Hi, Alice, how are you?' He glances over with a smile.

'Good thanks. You got your hair cut. Suits you.' His hair was always quite thick and wavy, but it started receding over the past year which is probably why he decided to cut it.

'Thanks.' He rubs the top of his head. 'Felt like a change. The kids have been doing double-takes all week.' Graham's the headmaster of the local junior school. The same school we all went to as kids.

'Where's Elizabeth?' I ask.

Mum looks up at the ceiling. 'In the office with your father talking about some legal thing at his work.'

My younger sister is a corporate lawyer. She's always been super-smart and super-efficient. We get on well, but we're not close. Well, not as close as we used to be. Her husband Graham is my ex-boyfriend. We started going out when I moved back to Ringwood after uni. We were only together for a couple of months, and were broken up years before she started going out with him, but things have been slightly awkward between me and Elizabeth ever since. Not on my part – I don't think of him in that way at all any more. She's the one who's been weird *about it. Not sure if she feels guilty or resentful. She always changes the subject when I've tried to clear the air with her. I thought my relationship with Elizabeth would improve once they were married but, if anything, we've grown further apart. Hopefully she'll relax once she hears that I'm about to marry Seth. I have butterflies at the thought of telling everyone.*

'Should be another half hour until lunch is ready,' Mum says. 'Shall we have a drink in the lounge? I've opened a new bottle of sherry.'

'Sounds good, but I'm driving,' I reply.

'We can drop you back,' Graham offers.

'Great. In that case . . .'

We troop into the lounge just as Dad and Elizabeth come down the stairs deep in conversation. Eventually, they notice me.

'Alice.' Dad nods.

'Hi, Dad.' I take a step towards him and we kiss on the cheek.

He claims his favourite spot in the corner of the sofa and Mum brings him a glass of Amontillado.

'Hi, Alice,' Elizabeth says, her gaze sweeping me from head to toe. 'Nice top.'

'Thanks,' I reply, touching my shirt. 'I got it in that boutique opposite the candle shop.'

She nods, not really listening. Her eyes narrow. 'There's something different about you.'

I'm hyper-aware of my engagement ring, but no one's clocked it yet as I already turned the diamond so it's facing inwards.

'Sit down,' Mum says gently. 'You're all making me nervous, hovering about. Elizabeth, sherry?'

'Yes please.'

We take a seat while Mum fusses around, setting down drinks and bowls of nibbles. Dad's reading the Sunday papers as usual and probably won't look up until lunch is served. It's down to the rest of us to make conversation. I was going to wait until dessert to make my announcement, but the news is fizzing in my chest, waiting to pop out. I'm going to have to ruin Dad's precious reading ritual.

'Alice, what's up with you? You're so fidgety.' Elizabeth is irritated with me. Honestly, I sometimes feel like she's the older sister, not me.

'Well,' I say. 'There is something actually.'

'Don't say you finally got made partner,' Dad says, peering over the travel section.

'I'm working on it,' I reply.

'Glad to hear it, because you've been at that firm a few years now. Maybe you need to move on if Faraday's dragging his heels.'

I don't want to get drawn into a conversation about work. I always feel like I'm doing pretty well until I talk to my father. He has this knack of making me anxious about my career. Like I'm not tough enough. Not driven enough. Like I don't measure up to Elizabeth. Although he wasn't exactly thrilled with my sister's choice of husband. When Graham was with me, he was a teacher. By the time he got engaged to Elizabeth, he was a deputy head. His recent promotion to headmaster has appeased Dad somewhat. Not enough for him to forgo the Sunday papers in favour of talking to him, though.

I think Dad will be happy about me and Seth, but I still feel slightly nauseous at the thought of telling him. At coming under his scrutiny. I've actually enjoyed keeping Seth separate from my friends and family because they're often too quick to pass judgements on my love life. Especially as they'd been nagging me for years to meet someone. Setting me up on all kinds of inappropriate blind dates that make me cringe when I think about them. In that respect, I was relieved to have met Seth because it meant my family finally stopped interfering in my love life.

'So, what's your news, darling?' Mum says, taking a seat herself, perching on the edge of the uncomfortable chaise.

I feel my face heat up. I realise I should be making this announcement with Seth present. But he couldn't come down to Ringwood this

34

weekend and I can't wait any longer. There are too many other people who already know. Mum would be mortified and Dad furious if they found out about our engagement from someone else. In fact, it's a miracle they haven't heard already. The local grapevine is usually way more efficient.

My throat has dried up, so I decide to show them instead. I wait until they're all looking my way, and then I slide my ring around and show them my hand.

'Is that an engagement ring?' Elizabeth asks.

'Seth proposed?' Mum says, putting her hands to her cheeks.

'Why haven't we met him yet?' Dad demands.

'Congratulations, Alice.' Graham comes over and kisses my cheek.

'Wow, congratulations!' Elizabeth turns to give me a hug, then takes my hand to examine the ring. 'That's gorgeous.'

'I'm so happy for you, darling,' Mum says, her eyes brightening with tears. 'I can't believe I'll have two married daughters. It only seems like yesterday you were at primary school.'

Dad sets down his newspaper. 'This is the endocrinologist chap, right? Seth Evans.'

'Yes, he's based in London right now, but he's got a job in Southampton Hospital starting next year.'

'When can we meet him and his family?' Dad asks.

'I'll set something up,' I reply.

'Good. Let's make it sooner rather than later. Don't let it derail your career, Alice. Remember what I told you girls – you need to be independent. Make your own money. You never know what's around the corner, so it's vital you're self-sufficient.'

Mum puts a hand on Dad's arm to stop him going off on one.

Normally, he wouldn't accept that from her, but today he stops lecturing me and clears his throat. 'Jane, fetch us a bottle of champagne from the chiller cabinet. We'll have a toast.'

Mum heads off to the kitchen. I've given up telling her not to be bossed around by him. She always says she doesn't mind. But I find it weird that Dad is all for me and Elizabeth being strong, independent women, yet he treats Mum like a skivvy. Okay, maybe that's a bit harsh. Not a skivvy, exactly, but certainly not as his equal.

'This is so exciting, Alice!' Elizabeth takes both my hands and squeezes them. 'Have you got a date in mind?'

'We were thinking of next spring or summer.'

She wrinkles her nose. 'That's not much time to arrange a proper wedding.'

'We don't want anything fancy,' I reply. 'As long as we can have it at the church at Ellingham, that's all that matters. I haven't got a clue about the rest of it.'

'You did such a good job as my maid of honour, I'm more than happy to return the favour and help you plan it.' Elizabeth gives an excited clap.

Thankfully, Mum returns to the lounge with a bottle of Moët to save me from replying. I'd already hinted to Daisy that she would be my maid of honour, but I guess I'm going to have to let her down, despite her knowing more about my life than my sister. Elizabeth will be really offended if I don't choose her. Family is family, after all.

Dad stands and expertly opens the champagne. He pours us each a half glass, the bubbles fizzing along with the butterflies in my stomach. Graham declines as he's driving, and toasts with lemonade instead. He seems a bit subdued. I hope everything's okay between him and Elizabeth.

'Congratulations, Alice,' Dad says, raising his glass.

I was hoping for a bit more of a speech. Maybe something inspiring or emotional, or at least a little warm. But 'congratulations' is something. I guess I should be thankful he isn't opposed to it. I only hope he gets on with Seth.

'Congratulations, Alice!' everyone toasts.

'Thank you,' I reply, relieved and excited.

'Gosh,' Mum says. 'I think that's the oven beeping. Elizabeth, do you want to give me a hand?'

'No, Lizzie, you stay,' I say, wanting time alone with Mum to see what she thinks about my engagement. I follow her back into the kitchen as everyone else takes their drinks into the dining room.

'Such wonderful news,' Mum says, opening the oven. Heat spills into the kitchen along with the smell of roast chicken and vegetables. 'I hope he's a good man.'

'He is, Mum. He's really well respected too.'

Since my break-up with Damian five years ago, Mum and Dad have been pushing me to settle down with a husband, but I've never felt ready for it. I never told them what happened with Damian. That he was emotionally abusive towards me. That, despite our short time together of only ten months, it's taken me years to be able to trust anyone again. That Seth is the first man I've fallen hard enough for to want to put my heart on the line again. To risk myself in that way.

Truth be told, in addition to my own relationship issues, the thought of turning into my parents gives me massive anxiety. But now that I'm with Seth, I really do feel like he's the one. I'm even quite confident about introducing him to everyone. Thankfully, Seth is pretty good with people. He knows how to size them up and win them over. When he needs to.

'Can you do the gravy?' Mum asks.

As we work together, I can't help wondering how many Sunday dinners we've had as a family. I also wonder what my married life will be like with Seth. Will we have kids and make our own Sunday dinner traditions? Is that what I want?

'You okay?' Mum asks, decanting the green beans into a serving dish.

'Yes, fine. Just daydreaming.'

'I haven't heard you talk much about Seth. You'll have to fill me and your father in on what he's like.' She points to the flowered

37

Portmeirion dish. 'Can you take the potatoes through to the dining room?'

Ten minutes later, all the food is laid out on a cream runner on top of the oval polished mahogany dining table that was the first large piece of furniture my parents bought after buying this house. The roast chicken has been placed in front of Dad, and he sits at the head of the table holding the carving knife and fork like he's the king of the castle. Which I suppose he is.

I detect a bit of an atmosphere in the room and see that Graham and Elizabeth are both quite stony-faced. They were fine a few minutes ago, so I wonder what can have happened between then and now.

Mum notices too. She frowns at them before glancing quickly at Dad who's now mid-carve, placing slices of chicken on each plate. 'So,' Mum says, turning to me. 'Tell us about this proposal. Did he get down on one knee?'

I proceed to tell them about Seth's helicopter proposal. Dad is quietly approving and Mum is visibly impressed, but I can tell that Elizabeth and Graham are only faking interest. Elizabeth is barely eating, while Graham angrily shoves food into his mouth. They've obviously had cross words about something.

I hope it isn't anything to do with me.

Chapter Eight

Now

I unplug the vacuum and somehow manage to wedge it back into the overcrowded hall cupboard. I've spent the whole morning cleaning, even though our characterful two-bedroom apartment is already spotless. It's the only way I can think of to keep my mind occupied. To stop myself from spinning out while I wait for my parents to arrive.

I've managed to put off seeing them since Saturday's disaster, but they've just messaged to say they're on their way over, so I can't get out of it – unless I refuse to answer the door. And even then, I get the feeling that Dad wouldn't be averse to letting himself in with the spare key.

I've been home alone for the past couple of days while Daisy's been at work. As a pharmacist, she puts in long, stressful hours, often seven days a week. We've been flatmates ever since we found ourselves back in Ringwood after uni. We started out renting a damp terraced house that we shared with two other girls. The two of us then moved to a cramped two-bedroom flat on a modern housing estate on the outskirts of town. Then, just over four years ago when our careers began taking off, we moved here to our dream flat just off the High Street.

It belongs to a friend of Daisy's parents so the rent is far more reasonable than it should be. I absolutely fell in love with the painted beams, picture rails and sloping ceilings, the wooden sash windows and chunky radiators. I had great fun moving in and decorating. Daisy wasn't that interested in that side of things, so I had free rein with paint colours and furniture placement, which suited us both just fine.

I was supposed to be moving out after the wedding, and Daisy's boyfriend Martin was going to move in. That's all been put on hold, but I know it's not fair on Daisy, so I'm grateful to her for having me back while I sort out a new place. I don't think I could face moving in with my parents.

Since my non-wedding on Saturday, Daisy and Laurence have been trying to get me to talk. To open up about what happened that day. But I've been feigning exhaustion and hiding out in my room, preferring not to engage. I know I'm going to have to face people at some point, but I'd rather do it later than sooner.

Knowing that fake Seth has my Seth's phone makes me terrified for my fiancé's safety. My first reaction was to call the police. But Laurence advised me that if I called them and explained that Seth is in danger, there's a strong possibility I could be sectioned under the Mental Health Act. Because no one else believes anything's wrong. They all think the man at the church is the real Seth. Even my parents are saying it's him. I'm the only person who believes my Seth is missing.

So, I'm trying to figure out what to do next. I don't think I've ever felt so alone in my life. My thoughts are a dark, swirling, frightening mess.

I tense at the shrill buzz of the doorbell. I feel like a trapped animal going to ground. I tell myself that the sooner I see my parents, the sooner they'll leave. I straighten up and walk across the hall to the front door where I press the buzzer. A few moments later,

Dad walks in, leans down and kisses my cheek. Smart as always, he's wearing dark jeans, loafers and a sage-green short-sleeved shirt.

'Alice,' he says, walking straight through to the airy living room.

Mum's immaculate in a soft blue linen dress and open-toe espadrilles. She gives me an appraising look. 'You look tired, darling. You should put on a little mascara and some lipstick, perk yourself up.' She gives me a hug and a squeeze and I usher her along the hall.

'Can I get you a drink?' I ask.

'No, we won't stay long,' Dad replies.

That's something at least, I think.

He makes himself comfortable on the sofa. Mum perches on one of the dining chairs, her gaze flicking from me to Dad and out to the view through the window. I remain standing just inside the lounge doorway.

Dad clears his throat. 'We're worried about you, Alice.'

'I'm fine,' I lie.

'Well, that's not really true, is it?' he says. 'Are you going to tell us what's going on? Come and sit down, talk to us properly.'

My parents have this way of making me feel about twelve years old again. I slouch and grow sulky. Muscle memory in action. But I do as he asks and sit on one of the dining chairs next to Mum, angling it around to face him.

'What do you want to know?' I ask. 'Other than what I've already told you. But no one wants to believe me.'

He takes a breath and grits his teeth, irritated by my attitude. Annoyed that I haven't tried to make everything smooth and perfect again, like I normally would. I hope he's only being this way because he's worried about me, but I'm pretty sure it's because I'm causing an inconvenient scandal. I'm being *difficult*.

'So you're still adamant you don't recognise your fiancé,' he says, as though I've purposely chosen to upend my life.

41

'I know my fiancé. I just don't know the man who was at my wedding,' I reply.

'Look, Alice, this has got to stop. You do realise that all this nonsense about not recognising him is in your head. You need to pull yourself together or get proper help. Moping about in the flat isn't going to get your life back on track.'

'Maybe you can patch things up with Seth?' Mum adds hopefully. 'Set another wedding date.'

'I can't imagine he'd want to get married now,' Dad retorts. 'Not after you humiliated the poor man in front of everyone. And if he does, I won't be footing the bill for a second wedding. You can do it quietly with just close family.'

I tune out while they air all their frustrations. I know they're only saying these hurtful and pointless things because they're worried about me, but it's not helping my state of mind. I breathe in and out, and try to picture my calm place – a cool, green forest with a clear stream and—

'Alice,' Dad says, cutting into my thoughts. 'Alice, are you listening to me?'

'Yes, of course.' I blink and reluctantly bring myself back to my surroundings.

'Right. Well, your mother and I, we feel that you need to see someone . . . professional. We have the number of a therapist who specialises in—'

'It's fine, I saw my GP yesterday,' I interrupt.

'You did?' He raises a sceptical eyebrow.

I knew that would shut him up. Honestly, I feel mean having these antagonistic thoughts towards my dad, but he can't help rubbing me the wrong way. I guess we've always clashed. He gets on far better with my sister. They're two peas in a pod.

Mum reaches out a hand to squeeze my shoulder. 'Well done for going to the doctor, Alice. What did she say?'

I shift in my chair, not wanting to recall the information, but realising I can't hide from it. 'She thinks I might have prosopagnosia, but I don't agree.'

'What's that?' My parents both look genuinely worried for a moment.

'It's a condition where you can't recognise faces,' I explain.

'*What?*' Dad looks sceptical. 'Is that a real thing?'

I shrug. 'Apparently.'

'How do you spell that?' He gets out his phone and starts tapping and scrolling, obviously looking for himself. 'Who did you see? A locum?'

'No, Dr Philips.'

'Oh, right.' He gives a small harumph and puts his phone down. Dr Philips is our family doctor. We've been with her for years, and I know Dad respects her.

'Anyway, it *is* a real thing,' I reply. 'I looked it up when I got home. But Dr Philips isn't certain I have it, because it's only Seth and his parents who I don't recognise. Whereas with prosopagnosia you generally can't recognise any faces at all.'

'How scary,' Mum says. 'I hope you haven't got that, darling.'

'Me too,' I reply. 'Dr Philips referred me to a clinical neuropsychologist and she's also sending me for an MRI scan on Friday, to be on the safe side.'

I think this might be the first time in my life I've seen Dad look genuinely shocked. Even at the church he was more angry than anything else. Whereas now . . . well, he can't exactly blame me if I have a medical condition. Although I'm sure he'll try to make it somehow my fault. Or maybe I'm not being fair.

I don't want to let myself think about the possibility that I might genuinely be ill. I stupidly did an online search for prosopagnosia and discovered that the scan will probably be looking for lesions on my brain. And now I can't stop thinking about them.

'Shall we come with you?' Dad asks a little more gently.

'No, it's fine.' I take a breath and try not to let my distress show. Ever since I came back from the doctor's I've been less and less sure that I can trust myself. My parents, my friends, basically everyone I know believes that the man I didn't recognise is my fiancé. Granted, most of them have never met him before, but what about all the people on Seth's side of the family? Surely they would have noticed something amiss.

It makes no sense that some random stranger would pretend to be my fiancé to trick me into marrying him. I mean, it's not as if I'm super-wealthy – my parents' money is theirs, not mine. Although I guess Elizabeth and I will inherit it one day. I'm not incredibly beautiful either. I'm nice-looking, have a good job and I'm usually decent company, but that's about it. I'm certainly not the kind of person someone would go to such extreme lengths to marry.

'I'm sure you'll be fine,' Mum says. 'They just do these scans as a precaution.' But her face is taut, her forehead lined with worry.

'I really think we should come with you to the hospital,' Dad persists.

I decide to ignore his request rather than giving him an outright no, and inviting another argument.

'You would have been leaving for your honeymoon today,' Mum says wistfully.

Seth and I had booked two weeks in Aruba at a five-star hotel. It was going to be blissful. Romantic and luxurious. I try to push away the thought. The regret.

'At least I wasn't paying for that as well as the wedding,' Dad grumbles. 'I hope Seth's got good travel insurance.'

I don't dare ask Dad how much money he lost on the wedding. My parents are wealthy, but Dad is frugal. He absolutely hates waste; it's one of his bugbears. I guess it's a hangover from scrimping for so many years.

Dad clears his throat and shifts in his seat. 'There's something else, Alice . . .'

I'm instantly alert.

Mum looks down at her shoes.

'What is it?' I ask.

'Well,' Dad says, trying and failing to be nonchalant.

'Tell me,' I press, already knowing by his tone of voice that he's going to say something I don't want to hear.

He looks at my mum and raises an eyebrow slightly before turning back to me. 'You haven't been returning Seth's calls or messages, so he contacted us and we met with him yesterday.'

'You met him?' I thought they might have done that, but it doesn't feel good to know they've been talking about me behind my back with this stranger.

'Yes,' Dad confirms. 'And we agreed that he should come over to talk to you.'

'No. Absolutely not.' My heart starts beating too fast and my throat tightens. I'm not ready to speak to him. I wouldn't know what to say. Wouldn't even know where to start.

'Be reasonable, Alice. You were engaged to the man. He has a right to know why you didn't go through with the wedding.'

'You *know* why, and so does he!' My skin turns clammy. I was already hot from pushing around the hoover, but the flat now feels completely airless. I walk shakily to the window and open it. An ineffective waft of warm air drifts in along with the buzz of midday traffic.

'I know you say you don't recognise him,' Dad says, getting to his feet, 'but I think the best way to get over that is to talk to him. See if some memories might start coming back.'

'Your father's right, Alice,' Mum adds. 'Maybe talking to him will jog your memory.'

I open my mouth to shoot down their suggestion, but then I close it again. Perhaps they do have a point. Much as I really don't want to see the man that everyone says is my fiancé, maybe if I talk to him, I can find out what his game is. Or maybe something will click. Perhaps I'll experience a flicker of recognition. A hint as to who he really is. *Anything.* But the thought of seeing that man again has made me literally start to shake. I need more time to prepare myself. Maybe I'll agree to see him after my scan, when I know more.

'I'll think about it,' I reply, needing my parents to leave so I can be by myself and process my thoughts. I'm desperate to be alone right now.

'You better think fast,' Dad says, heading towards the door with my mum. 'Because Seth's waiting outside.'

His words take a moment to register, but when they do I feel physically sick.

Chapter Nine

THEN

The Old Bell is always busy, especially on a Thursday. I'm not normally one to go out drinking on a week night, but I'm off to London at the weekend and my friends all want to celebrate my engagement here in Ringwood. I'm already feeling quite tipsy thanks to the two Martinis Daisy forced on me before we left home.

The warm, welcoming scent of beer and chips hits me as Daisy and I walk into the pub and head over to the crowded bar, glancing around to see if any of our group have arrived. I catch sight of a few school friends – Janey, Madeline, Danica and Kieran – over at a large trestle table in the corner. They wave and call over to us. I grin and wave back, feeling unexpectedly nervous at the thought of introducing everyone to Seth tonight. I hope they all get along. It's important that my friends like him. I can't believe they haven't met yet, but with Seth leading such a busy life in London, there just hasn't been the opportunity. So tonight feels like a big deal.

I glance at my phone, and see it's just after six thirty. He should be leaving work about now, and the drive from London will probably take around an hour and a half. Maybe two hours if the traffic's heavy. It's a shame there's no train station in Ringwood – that would make things so much easier.

'What are you having?' I ask Daisy.

'No, I'm getting these,' she says, fumbling in her bag for her card.

'You don't have to—'

'This is your night,' she says, cutting me off. 'You shouldn't have to put your hand in your pocket.'

'Oh, well, thank you.' After her initial lack of excitement at my news, Daisy seems to have had an abrupt change of heart. She's now become almost enthusiastic. She thinks my engagement might possibly spur Martin on to make more of a commitment to her. She wants the four of us to double date and even mentioned going on a mini break together. I'm not too sure about that. I don't think Martin and Seth will have that much in common. But we'll see what happens after tonight.

It was Daisy's idea for us to go out for a celebratory drink. She arranged the whole thing. Drinks at our local pub with everyone, followed by a curry in town. Not the most original or classy night out, but I don't want a big fuss and Seth was happy to keep it low-key.

'Mine's a pint.'

I turn at the sound of Laurence's voice. He and Francesca are standing behind us, bundled up in coats and hats, smiles on their faces.

Fran leans in for a hug. 'Congratulations, Alice. So happy for you.'

'Ahh, thank you. It all feels a bit surreal actually.'

'I bet it does. Exciting though. Is Seth coming this evening?' she asks.

'Yeah, he should be on his way now,' I reply.

'Hope he's prepared to be grilled by everyone,' Laurence says.

'We're not going to be interrogating the poor bloke,' Fran replies, taking off her bobble hat.

'You will go easy on him, won't you?' I give Laurence a pleading look.

He raises his hands, laughing in mock surrender.

'Fran, did you get your hair cut?' I ask.

'Just a trim.' She runs a hand through her shinier-than-usual brown hair.

'Looks really good,' I say. 'Loving the layers.'

'Thanks. I don't usually make this much of an effort. No need to worry about looking good when you work with animals all day. I much prefer animals to humans. Less judgemental.'

'I know what you mean,' I reply. 'I'd love to get a pet, but we're not allowed one in our flat.'

Daisy glances back at us. 'Hey, guys. Pint for you, Laurence. And what are you drinking, Fran?'

'I'll have a pint, too.'

'Nice hair, by the way,' Daisy comments.

A couple of minutes later, we're all walking over to the table with our drinks. Martin shows up at the same time and slings an arm around Daisy, kissing her cheek as she passes him his beer.

'Thanks, babe,' he says. 'Congrats, Alice.'

'Thank you,' I reply.

'Sure you want to be tying the knot? Next thing you know it'll be mortgages, kids, grey hairs . . .'

'Shut up, dickhead. Course she's sure,' Daisy replies, nudging him in the ribs with her elbow and almost spilling his drink.

'Careful, Dais!'

I shake my head at Martin's teasing, but Daisy isn't too thrilled with his comments. She slides out from under his arm and goes over to sit with Janey and Madeline.

Martin shrugs and starts chatting to Laurence.

Once I reach the table, everyone offers their congratulations. It's so nice to be surrounded by warmth and good wishes. Daisy makes me tell everyone how Seth proposed and I notice her watching Martin as I recount my story. I don't think she's happy with his reaction, because her expression is growing cloudier as everyone apart from Martin becomes caught up in the romance. He's sipping his pint without comment.

I'm pleased how everyone seems really keen to meet Seth, especially as he'll be moving down here next year and becoming part of our social circle.

My phone pings and I see it's a voicemail from him. I guess he was calling to let me know his ETA. I hope he makes it down before we move on to the Indian restaurant. Actually, even if he's a bit late, it won't matter. I'm just dying to introduce him to everyone.

I stick a finger in my left ear to try to block out the pub noise, and listen to his message:

'Alice, I'm so sorry, but the car's playing up. I think it's the starter motor. I can't risk coming down 'cause I have to be at work by ten tomorrow morning. I'm really sorry. I feel terrible about missing it. Have a lovely evening and I'll see you tomorrow night, okay? Love you.'

Disappointment drops into my stomach like a rock. I take a huge swig of my Martini and try not to let this feel like the end of the world. I guess it's not Seth's fault that his car's playing up, but I can't help feeling frustrated and a little angry. I've asked him to meet my friends so many times, but there's always something stopping him. Mainly his job. I just hope his work–life balance will be better once he moves down here. I thought I was a workaholic, but his hours are crazy.

'Everything okay?' Laurence asks.

After a moment, I realise he's talking to me. I feel a bit embarrassed at the thought of telling everyone my fiancé can't make it to his own engagement party. I lean closer to Laurence and mumble that Seth's car's broken down and he won't be coming. Stupidly, I realise I'm about to cry. I sniff back my tears and tell myself not to be so oversensitive.

'Damn.' Laurence puts his pint down and gives my arm a squeeze. 'That's a bit shit. Sorry, Porter.'

'Oh well, what can you do?' I reply, trying to put on a brave face. 'Hey, guys,' I say, raising my voice. 'Seth's car's broken down so we'll be celebrating my engagement without him.'

Everyone is quiet for a moment before making sympathetic noises.

'Shall we reschedule for another night?' Fran asks, concern in her eyes. 'How about one night next week?'

50

'No, that's okay. Seth is just so busy at the moment. I'll let you all know when he finally makes it down, and then we can try again.'

'Sure. Okay. You must be disappointed though.'

'I'm fine,' I reply, taking in a deep breath through my nose, determined not to let this ruin the evening. After all, I'm still engaged. It's not as if he didn't want to come.

'Why don't you send him some photos of the night?' Fran suggests. 'That way, at least he'll be able to kind of see you.'

'That's a great idea.' I lean in towards Francesca and we blow kisses to my phone camera. I caption it: *Two Hot Babes* and send it to his WhatsApp with a kiss emoji.

'There's only one thing to do in these kinds of situations . . .' Danica says, shaking her head.

Everyone waits for her words of wisdom.

'Get hammered!' she cries, holding up her glass.

We cheer and I can't help laughing, even though it's slightly hollow. Right now I feel so thankful for my friends. I don't know what I'd do without them. I've known most of these girls since primary school. We've had our ups and downs over the years, but now we're all adults I appreciate our shared history. It's nice. Comforting.

The evening passes quickly in a blur of laughter and alcohol. At ten to nine we all decamp to the Indian restaurant and order pretty much everything on the menu, along with more drinks. I'm trying not to think about work tomorrow. Miriam couldn't make tonight as she had a family dinner to go to, but I already know she's going to love teasing me when I crawl in tomorrow morning with the mother of all hangovers.

Throughout the evening, I make sure to take lots of photos and send them to Seth with silly captions. Hopefully that way he won't feel like he's missing out too much and he'll know I'm thinking of him.

'Kennedy, come here and have a selfie with me!' I call out to Laurence across the table.

'Do I have to? I can't move. Shouldn't have ordered those extra onion bhajis.'

'Fine, I'll come over there then.' My words are slurring, but I'm still in that nice fuzzy stage of drunkenness before the spinny head hits. I stand and make my way around the table to where Laurence and Martin are seated. I crouch between them and take our photo as they plant a kiss on each cheek.

I caption the photo: Two New Friends and press send.

'Shall we get the bill?' Daisy asks.

'What's the time?' I reply.

'Almost half eleven.'

'Yeah, s'get th'bill,' I reply.

My phone buzzes with a text from Seth. I'll check it in a minute.

'Alice doesn't have to pay, because it's her night,' Daisy declares. She's always generous when she's had a few to drink.

'Fine, but she has to work out what everyone else pays,' Laurence says, 'because she's . . .'

'The accountant!' everyone chants.

I laugh and hold up a hand. 'Fine, I'll do it.'

While I wait for the waiter to bring over the bill, I eagerly check my text from Seth to see if he's been loving my photos and little messages. But when I open up WhatsApp to read his reply, I'm confused for a moment. Then my stomach knots.

What the fuck, Alice. Are you trying to rub in the fact that I'm not there? Who are those two blokes?

He's obviously misread the situation. He thinks I'm playing some kind of game, when I'm absolutely not. I'm suddenly very sober and very worried.

Hey, Seth. I was just trying to involve you in the evening as you couldn't make it. Didn't mean to upset you. Thought you'd enjoy the pics xx

Being sent photos of random men kissing you isn't enjoyable for me.

Not random – the last photo was of Laurence and Martin. I was saying they could be your new friends.

Yeah. That's doubtful.

Please don't be angry. Shall we chat?

I get that you're upset, Alice. I'm sorry I couldn't make tonight, but it wasn't my fault. Bombarding me with all those photos was pretty childish, don't you think? Look, it's late. I'm going to bed. Night.

I actually feel sick now. I need to fix this.

Can we please talk? xx

I wait for Seth to reply, but it doesn't look like he's seen my last message. The ticks next to it haven't turned blue yet. Or maybe he has seen it, but he's purposely not clicking on it.

'Here's the bill, Alice.' Daisy passes me the plate with the print-out on it.

'You're not allowed to use a calculator!' Janey calls out.

'In a minute,' I say, turning away and hunching over my phone. My heart hammers as I try calling Seth, but it goes straight to voicemail. I end the call and try again. Same thing – straight to voicemail.

'Seth, can you call me? I didn't mean anything bad. Fran thought it would be cute if I sent you photos of the night seeing as you couldn't make it, that's all. I'm sorry you misunderstood. I've missed you tonight. Please ring me back.' My voice catches on the last word. I end the call feeling devastated. I just want to talk to him so we can sort this out, but I get the feeling he won't be returning my call tonight.

Chapter Ten

Now

'You're joking, right?' I reply, knowing full well that my dad is not in a joking mood. I can't believe he's arranged this meeting without consulting me. It's not his place to do it.

'You wouldn't call Seth, so we had to intervene,' Dad replies. 'Far better to talk things through than pretend nothing's wrong.'

That's easy for my father to say. He isn't the one who has to do this. He isn't the one who feels as if his body is going into shock and he might be losing his mind. I really don't think I have it in me to face 'Seth' right now. What if he's dangerous?

'It's for the best, darling,' Mum says with worry in her eyes, like she doesn't actually believe it's for the best, but just wants to go along with Dad for a quiet life.

Why couldn't I have more understanding, gentle parents? Why are they so keen to keep pushing me into things they think I should be doing or feeling or thinking? I wish that for once they would just let me be. But explaining all that to them right now would take more energy than I have. My terror at seeing 'Seth' again is beginning to be replaced with a quiet fury.

'Fine,' I reply, through gritted teeth. Even though I feel sick at the thought, maybe this will be an opportunity to get the answers I'm looking for.

Dad gives a satisfied nod, ignoring my tone. 'We'll go downstairs and send him up. Now, Alice, when he gets here, be nice. Tell him about the scan and explain that everything happened because of a medical issue. Nothing to do with you changing your mind. I think that's the best way to make him understand.'

I nod. I have no intention of begging the man to forgive me or take me back. I'm more concerned with discovering what's going on. With finding out where the real Seth is or if there's something else at play here.

'Good luck. It'll be fine,' Mum says, kissing my cheek before they head across the hall to the front door.

Once they've gone, I let go of my fury for a second and savour the emptiness of the flat, clinging on to my remaining moment of peace, wishing it didn't have to be interrupted again. My brain is buzzing and my fingers and toes are tingling at the thought of my imminent visitor. I briefly consider not letting him in, but that would only delay our inevitable meeting and anger my father. I sigh, realising that I may as well get it over with.

A tap at the front door makes me jump. I appreciate that he didn't press the bell at least; its harsh ring would have been even worse for my nerves.

I glance in the hall mirror at the unruly black curls springing around my face, at my make-up-free skin. Mum was right – a bit of lip gloss and mascara might have prepared me better. I debate whether or not to change out of my sweats and do something to make myself more presentable, but I wouldn't know where to start so I don't bother. I breathe into my hand. At least my breath is fresh.

I stand before the front door trying to get my emotions under control, wondering who I'm going to see on the other side of the door – my Seth, or the stranger? Please God let it be my fiancé.

I turn the handle and pull open the door.

'Alice . . .'

My heart sinks and I honestly feel like crying.

This man is the same stranger from the church. Tall, dark-haired, dark eyes, broad-shouldered. He's handsome by anyone's standards, in jeans and a short-sleeved grey shirt. But I'm not attracted to him. In fact, I feel uneasy and odd around this man. Not afraid, exactly. More like I just want him to leave.

'Hello,' I say, biting my lower lip and looking down at the carpet. The urge to close the door in his face is strong, but instead I say, 'Come in.'

He follows me back along the hall to the living room where I gesture to the sofa. He picks the same spot where my father was sitting moments ago. I choose to sit on the dining chair furthest away from him, trying to keep my panic at bay.

I don't know what to say, and, by the looks of it, neither does he. I'm embarrassed and uncomfortable at this whole situation and I could kill my father for putting me in this position before I feel emotionally ready to deal with it.

'Well, this isn't awkward,' he says, raising an eyebrow. He's well-spoken, his voice deep and soft, but it doesn't trigger any kind of recognition in me. I think he wants me to respond, but I don't know what to say. He sighs. 'What happened at the church, Alice? Everyone's been saying you didn't recognise me. I don't even understand what that means.'

I clear my throat, but it feels tight and scratchy. I massage it with my fingers.

'Are you going to tell me what's going on?' he asks. 'Have you changed your mind about getting married? You know you can talk to me, right? I'm really worried about you. About *us*.'

I force myself to look at him, trying to work out if it's really Seth, and if it is, why I don't recognise him. His voice, his mannerisms, everything feels alien. If what the doctor says is right and I might have some sort of face blindness, then I guess I owe him an explanation. But despite the possibility that it's true, I don't really believe it. It's not just his face I don't recognise; it's his whole persona. There's just something that's off about him.

'I cancelled the honeymoon,' he says.

'Sorry,' I croak.

'What are you actually sorry about?' he asks, an edge creeping into his voice. 'Are you sorry about the honeymoon? The wedding? Us? *What?* I need some kind of explanation, Alice. You owe me that, at least.'

I rub my upper arms, wishing I could be anywhere else than here with him. This fake Seth. I don't understand the disconnect between what I'm seeing and what everyone else believes. It makes no sense. Am I losing my mind? Could I be wrong? Could this actually be the real Seth? I force myself to look at him again and recoil as his eyes bore into mine. No. I absolutely 100 per cent do not know this man.

'I . . . I was excited about the wedding. I wanted to marry Seth . . . *you*. But when I saw you in the church, I didn't recognise you. You honestly look like a stranger to me.'

'You didn't recognise my face?'

I nod.

'Have you heard of prosopagnosia?' he asks.

'It's what my GP thought I might have. But she's doubtful because it's only you and your parents that I don't recognise.'

'Do you still believe I might not be Seth?' he asks.

I shrug. Inside, I feel like I should be shouting at this imposter, asking him who he is and what he's done with Seth. But I feel paralysed. Terrified.

'So that means you're still unsure.' He takes out his phone. 'Why don't you come and look at these photos.'

I hesitate, unwilling to get that close to him.

He's scrolling through his phone, waiting for me to come over.

I take a breath and walk across the living room, my brain swimming, legs shaky, like I'm approaching a cliff edge with a sheer drop. As I draw nearer to him, a strong sweet smell invades my nostrils and makes me gag, but I manage to ignore it and sit on the sofa, leaving a couple of handspans between us.

He looks across at me and I press a hand to my chest trying to calm my breathing. 'Here.' He hands me his phone.

I take it and edge away slightly. The photo he shows me is of the two of us out in a bar in London. I remember the night very well as it was my first trip there to see him, just one week after we first met. He has his arm around me and our heads are tilted together. I was glowing, happy, almost in love by that point. But the man in the photo is the same stranger sitting next to me on the sofa. It isn't *my* Seth. It's the weirdest feeling ever to see this familiar memory overlaid with the image of someone else. It makes me want to cry.

He leans across and swipes the screen. The next photo is of us in the garden of Seth's parents' holiday home in Rockford, a small hamlet just outside Ringwood. Again, the man who should be Seth, isn't my Seth. Brook Cottage was his parents' wedding gift to us. We were due to move in after we were married. But, of course, that's not going to happen now. All our plans have disappeared down the drain like dirty dishwater.

'Do you remember these photos?' he asks, swiping again to show more images of us; these ones are from our holiday in Portugal earlier this year.

'I remember the photos, but not you,' I reply quietly. The first thought that comes into my mind is that he could have

Photoshopped them. I stare at the images trying to see if I can spot whether they might be fake, but I can't see anything obvious, although that doesn't mean anything. He could have paid a professional to alter them. But why would he do that? What would be the point?

I realise that the easiest way to check the photos' validity would be to look at the photos on my own phone. In fact, why the hell haven't I done that already? Probably because I've been wandering around in some kind of dazed shock for the past three days. Now that I've had the idea, I'm desperate to check my phone album, but I don't want to do it while he's still here.

He retrieves his mobile and we resume our awkward silence for a moment. I don't want to offer him a drink because that will only prolong his visit.

'So,' I say without actually looking at him, 'my GP has referred me for a brain scan later this week.'

'That makes sense,' he replies. 'Hopefully they'll find out what's wrong and we can get our lives back.'

'Mm,' I reply noncommittally. 'But . . . in the meantime, I think it's probably best if we don't see one another. Not until after I get the results.'

'Really?' He frowns and gets to his feet. 'Alice, do you honestly not know me?'

'No. I'm afraid I don't. I'm sorry.'

He shakes his head and runs a hand through his hair. 'Seeing as the honeymoon's off, I'm staying at Brook Cottage. I don't start my new job at Southampton until next month, so I thought we could spend time together. Work out what's happening here. I thought it would be a good idea for us to spend *more* time together, not less. In case something jogs your memory. I mean, how are we supposed to get through this if you don't even want to see me?'

I clench my fists. 'It's not that I don't want to, it's just that it feels too weird.' I stand and start pacing the lounge. 'I can't deal with it. With *you*.' I stop and turn, making myself look him in the eye. 'I'm sorry if that sounds harsh.' But I'm not sorry at all, and I don't understand why I'm being so polite to this man.

'So, what? You want me to leave?' His jaw muscles flex and his eyes harden.

'I'm sorry, but yes, I do.'

He looks taken aback. Gutted. He blinks. 'Fine.' He starts towards the door and then stops and turns around. 'I don't know what's happening here, Alice, but I want you to know that I love you. I still want to spend the rest of my life with you even if you don't. I really hope this is fixable. That this isn't some . . . I don't know . . . some elaborate plan to get out of marrying me?'

I shake my head. 'It's not any kind of plan. Believe me, this is the last thing I wanted.'

'Good.' He takes a step towards me but I instinctively cringe backwards. He stops where he is and throws his hands up in despair. 'Okay, I'll leave. But please don't shut me out, Alice. You can call me any time, and don't ignore my messages, okay?'

'Okay,' I reply, unsure whether I'll be able to keep my word on that.

He pauses for a moment and stares at me, trying to convey something with his eyes. But his gaze leaves me cold. He turns and leaves the apartment.

As soon as the front door closes, my legs turn to jelly and I sink down on to the sofa, trembling. This whole situation is so screwed up. I feel as though I've stepped into an alternative reality.

My phone! I need to check my photos. I reach forward to snatch it up off the coffee table, the screen still a maze of cracks from when I dropped it on my wedding day. There are several more messages and missed calls from friends and family, but I ignore them all, going straight to my photo album. Please let my photos show the real Seth. Let this not be down to some terrifying brain condition or breakdown. I need to see a photo of my actual fiancé. An image of the man I love.

I scroll through my photos with trembling fingers, looking for the ones of me and Seth. There are none from the past few months, which is strange because I'm sure I took a few selfies of us when we were looking round the wedding venue. I scroll back further, but can't seem to find any photographs of us at all. Maybe I'm going too fast. I slow down my search and glance at every single image individually. After several minutes of painstakingly trawling through, I realise there are none of me and Seth. Not one. I'm so confused.

Where on earth have they gone?

Chapter Eleven

As I leave the flat, my nerves are jangling. Why is it so hot out here? This is England, for goodness' sake, not the South of France. The sun is beating down. There's no shade at all. I put a hand to the top of my head – boiling. I wish I'd worn a hat. I'd better not get sunstroke.

I stop walking for a moment, place my hands on my hips and try to breathe. Try to gather my thoughts and keep up the positivity I've had all week. There's no reason to lose hope now. All I need to do is get a better handle on what's going on. I'm pretty certain the wedding's still off, but I need to make sure it stays cancelled for good or this whole thing will have been for nothing.

And I absolutely can't have that.

Not after everything I've been through.

Chapter Twelve

THEN

I'm normally one of those annoyingly chipper people who loves a Monday morning. Keen to get the day going, fired up by the challenges ahead.

Not today though.

It's only nine thirty and I'm sitting at my desk having achieved precisely nothing while already contemplating my third coffee of the day.

It took my whole weekend in London to get Seth to forgive me. For him to believe that I truly didn't mean anything by sending him that photo of Laurence and Martin kissing me on the cheek. I don't know what I'd been thinking. Actually, I think the point is I wasn't thinking. I was drunk. I immediately realised how insensitive I'd been and I apologised. But Seth didn't want to accept my apology straightaway.

He asked what if it had been the other way around. Told me to imagine if I hadn't been able to make it to London to see him and he'd then sent me a photo of two girls kissing him. When he put it like that, I was mortified. Still, I spent two days grovelling to a very moody fiancé before he finally forgave me. By then, it was Sunday evening, and time to get in the car and drive home. Consequently, today I'm exhausted.

'Everything all right, Alice?' Paul asks as he walks past my desk, his grey suit pristine. It's not a concerned question, more an irritated one. He's caught me zoning out.

'Yes, fine, thanks, Paul. Just working out which clients' accounts take priority today.'

'Hm, okay.'

My mobile buzzes on my desk and I glance at the screen. Paul follows my gaze and I'm embarrassed to see the florist's details flash up.

'Wedding plans?' Paul asks with a smile, trying to be nice. But I've already noticed his jaw tightening and the vein above his left eyebrow beginning to throb.

'Oh, no, I haven't started planning yet,' I lie. 'This is hopefully a possible new client.'

Paul looks at me over the top of his glasses and I squirm internally. I'm so stupid. It's obviously a call to do with my wedding. Why didn't I just admit it? I blame my ill-judged response on a lack of caffeine.

'Alice, would you mind taking a look at this payroll for Barker and Sons?'

I look up to see Miriam beckoning me over with a sly wink to let me know she's saving me from my boss's scrutiny.

I glance back at Paul. 'I'd better . . .' I gesture to Miriam.

'Yes, yes, of course.' He walks back to his desk where Charlotte's hovering with a cup of brown-nose coffee for him, her complicated plait draped over one shoulder like a giant shiny slug.

My hackles rise as I overhear her mention my name along with the words 'away with the fairies'. Bloody Charlotte never misses any opportunity to twist the knife. I realise it's probably just her insecurity, but that doesn't make it easier to bear.

The morning drags on after that. Paul is right to be irritated, but my vagueness is totally out of character, so I do think he could cut me some slack. No one's perfect all the time.

I decide to take an early lunch so I can get some fresh air and give myself a talking to. Get my productivity levels back on track. I normally eat at my desk, but I need to get out of the office today. I close my laptop, grab my bag and coat and head for the door.

'Want some company?' Miriam asks. 'No worries if not.'

'Actually, yes,' I reply. 'That would be lovely.'

We battle the icy rain and head to Bites & Beans, our favourite relaxed lunch spot situated a few doors down from the office. It's packed, as usual, but my friend Danica's younger sister Tabitha works here and she manages to magic two spare chairs and a patio table out of the back room for us. Within five minutes, Miriam and I are brought two piping hot bowls of spicy parsnip soup and a couple of sourdough rolls. Aside from the great food, part of this place's appeal is the fast service – essential for the lunchtime crowd.

Miriam picks up her spoon. 'How was your weekend with Seth?'

'Don't ask,' I reply.

'Oh dear. Sounds bad.' She blows on her soup and takes a huge mouthful. 'Mm, so good. I'm starving.'

'We had a bit of a falling out over this whole photo debacle, but it's all sorted now.' I skirt over the details, not wanting to rehash it again.

'Glad to hear it's sorted,' she replies. 'It's hard doing the long-distance thing. Bet you'll be relieved when he finally moves down here.'

'Tell me about it,' I answer with feeling. 'But anyway, how was your weekend?'

'Blissful,' she replies, closing her eyes with a smile.

'Ooh, now I'm intrigued.' I lean forward, waiting for her to elaborate. 'Is there a new woman in your life you haven't told me about?'

She snaps open her eyes. 'Nothing as exciting as that. Just a lazy couple of days, eating, reading, bingeing Netflix and Prime.'

'Okay, that does sound blissful.'

'It really was.'

'Oh, and thanks for rescuing me earlier,' I say. 'Paul's been off with me ever since I announced my engagement.'

'Maybe it's because he lurrrves you and you've broken his heart.' She laughs her head off at this.

I give Miriam a mock glare. 'Very funny, but absolutely not. If he loves anyone it's suck-up Charlotte with her holier-than-thou attitude *and designer suits. And, sorry, but I'm pretty sure she must get up at four a.m. every morning to style her hair. There's no way that mermaid plait took less than two hours to construct.'*

'Don't let her get to you,' she replies.

'I wouldn't normally, but why can't she just be nice, instead of bad-mouthing me to Paul all the time. It's making me crazy. Wow, this soup's good.'

'I know, right.' Miriam tears off a chunk of sourdough and dunks it into her bowl.

'Actually,' I say, making a snap decision, 'there's something I wanted to ask you . . .'

Miriam's dark eyes widen with interest as she finishes chewing. 'Now it's my turn to be intrigued.'

I banish Charlotte and Paul from my head and give my friend a smile. 'Do you think you might like to be one of my bridesmaids?'

Her mouth drops open and then she beams. 'Really? I've never been a bridesmaid before!'

'And I promise I won't make you wear anything horrible. No flouncy, frumpy lacy stuff.'

'I'd love to. Thank you, Alice.' Miriam's eyes glisten and I'm thrilled she's so touched.

'Daisy and Francesca have also said yes to being bridesmaids, and my sister will be maid of honour. So she'll basically be the one bossing all of you around.'

'I'd like to see her try,' Miriam replies with a grin, folding her arms across her chest.

I think back to my conversation with Daisy last week. I knew she'd be disappointed when I didn't ask her to be my maid of honour, but I couldn't snub Elizabeth. My sister's already a bit sniffy with me about something or other. Not sure what. I'm going to have to get to the bottom of that situation. I don't understand why so many of my friends and family are being difficult right now. Is there something about weddings that turns people into a nightmare? I thought I was supposed to be the bridezilla, not everyone else.

'You okay?' Miriam asks, noticing my sudden frown.

'Yeah, just family dramas on my mind.'

'Oh, that sucks.' Miriam throws me a sympathetic look. 'Well, don't stress about Paul or Charlotte. You're great at your job, so you've nothing to worry about there. Paul wants a successful business and you're better with the clients than Miss Hairdo so you'll always be the favourite.'

'Thanks. I just want to be made a partner, like he promised when I joined. Otherwise, why am I breaking my back, working all the hours?'

'You definitely put the hours in,' Miriam agrees. 'Trouble is, so does Charlotte – only she gets half as much accomplished in the same amount of time.'

I nod. 'I wouldn't mind, only she's always stirring things. Dropping snide comments into Paul's ear. It's really frustrating.' I give a little growl.

'Maybe you should call her out on it?' Miriam says.

I baulk at the thought of causing a scene. 'Maybe. I just wish he'd realise what she's up to, without someone else having to say something.'

'Oh, he won't realise. He needs to be hit over the head with the truth to see it.' Miriam mops up the last of the soup with her roll, then wipes her generous mouth with a napkin.

I'm still only halfway through my lunch, but I check the time and note that we should probably be getting back. Too much talking, not enough eating. I dismiss the idea of bad-mouthing Charlotte to Paul. No. I think the best way to deal with Charlotte is to outshine her. I need to get back to the office and work my arse off.

Momentarily buoyed up by my plan of action for the afternoon, I shrug on my coat and we head back. But despite my solution for dealing with my tricky work colleague, the closer we get to the office, the quicker my optimism deflates – working my arse off is my default behaviour and it doesn't seem to be getting me anywhere. In fact, the harder I work, the less recognition I seem to get.

Chapter Thirteen

Now

It's one of those summer evenings when the air is warm on your skin and there's no hint of a chill. It's seven thirty on a Friday so Ringwood is busy with people heading out for dinner and drinks. I suppose I'm one of them, but I feel set apart from everyone. Like I'm watching from the fringes. Chatter and light spills out from pubs and bars along with the scent of flowers from hanging baskets and wafts of garlicky food, coffee, and alcohol. It all floats by as I move towards my destination. My trainers are silent on the pavement as I walk through town like a spectre. Invisible.

On the opposite side of the street, a group of women exit a taxi. They're loud. Happy. Excited. I realise it's a hen night. The bride-to-be wears a cheap veil. An L-plate hangs around her neck. I walk faster so I don't have to look at them or think about my own hen weekend. My failed wedding. It's too depressing a thought.

Attempting to let my mind go blank, my gaze snags on a figure coming towards me. A man in green cargos and a black T-shirt. He's looking down at the pavement as he walks. His outline feels familiar, but I can't place him. Until he looks up and catches my eye.

I freeze.

He walks past and I open my mouth to say something, but nothing comes out. I feel winded, like I've been punched in the chest.

Was it him?

No. Surely not.

I pivot around to see if it's true or if my eyes were playing tricks on me, but I can't spot him any more. He's disappeared. I blink and take a step in the direction he went, but I catch what I'm doing and stop. I give myself a shake. I'm being stupid. Of course it wasn't him. It's dark, I'm tired, and I haven't seen my ex-boyfriend, Damian, for years.

My mind isn't exactly the most reliable at the moment. Not after everything that's happened with Seth. I attempt to shrug off my momentary fears. I have enough to worry about without imagining unwelcome ghosts from my past.

As I draw closer to my destination, I cast a few glances around the vicinity, just to make sure he's gone. Thankfully, the man – whoever he was – is no longer in sight. I pause outside Hibiscus, my favourite Mexican restaurant, before pushing open the door. Even its cheery bright-blue and burnt-orange walls aren't able to completely banish my jitters.

I spot Daisy straight away sitting at our usual table in the window, wearing a flowery maxi-dress and gold hoop earrings, her blonde hair tumbling over her shoulders in loose waves. I feel crumpled and worn by comparison in faded jeans and a plain black T-shirt – the first items of clothing I grabbed from the wardrobe earlier today – having come straight to the restaurant after my appointment with the neuropsychologist.

Daisy takes a sip of beer and gives me a wave. 'Hey, how have you been?' she asks tentatively as I come over. I grip the back of the chair opposite her, trying to get my breathing under control. To slow my heartbeat and shake off the shock that's still trying to take hold.

'Is everything okay?' she asks, her forehead creasing.

'Umm . . .' I swallow. I'm on the verge of telling her that I think I just saw Damian.

'Have you sorted things out with Seth yet?' Daisy asks, interrupting my train of thought.

At her mention of Seth, I decide not to bring up Damian, unwilling to let my mind linger on that distressing subject. Instead, I answer her question. 'Not yet, no.'

'Oh, *Alice.*' She shoots me a sympathetic look and then gestures to the glasses and bottles on the table. 'I got us some beers and tequila shots. In case you need them.'

'I definitely do,' I reply, finally sitting down heavily, exhaustion cloaking me.

We tip our shots straight back and I welcome the fiery burn in my throat followed by the slow spread of numbing alcohol into my bloodstream.

'That's better,' I say, shaking my head a few times while my brain adjusts to the tequila.

Daisy's been staying at Martin's this week, so this is the first time I've talked to her properly since the weekend. She said she was giving me space, but I think she left because she felt awkward around me. To be fair to Daisy, I'd been shutting myself away in my room, not talking, so there wasn't really anything she could do to help.

'Thanks for dragging me out,' I say.

'I wasn't sure you'd come, but I couldn't have you moping around on a Friday night, could I?'

I think back to this time last week – the evening before my wedding day. It seems like a lifetime ago. It doesn't even feel like that excited bride-to-be was me. There's no point in torturing myself thinking about it. That was then and this is now. My current reality is not what I was expecting, but I'm going to have to deal with it or fix it. Somehow. I miss my Seth. I want him back.

We sit sipping our beers for a moment, unsure what to say next. I never have awkward silences with Daisy, so this feels strange. I feel like it's up to me to make the effort.

'I went to see a clinical neuropsychologist this afternoon,' I say.

'Wow. Really?' Daisy's eyes widen. 'That's . . . good, right? So what happened? Did it go okay?'

I pull a face and waggle my hand from side to side. 'Yes and no.'

'What do you mean?'

'Well, it was all a bit vague.'

'Vague? How? Oh, I've already ordered your usual – chilli-cheese veggie fajitas, right?' She takes a swig of beer.

'Great, thanks.' I shift in my seat, trying to get comfortable. 'Well the doctor seemed really nice. She did a series of tests to see if I'm suffering from face blindness.'

'Oh.' Daisy sets her beer bottle back down. 'I've heard of that. Is that what she thinks you have?' Her eyes fill with concern. 'Is that why you couldn't recognise Seth?'

'My GP thought I might have it so she referred me to see this neuropsychologist.'

'And?' Daisy leans forward, her eyes widening further.

I wish she didn't seem so eager to get all the gory details. I feel as though I'm in some lurid reality TV show where everyone can't wait to watch the next instalment. But this is my *life* that's falling apart. Seeing Daisy so interested makes me realise that everyone must be talking about me. I can just imagine the Ringwood rumour mill in action. Everyone gossiping and speculating about what really happened. Have I had a mental breakdown? Did I catch Seth cheating? Have I met someone else? And it's not like anyone would be doing it maliciously (apart from maybe Charlotte) but they would still get an illicit thrill from talking about it.

I shouldn't let it worry me. After all, people's opinions aren't going to ruin things further or make things better. It's simply throwaway gossip. But the thought of them doing it is yet another anxiety on top of everything else. I've been ignoring all the messages I've received this week because I can't face the prying and pitying. And also because if I don't know what's going on, then what am I even supposed to tell people?

As well as all the messages from friends, my parents also won't stop calling. I've sent them a few texts keeping them up to date with my appointments, but I don't have the energy to face them again. Not after the stunt they pulled last time, ambushing me by bringing 'Seth' over to the flat.

'You don't have to talk about it, if you don't want to,' Daisy adds, sensing my reticence.

'No, it's fine,' I lie. 'The neuropsychologist is pretty sure I don't have face blindness.'

'Really?' Daisy inhales. 'Well that's good news, isn't it?'

'I don't know. Maybe. But if it's not that, then what is it? They're still going to do a brain scan to be on the safe side.'

'Right. When's that?'

'Next week.' The thought of it makes my whole body tense up. I reach for my bottle of Corona and take a swig. Despite the doctor feeling confident that I don't have prosopagnosia, I still feel really wobbly about everything.

'It'll be okay, Alice. I'm sure they'll get to the bottom of things.'

'Hope so,' I reply. The psychologist also recommended that I see a colleague of hers who she said might be better placed to help me, but the thought of talking about it all with another unfamiliar doctor makes me want to curl up and sleep for a hundred years.

A young waiter comes over with our order, the plates piled high with colourful food, but, despite an empty stomach, my appetite has almost disappeared.

'One chilli-cheese fajita with roasted veggies and one sweet-potato and feta taquito with a side of fries and a green salad.' The waiter sets the plates down in front of us. 'Can I get you any more drinks?'

'This looks great,' Daisy replies. 'Two more Coronas please.'

We thank the waiter who nods and leaves.

'You okay, Alice? You look exhausted.'

'Probably because I am,' I reply. My head feels tight where I scraped my hair back into a bun earlier. I reach up and twist off my elastic hair tie, freeing my curls and easing the tension in my head a little. I must look an absolute sight, but I honestly don't care. 'Anyway, enough about me,' I say, nibbling on a French fry. 'How are things with you and Martin?'

Daisy exhales noisily. 'Yeah, fine.' She starts cutting into her crispy taquitos.

'Doesn't sound like it.' I give her an enquiring look.

'No, it's just the usual. He's studying, I'm working, his flat-mates are annoying, blah, blah, blah. But it will be fine. We're still madly in love with each other so it'll all be worth it in the end.' Her face reddens as she realises she might have been tactless.

I skip over her embarrassment. 'Sorry I wrecked your plans for him to move into the flat with you. I'll try to find a new place soon, I promise.'

'No rush,' she says, but I can tell she doesn't mean it.

'Look, I don't mind if he wants to move in with you now. I'm in my room most of the time anyway.'

'Are you sure?' Daisy asks, hope lighting her eyes.

'Of course,' I reply. But the thought of sharing the flat with a loved-up couple fills me with dread and I have to gulp down the urge to sob. Despite all this concern from friends and family, I still feel like I'm on my own. Everyone thinks I'm having some kind of breakdown and perhaps they're right, but I wish there was someone I could talk to who made me feel safe. Or at least heard.

73

'How's your food?' Daisy asks, unaware of the turmoil in my head. 'Mine's amazing. Want to try some?'

'No thanks. Mine's good.' I place the tiniest forkful of fajita into my mouth. But it tastes of nothing. Like I'm chewing polystyrene. As I take a swig of beer to wash it down, I remember the main reason I agreed to step out of my misery pit and come out with my friend this evening. 'Daisy . . .'

'Hmm?' She looks across at me, still rapturously chewing.

'Do you have any photos on your phone of me and Seth together?' My heart rate increases as I wait for her reply.

'Photos of you and Seth?' Her forehead creases. 'I didn't get a chance to take any at the wedding . . . Oh. Sorry.' Her face reddens. 'Didn't mean to bring that up.'

'It's fine. But no, not at the wedding. Before that. Photos of me and . . .' I almost say, *the real Seth*, but I don't want Daisy to think I'm losing my mind any more than she already does so I amend my sentence. 'Photos of me and Seth from before the wedding.'

'Um I think you might have sent me a few on WhatsApp, but they're probably the same ones you posted on Instagram and Facebook.'

'They're not there any more,' I reply.

'You took them down?' she queries.

'Um, well that's the thing. I didn't take them down, but all my photos of him are gone.'

She stops chewing for a moment. 'Gone?'

'Yeah. I looked for them in my phone and they're not there any more. So I checked social media, but those have all disappeared too.'

She gives me a doubtful glance. 'How can they have disappeared?'

'I don't know,' I reply, choking back a sudden wave of nausea.

'You sure you didn't delete them?' she asks. 'Maybe you just don't remember.'

'I think I'd remember deleting pictures of me and Seth!'

Daisy's lips clamp together.

'Sorry, didn't mean to snap,' I reply, cursing myself for taking my distress out on my friend.

'It's fine.' She waves away my apology.

'Seth's not on social media at all,' I continue, 'except Twitter, but he never tweets anything and his profile pic is the NHS rainbow thing.' I try to slow my breathing. Every time I talk about or think about Seth, I feel sick and dizzy, like I'm not even here.

'Hang on, let me have a look.' Daisy picks up her phone and starts scrolling. Within seconds, she passes it across to me. 'There.'

I take the phone with trembling fingers. Daisy notices, but quickly covers her shock at my nervous state with a forced smile. I hungrily transfer my gaze to the screen, willing it to be a photo of me and my real fiancé.

'I think that was the first time you went up to London to meet him,' Daisy says. 'You sent me that photo because you wanted to show me how hot he was.' She grins.

It's a photo of him on his own, sitting on a blanket in Regent's Park, giving me a sardonic smile. I remember taking the photo. But this image is of the strange new Seth, not *my* Seth. How is this possible? My head swims and I get up from my seat. 'Back in a minute,' I mumble before rushing to the back of the restaurant where I barge into the loo, fumble with the door lock and throw up down the toilet.

It's mainly tequila and beer. I haven't eaten any proper food since breakfast which, granted, was at around 1 p.m. when I had a couple of slices of toast and a Snickers bar.

I rinse my mouth with tap water and sit on the lid of the toilet, trying to get the whirl of thoughts in my head to slow down. Everything is jumbled. Everything is strange. As though I've stepped into an alternate universe where nothing makes sense.

I glance up at a light tapping on the door.

'Alice? It's Daisy. You okay in there?'

I inhale and get to my feet. 'Yep, fine. Be out in a minute.' My voice sounds strange to my ears. I fight the urge to break down into a heaving, sobbing mess. Instead, I splash my face with water and dab it dry with a paper towel that smells of stale chemicals.

Back out in the restaurant, I'm almost shocked by the normality of the place – the salsa music, the chatter, laughter, clink of cutlery, the warmth and buzz of everyone enjoying themselves on a Friday night. I try to cling to that normality. To let it anchor me and keep me from being pulled under again.

'Are you ill?' Daisy asks. 'Is your food not good?'

'I think it's just the alcohol on an empty stomach,' I reply with a fake laugh. 'I haven't been eating much this week.'

She reaches over and squeezes my hand as I sit back down.

I push my full plate away, unable to bear even looking at the food.

'Alice, I'm worried about you. Are you sure you're okay?'

Annoyingly, a tear has slid down my cheek. I swipe it away with the side of my forefinger. 'No, not really.'

'Was it the photo that upset you?' she asks.

I nod.

'Seeing a picture of Seth? Was it . . . ? I mean . . .'

I answer her unasked question. 'The man in that photo you showed me was the same man at the church last week. I don't know him, Daisy. It's not Seth.'

Her eyes widen and I see her brain working. Daisy's being kind and helpful, and saying all the right things, but I know what she's like. Part of her is loving the drama. I can't help feeling bitter and annoyed that she wants all the details. But it's not her fault. I'm also annoyed at myself for feeling this way. For being upset with

Daisy for simply wanting to know what's going on with me. She's my friend. Of course she's interested and wants to help. I have to get over this fear of talking about it. I need to trust my friends and family. Let them know what's going on in my mind instead of keeping all my fears bottled up.

'I . . . I was wondering if I should go to London. See if Seth's there. In his flat. Or if anyone at work knows where he might be.'

Daisy can't keep the doubtful expression off her face. She bites her lip. 'Are you sure that's a good idea?'

'No. I'm not sure of anything. But it's got to be worth a shot, hasn't it? Maybe he's in his flat. In trouble, or in danger, or . . . I don't know.' I slump in my seat.

Daisy reaches over and places her hand over mine. 'If you think that might help, then . . . maybe you should go. Put your mind at rest.' Her words are encouraging, but her expression is still sceptical.

'I honestly think I might be losing it,' I whisper.

'Don't be daft. Course you're not. You've just had a traumatic experience and it might take a while for things to get back to normal. Maybe you should talk to someone about it. Another psychologist or someone?'

I shrug. 'Maybe.' I don't want to go to another psychologist, but I can't think what else to do. Perhaps that really is my best option.

'I know!' Daisy fixes me with a triumphant look.

'What?' I'm not optimistic about whatever it is she's excited about.

'Why don't you talk to Laurence?'

'*Our* Laurence?'

'Yeah, why not? He's a counsellor, and he knows you. He'd be perfect.'

'Would he be allowed to work with a friend?'

77

'I don't know, but if you asked him I'm sure he wouldn't say no. If he did turn you down, I'd have to have a serious word with the boy. Why don't I call him now? Set up a time for this weekend.'

My first instinct is to say no. I mean, it's *Laurence*. It would be weird to spill my guts to a friend in his professional capacity rather than as mates having a heart-to-heart. But I'm so lost and scared right now that I can't think of any better alternative.

'Okay,' I reply. 'Do it.'

Chapter Fourteen

THEN

'Table for six under the name Porter,' Dad says to the dark-suited greeter at the nineteenth-century Manor House. Nestled in the forest on the outskirts of Ringwood, this fancy hotel and restaurant used to be an abandoned, fenced-off haunted house of a place, until a swanky hotel chain bought it up a few years ago and restored it to its former glory with the addition of a Michelin-starred chef.

It's Graham and my sister's one-year wedding anniversary so we've come out for a celebratory dinner – our parents' treat. The only problem is that I can't get hold of Seth. He should be arriving here any minute but I'm already getting déjà vu. I have a sick feeling in my stomach that something is going to prevent him from showing up, same as last time at our impromptu engagement party.

I smile distractedly as the rest of my family oohs and aahs at the beautiful hotel foyer decor. It's been decked out for Christmas with fresh garlands of fir, holly and ivy, bowls of winter flowers, white twinkling lights, and a twenty-foot Christmas tree reaching up to the stained-glass domed ceiling. But all that is just a backdrop to my growing apprehension. I check my phone again, but there are no messages. Which is a good thing. At least Seth hasn't cancelled, so this must mean he's on his way.

We're shown to a circular table set into a deep bay window that looks out over a floodlit ornamental garden. I let everyone else choose where to sit before taking a seat next to my sister. The chair to my right is conspicuously vacant. Next to Seth's empty chair is Dad, then Mum, then Graham. Thankfully, I have a bird's-eye view of the restaurant entrance, so I'll be able to spot Seth as soon as he arrives.

'Where's this fiancé of yours?' Dad asks bluntly. Loud enough to make the foursome at the next table turn to glance over at us briefly, curious.

'On his way,' I reply with a tight smile, hoping that's truly the case. 'You know what the traffic's like on Fridays.'

'Hmm,' Dad replies, turning his attention to our server, a gorgeous twenty-something woman with red hair.

'Hi, I'm Sienna. Would you like to see the wine list?'

'We're celebrating,' Dad replies. 'We'll need champagne.'

'Lovely,' she replies with a smile. 'What's the occasion?'

'Our wedding anniversary,' Elizabeth says, grinning at Graham.

'Our first year of marriage,' Graham adds, kissing my sister on the cheek.

Sienna puts a hand over her heart. 'Aw, congratulations. A bottle of the Veuve Clicquot?'

'Lovely,' Elizabeth replies.

'Are we still waiting for one of your guests?' Sienna asks, pointing to the empty chair. 'Or shall I clear away this place setting?'

'He should be here any minute,' I reply.

She gives me a cool nod. 'Great, I'll get that champagne for the table.' She leaves and I try to relax my shoulders and enjoy myself. We're here for my sister and Graham, not for me.

'Can't believe it's been a year,' I say. 'It was such a gorgeous wedding day with that dusting of snow when you left the church.'

'It really was,' Elizabeth replies dreamily before turning to look at me. 'That will be you soon, Alice. Are you going to book the church at Ellingham?'

'Definitely. But I was wondering about maybe having the reception here. Of course, I want to see what Seth thinks first.'

'Oh, yes,' Mum says. 'A reception here would be lovely.'

'You could probably get married here too,' Elizabeth says. 'Have it all in the one place.'

'No, just the reception. I really want the church for the service. But lunch and a party here afterwards would be amazing.'

Dad grunts and I see Mum bat his arm to be quiet. I can read him like a book. Dad will be wondering about the cost.

'Just to let you know,' I say, aiming my words in my parents' general direction without any actual eye contact, 'Seth and I would like to chip in for our wedding. His mum and dad want to put something towards it too.'

'No, no,' Dad replies. 'We did your sister's, we'll do yours too.'

I take a breath and try to think calming thoughts. How does my father always manage to make me feel so guilty? 'Okay, well, thanks so much. That would be incredible.' I shift in my seat. The only problem with my parents paying for the wedding is that Seth and I will have to rein in what we want. I'm not too concerned with having a lavish wedding, but I know for a fact that Seth and his parents want to splash out on a big event. I check my phone again. Still no message.

Our waitress returns with a bottle of Veuve and six champagne glasses. She pours one for each of us, and I give my sister a happy glance. But I can't help eyeing Seth's empty glass, then throwing another hopeful look at the entrance.

Still no sign of him.

I press a hand to my abdomen, trying to quell the sloshing mix of disappointment, anger and anxiety. But it doesn't work. I don't think he's coming.

'Are we ready to order?' Sienna asks brightly.

I haven't even picked up my menu yet. I fumble for it and slide my gaze down the page, the words blurring slightly.

'I'll have the Portland crab to start and the duck to follow,' Dad announces.

'Shouldn't we wait for Alice's fiancé?' Mum asks tentatively.

I shoot her a grateful smile.

'I'm pretty hungry,' Graham says.

'Me too,' chimes in Elizabeth.

'No, of course,' I reply. 'Let's order.'

Sienna gives me a clenched-teeth smile like she's sharing an awkward moment. But I pretend not to notice.

'The spinach gnocchi please,' I say, picking the first thing I see on the menu.

'Any starter?' Sienna prompts.

'Oh, just a salad or something.'

Elizabeth frowns at me. 'Don't sound too enthusiastic, Alice.'

'Sorry.' I blink rapidly and try to focus. 'I just meant there's so much choice. It all looks so good. Umm . . .' I frantically scan the menu. 'The asparagus. I'll have the asparagus to start.'

'Do you think your fiancé's actually coming?' Graham asks. 'Only it doesn't feel like we can really relax until he gets here.' He whispers something to Elizabeth who hisses something back at him.

I take a breath and exhale shakily while Mum gives her order. Then we all wait while Graham and Elizabeth finish their whispered conversation that's obviously about me and Seth, but I'm not sure exactly what it is they're saying. They both order in polite, clipped tones while I wish I could hide under the table.

Oblivious to the abruptly strained atmosphere, Dad is now asking our waitress about the wines. Mum is sipping her champagne while glancing anxiously from me to Elizabeth and back again.

'Back in a minute,' I mutter, lurching to my feet and leaving the table. I head straight for the exit in search of the loos. After a few wrong turns, I spot the door and let myself into the plush marble bathroom *where I allow myself to breathe. Then I take out my phone and call Seth. It rings once before going to voicemail.*

'Hi, Seth, it's me. Just checking you're almost here. We're at the restaurant. I texted you the details. Let me know if you've been held up. Hope everything's okay. Love you.'

I look at my reflection in the long mirror above the sinks. I went to the salon after work today so my hair looks good – my dark curls thick and glossy, my eyebrows freshly shaped. I jump as the phone shrills in my hand.

Thank goodness. It's Seth.

'Hey,' I say, trying to be laid-back and non-critical.

'Alice! I'm so sorry. I've been stuck in a meeting.'

'But you're almost here, right?'

An older woman comes through the door, gives me a nod and goes into one of the stalls.

'No,' Seth replies. 'That's the thing. I literally just got out of the meeting.'

'What?' My heart shrinks and a sudden lethargy blankets my body.

'I know, I know, it's your sister's anniversary bash. You'll have to celebrate without me, I'm afraid. No way will I make it in time.'

'Couldn't you have messaged earlier? Let me know you couldn't make it.'

'I would have if I could, but it was an important meeting. I was stuck in there for over two and a half hours and couldn't get a message out. I'll make it up to you. Promise.'

'Okay, we'll talk about it later.' I don't have the time or energy to get mad with Seth right now. I need to go back to the table and smooth things over with my family.

'You sure you're okay?' he asks.

'Fine,' I reply, knowing full well I sound anything but.

The woman in the stall comes out and washes her hands. Re-applies her peach lipstick and fluffs up her hair.

83

'I really am sorry,' Seth says. 'You're still coming tomorrow, right? We've got tickets to the theatre.'

'Yeah,' I reply. 'See you tomorrow.'

The bathroom door opens again and Elizabeth walks in.

'Love you,' Seth says.

'Love you too.' I hang up and try to gauge my sister's mood.

'What are you doing in here?' she snaps, tucking her hair behind an ear.

'Are those Mum's diamond earrings?' I ask.

'She said I could borrow them. Why are you skulking about in the loo? Was that Seth on the phone? Is he almost here? Graham's not happy and, quite frankly, neither am I.'

'I know, I'm so sorry. Seth got stuck in a meeting at the hospital. He's not going to make it.'

Elizabeth shakes her head.

'We can have a lovely evening without him,' I say, trying to lift her mood. 'It's your one-year anniversary!'

She draws in a long-suffering breath.

'What's wrong?' I ask, hoping she says nothing.

'What's wrong is that this is supposed to be a celebration of our wedding, but it feels like the Alice Show.'

'That's not fair! I'm sorry about Seth, but this is hardly my fault. I want you to have a lovely evening, Lizzie. Can't we go back out there and start again? Look, the food hasn't even arrived yet, we haven't done the toasts, we're in a beautiful place . . . let's just enjoy ourselves, have a few drinks and celebrate you and Graham being in love.'

'Yeah, well . . .' Her shoulders sag. 'Graham's in a terrible mood and I feel like I just want to go home.'

'What's wrong with Graham?'

'Nothing. I don't want to talk about it. Now, are you coming back to the table, or what?'

'Yes, I'm coming, but tell me what's—'

'I said I don't want to talk about it,' Elizabeth retorts.

I flinch backwards at her hostile expression.

She looks contrite for a millisecond before hardening her face again. 'The more I talk about it, the more upset I get. The last thing I want is to go back to the table with tears running down my face.'

'Tears?' I question. Wondering what on earth Graham could have said to make her so upset.

But Elizabeth has already turned away from me. She's opening the door and leaving.

I follow her, disappointment and anxiety vying for first place in my gut. As I stare at the stiff set of my sister's shoulders as she strides back to the table, I realise it's going to be a long and painful evening.

Chapter Fifteen

Now

Trudging up the gravel path, we come across a couple of grey and white donkeys. Laurence strokes one on the nose and gives the other a scratch behind the ear. I can't help wondering what it would be like to be a donkey or wild pony grazing my way around the forest with no complicated problems or desires. These two decide to follow us part of the way. I think they're hoping we might have a carrot or an apple for them, but sadly there's no food in my bag.

It's Saturday morning, and Laurence and I have met up at Linwood – a pretty hamlet in the New Forest – for our first counselling session. He first suggested we meet at his office. He works from home in his spare room. It's all done out with a smart desk and comfy chairs, certificates framed on the wall. But I'm not comfortable talking to him in such an official capacity. Not while things are already so odd in my life. The thought of such formality made me feel claustrophobic and panicky. Thankfully, Laurence agreed and suggested going for a walk instead. Linwood is reasonably close to Ringwood, the weather is sunny and there are hardly any people around so it's private, yet open. The plan is to walk and talk for an hour and then finish up at a nearby pub for lunch.

After fifteen minutes or so, we reach the top of the path and take a right towards one of my favourite viewpoints before coming to a gradual halt. In silence, we drink in the vast open plain of grass and bracken, clusters of trees, breathtaking views of the silver lake and low hills beyond, and above us the wide azure sky. I've been here a hundred times or more, but I could never tire of it. The only sounds are birdsong and the soft rustling of the breeze sweeping through leaves and grass.

Our donkey friends have wandered off towards a distant stand of trees and I realise Laurence and I haven't even started talking yet. I like the fact he hasn't pushed me. He told me to open up in my own time and then to talk freely. I'm hesitant to spoil the tranquillity and peace of this place with my woes, but I suppose that's the whole reason we're here.

'Thanks for doing this, Laurence,' I say, wrapping my arms around myself.

'Thanks for trusting me.' His blond hair is even more tousled than usual and he has a bit of unshaven scruff on his jaw and chin that he scratches as he gives me an encouraging smile. As he does so, I'm reminded of how he looked as a young boy when it was me, Daisy and him running around together in the school playground – the three amigos.

We walk around the heathland in a wide loop, loosely following the grassy tracks, startling rabbits who zigzag away from us, and passing the occasional dog walker with a friendly *hello*. At some point, I begin talking. I start off slowly, hesitantly, but it soon comes rushing out in a torrent. I tell Laurence everything, from the start of my wedding day disaster right up to my appointment with the neuropsychologist yesterday. He doesn't interrupt me at all, other than to clarify a couple of things and reassure me that he's still listening. I try to explain how I felt when I saw a stranger standing at the altar rather than my fiancé. And how even the *thought* of seeing him again makes me anxious.

I tell him how I feel like fate has slapped me down. Like it heard my self-congratulatory thoughts on my wedding day and decided I wasn't supposed to have so much happiness. I hate how I've started to sound so self-pitying, so I stop myself going down this track. I mention the missing photos, explaining that I can't seem to locate any images of *my* Seth, only those of the new Seth. Finally, I stop talking. I'm mentally drained, but it's a relief to have unburdened myself.

'That must have been difficult, Alice,' Laurence says after a few beats of silence. 'Going through all that trauma, and then talking about it so honestly.'

I nod, his empathy bringing a lump to my throat. I realise I didn't speak this freely with my GP or the psychologist. With them, I recounted bare facts rather than including my deepest, darkest fears and emotions.

'So when you walked down the aisle,' Laurence says, 'that was the very first time you didn't recognise Seth?'

'Yes,' I reply, stepping over a drying patch of mud. 'Everything was normal up until that moment.'

'And you didn't recognise Seth's parents either?' Laurence takes my arm as I stumble.

'Thanks. No. They were the only three people I didn't recognise. But the thing is . . .' I pause.

He doesn't prompt me. Just waits.

I inhale. 'This is going to make me sound like some sort of conspiracy theorist.'

'Look, Alice. You don't have to tell me anything you don't want to. Just know that I'm not going to pass any judgements. This conversation will have no bearing on our friendship, and I won't bring any of this up again unless we're in a counselling session, or unless you want to.'

I take in his words and decide that I do want to open up to him because the alternative is to have these crazy thoughts grinding through my brain every minute of every day with no escape. 'Okay, so the thing I can't stop thinking about is whether this might all be some kind of elaborate hoax.' Saying the words out loud makes me cringe inside.

'In what way?' Laurence asks with no judgement in his voice.

'In the way that Seth and his parents could be three lookalikes who are doing a bloody good job of convincing everyone I've lost my mind!' As I blurt out my darkest fear, I feel a mixture of relief and horror. Surely, after that, Laurence will think I need serious help. 'I know how it sounds,' I add. 'I can't believe I'm even thinking these things, let alone admitting them to someone else, but at this point I can't find any other explanation that makes sense. All I want is to find out where my fiancé went. What's happened to him?'

I stop walking for a moment and stare out at the wide blue sky, wishing I could make sense of my life right now.

Laurence comes to a halt and turns, waiting for me to continue.

I shake my head in frustration before continuing to spill my guts. 'I'm genuinely worried about Seth right now. About where he is, what he's thinking . . . Did he pull this stunt to get out of marrying me? Is there someone else in his life?' As I air my fears, thoughts of Damian flit through my mind. I think of all those times he told me I was lucky to have him. How no one else in their right mind would ever want me. That I was essentially unlovable. The rational part of me knows that's not true, but his past words have a way of seeping into my present thoughts like a dark, sticky poison with no antidote. Was Damian right? Has Seth somehow concocted this horrible situation to get out of marrying me?

Silence flows between me and Laurence, the warm air heavy and expectant. Waiting for enlightenment that refuses to come. 'I honestly feel like I'm going crazy,' I add, my voice cracking. I clear my throat. 'My fiancé has disappeared and no one else seems to care. No one believes what I'm telling them.' I start walking once more, lengthening my strides as though I can out-walk my fears.

Laurence matches my pace. 'It's okay, I understand,' he replies calmly.

'You do? Because I'm not sure *I* would if I heard someone say it.'

'Of *course* I understand,' he says gently.

'You understand that I truly believe that man at the church was not my fiancé?' I ask, wanting him to really know how I feel. 'You already mentioned that the police might recommend sectioning me if I reported Seth missing. But what do you genuinely believe? Do you think I'm losing my mind?'

'Alice,' he replies, 'I'd be terrified if the person I loved suddenly became a stranger to me.'

'That's exactly how I feel,' I cry. 'Since it happened, I just feel terrified all the time. My whole reality has shifted. This . . . *thing* has been so out of the blue. I just . . . I don't know what to do.'

'We'll figure it out,' he replies.

'Will we?'

'Yes.'

'I hope so.'

'I know so.' He bumps me with his elbow, and although I realise that he hasn't exactly said he believes my theory, I still thank God I have Laurence as a friend because right now I'd be lost without him.

We come to another halt, already finding ourselves back at the top of the gravel path that leads down to the car park.

'Shall we go down?' he asks. 'Get some lunch?'

'You've earned it,' I say. 'Listening to my mad ramblings.'

'They're not mad ramblings. You've had a traumatic thing happen to you, and I'm honoured that you chose to share it with me.'

'I don't know what I'd do without you, Laurence.'

'Yeah, well, I am pretty great.' He buffs his nails on his T-shirt and grins.

I give him a playful shove and we make our way back down the path.

'So you've only met with Seth the one time since the wedding?' he asks.

I wince at his use of Seth's name for this stranger, but I don't correct him. 'Yes. When my parents brought him round to the flat.'

He nods thoughtfully. 'Are you planning on seeing him again?'

'I know I should, but I'm not keen.' Laurence and I move to the side of the path to let a couple of ramblers march past us, their hiking boots crunching over the gravel in military time.

'Why aren't you keen?' he asks.

We start walking again, the ramblers already disappearing out of view.

'Just, you know, the whole feeling-anxious-whenever-I'm-around-him thing.'

'Hmm. Okay.'

There's a beat of silence.

'You think I should see him again, don't you?' I say, my pulse sliding up a gear.

'Not necessarily. I'm just not sure how you can move forward in your life without resolving things with him one way or another. But you can do it in your own time. You don't need to feel pressured by family or friends, or by him.'

I give a loud sigh. 'I know I *should* see him. I know I'm not going to fix anything by ignoring him. But I just can't get the whole conspiracy idea out of my head. I can't help thinking I'm talking to an imposter. Which I know is ridiculous.'

We walk in silence for a while and I wonder if Laurence is waiting for me to say something else. Finally, he responds. 'Okay, so there is one thing you could do when you get back home. One thing that could help you try to make sense of things . . .'

My stomach flip-flops with nerves. Ever since the wedding, every time I talk to someone, I feel like I'm tiptoeing through a war zone. Every conversation is laden with landmines and sniper fire. Any suggestion or new information could trigger me. I trust Laurence, I really do, but it doesn't stop me feeling terrified at what he's about to say. Making our way down the path back towards our cars, I tell myself not to be so dramatic. Laurence is here to help me, not to shock or trip me up. I need to trust him. But it's hard to trust anyone when I can't even trust myself.

'What's your suggestion?' I ask, reluctantly.

'It's just a little exercise that might help you clarify things,' he replies.

'Okay, but what is it?'

'I think it could be helpful to think about what *your* Seth looks like, compared with the new Seth. Try to pinpoint the physical differences between the two. Maybe even do a couple of sketches of each of them, seeing as you've got no photos of your original Seth.'

'Have you seen my drawing skills?' I reply, trying to sound lighter than I feel.

'This isn't about being the next da Vinci,' he says with a smile. 'It's just an exercise that might be helpful. You don't have to do a sketch; you can make a list of their features if you prefer. Or write down a description of each face.'

'Hmm. Okay. I'll give it a go.' I'm not sure what the purpose of it is, but Laurence is the expert. He's giving up his Saturday morning to help me, so the least I can do is try it.

'Like I said, I think it might give you some clarity. Then we can make another date to meet up.'

'Great, okay. Thank you. It's honestly been such a relief to be able to talk like this. You don't know how much lighter I feel.'

'Come here.' He gives me a hug. 'You know I'm always here for you, Alice.'

We break apart and carry on walking.

'There's one other thing I didn't tell you,' I say, my heart beating faster as I remember last night.

Laurence doesn't reply, just quirks an eyebrow at me.

'I was walking to Hibiscus to meet Daisy, and I thought I saw Damian.'

Laurence freezes.

I stop and turn.

'You saw Damian?' His face clouds over. 'Damian Carter?'

'Well, that's the thing. I might have been mistaken. It was dark when he walked past me. He caught my eye and I thought I was going to have a heart attack. But then he just kept on walking and I realised it probably wasn't him. Just someone who looked similar.'

'Okay,' Laurence says, relaxing slightly. 'I thought he moved away, didn't he?'

'Last I heard he was living in Wales,' I confirm.

'Good. So it probably wasn't him. But I'll check it out anyway. Make sure he isn't back on the scene.'

We both exhale at the same time. It was Laurence who gave me the courage to leave Damian in the first place. He made me see what my ex was doing – gaslighting me into believing I was a bad girlfriend, making out that I was neglecting him in favour of my friends and family when, in reality, Damian just wanted to keep me all to himself so that he could control me. Limiting when I could go out and who I could see by guilt-tripping me. Saying that I didn't care about him. That I was a thoughtless, selfish person who did what I wanted without thinking about how it made him feel.

Every time I planned to do anything without him – attend a works do, go to a family gathering or meet up with friends – Damian would sulk. I would make the mistake of asking what was wrong and, all the while, I'd have this dread in the pit of my stomach, knowing how the conversation would end: in a huge blow-up with me apologising, reassuring him that of course I wouldn't go to whatever event had got him so insecure, soothing his rage until he forgave me.

Laurence helped me to see that this was how my ex manipulated me. Making me think I was in the wrong for simply wanting to live a normal life that didn't revolve completely around him. It was a horrible, horrible time and the thought of Damian coming back on the scene again brings me out in a cold sweat.

'Don't worry,' Laurence says, pulling me in for another hug. 'I doubt it was him you saw. And even if it was, it's all ancient history. You're not with him any more. He doesn't have any hold over you or bearing on your life.'

I step back and nod. 'You're right. Of course you are. I'm just being silly.'

So why do I still have that prickle of unease crawling over my skin?

Chapter Sixteen

THEN

Seth opens the passenger door to his blue BMW Z4 Roadster and I step out on to the carriage drive in front of the Manor House Hotel. The drive here was fun. Seth and I haven't stopped laughing since he arrived at Brook Cottage this morning. I'm so full to the brim with love for this man. I absolutely cannot wait for us to get married.

It's one of those rare crisp December days where the sun is lemon bright and the sky is at its cleanest freshest blue. An icy snap in the air catches in my throat and clears my head of all thoughts other than how lucky I am to be alive on such a beautiful day.

Seth hands the keys and a hefty tip to the valet and we stand in front of the building gazing back down the tree-lined avenue.

'I can see why you brought me here,' he says, shading his eyes and taking in the sweeping drive, the manicured lawns and the herd of deer grazing in the meadow beyond. The stag raises his head and stares in our direction, as though he knows he's being admired.

'I knew you'd like it,' I reply. 'We're so lucky they had a cancellation. Otherwise, the waiting list is two years.'

'I'm not waiting two years to marry you,' he says, leaning down to kiss me.

I decided not to bring up Seth's absence at Elizabeth and Graham's anniversary dinner. The two of us have had enough miscommunications and mini fallouts since our engagement; I don't want any more. I'm treating today as a clean slate.

'Let's take a photo in front of the hotel,' I say, pulling my phone out of my handbag.

'You and your photos,' he teases, poking me in the ribs.

I laugh. 'Stop! I'm ticklish there.'

'I know.' He grins and tries to do it again while I squeal and dodge out of the way.

We're both dressed smart-casual for this visit – me in black jeans, stiletto-heeled black boots, a cream cashmere polo neck and a short faux-fur jacket. Seth in dark-wash jeans, Adidas trainers, white shirt, grey sweater and a black wool jacket. We position ourselves a short way in front of the arched entranceway, lean into each other and smile at the screen. I'll probably post it on Instagram later with a retro filter and a well-thought-out caption. Seth isn't one for social media. Too busy for all that shit, he likes to say with a smile.

'Come on, let's go inside,' he says, rubbing his hands together impatiently.

We walk up to the polished wooden desk and tell the receptionist we're here to have a wedding tour. I feel like the luckiest person in the world. Here I am with this gorgeous, funny, kind man. We're at this stunning venue, on the verge of being together for the rest of our lives. I ignore the little niggles in my head – the fact that he still hasn't met my friends and family, that his work often means he can't honour commitments, that, so far, he's been the one to make all the major decisions in our relationship. The thing is, we're pretty much on the same page about everything, so I guess there's no real problem there.

Moments later, a stunning woman walks into the foyer, her heels clip-clipping across the marble floor. As she draws closer I frown in partial recognition.

She thrusts out a hand. 'Hello! I'm Sienna Doyle, the Manor House wedding coordinator.'

'Alice Porter.' I shake her slim hand. A no-nonsense handshake, firm and brief.

'Do I know you?' I ask Sienna. She looks and sounds oddly familiar with her flame-red hair and raspy voice.

She stares at me critically for a couple of seconds, and then recognition dawns. 'Yes! You were here last weekend with your family,' she says. 'I was your waitress.'

'Oh, that's right.' It clicks into place. I didn't really take to her at the time, but that might have been because the whole evening was awful. I wasn't in the right frame of mind to be friendly to anyone.

'The restaurant was short-staffed that night so I stepped in,' she adds. 'One of your party didn't show up. I'm guessing that was you, Seth.' She turns to him with a pretend-stern expression on her face. A smirk lying beneath it.

That's a bit overly friendly. Using his first name without Seth even introducing himself.

Sienna tuts and holds out her hand for him to shake. 'Standing up the bride-to-be? We can't have that.'

I turn to Seth to see his expression, but instead of being bemused by Sienna's forward behaviour, he shakes his head with a flirty smile. A smile he normally reserves for me.

'Sienna?' He says her name as though he's just found the holy grail. An exhalation – part question, part answer. 'Sienna!' he repeats, this time with more lightness. 'No way. It is you! You dyed your hair.' Seth steps forward and I watch in dismay as the two of them hug. I'm not the jealous type. I always believe there's no point being in a relationship with someone if there's no trust. But this fizz of chemistry between them is really pissing me off. Especially as this is supposed to be our wedding tour.

I realise that instead of Seth and I having a loved-up afternoon, I'm about to compete with this stunning woman for his attention. I wrack my brains to think of a good enough excuse to cancel on the spot, but my mind comes up empty. Anything I said would make me look jealous and petty. Insecure. Which, at this precise moment, would be right. I tell myself not to be so silly. This isn't like me.

'Can't believe you're getting married,' she says to him before giving me a smile that's verging on patronising.

The subtext of that sentence is that she can't believe he's getting married to me.

'Alice,' Seth turns to me. 'Sienna and I go way back. Her parents live just up the road from Brook Cottage.'

'Do you remember that time we went drunk-paddling in the stream in your garden and woke up your parents?' Sienna touches his shoulder and laughs.

'Don't remind me. Dad still hasn't forgiven us for opening his precious bottle of Macallan whisky.'

'Oh no, does that mean I'm banned from the cottage?' she asks, a twinkle in her blue eyes.

'Actually, Seth and I are going to be moving into Brook Cottage after the wedding,' I say, hoping I don't sound too territorial, but realising I probably do.

'Oh, nice.' She turns back to him. 'I hope you've updated the plumbing.'

'Two years ago. Complete overhaul.' Seth gives her two thumbs up which is quite dorky and out of character for him. Is he nervous?

'So, we're really excited to look round the hotel,' I say, trying to steer the conversation away from their shared history and back to our wedding day. I throw in my warmest smile. I can't let this woman get to me. I need to pretend she's my new best friend.

'Of course!' she exclaims. 'You're going to love it. I'll walk you through what your special day could be like. Come this way. We'll get you both a drink first.'

The afternoon passes painfully slowly while Sienna gives us a tour of the hotel along with constant references to her and Seth's shared history. Despite my best intentions to be relaxed and friendly, I'm finding it really difficult to stay upbeat. Sienna's shameless flirting is wearing on my nerves.

The rough gist of the tour is the choice between a stunning wood-panelled hall inside the hotel, or a rustic barn next door to the main building. Sienna explains about the various catering packages, and shows us examples of the different suites available for us and our guests. Instead of giving the hotel all my attention as I'd planned, I barely take in any of the details. Anyway, there's no point. I've already made up my mind that we won't be having our reception here. Especially after Sienna reassures us that she'll be on hand throughout our special day to ensure everything runs smoothly. Yes, I'm sure she will.

I'm wondering if she and Seth were just friends, or if there was ever something more to their relationship. My jaw aches from fake-smiling and I'm getting the beginnings of a tension headache.

Finally, we return to the foyer where, instead of the professional handshake she started with, she leans in to kiss us on the cheek in turn, lingering longer on Seth.

'Now that you're moving back down, you better keep in touch,' she says to him. 'I'm in Lymington now, so not too far away.'

'Definitely,' Seth replies.

'Are you still on the same number?' she asks him.

You've got to be kidding me. I restrain the eye roll that's trying to force its way out.

'Yes, same number,' Seth replies.

'Great.' She beams.

I give a wan smile, desperate to leave now.

Finally, Seth and I leave Sienna to the rest of her day and make our way back outside. The sun has dipped behind the trees and the air *is cold enough to steal our breath. The valet has already fetched Seth's car and I slip gratefully into the passenger seat, massaging my temples.*

'What a fantastic venue,' Seth says, getting into the car and pulling the door closed. 'It's a "yes", right? We should call and tell Sienna tonight. Don't want anyone else snapping up that date.'

'I'm not really feeling it,' I reply apologetically, pulling my seatbelt across.

'You're joking, right?' Seth turns to me, his brow creased in confusion. 'You were the one who wanted me to come here in the first place.'

'I know, I know. Let's just take some time to think about it,' I reply. 'There's lots to mull over.'

Seth's frown deepens. 'Really? But I thought—'

'That was a coincidence – your friend working there,' I interrupt his protest.

'I know. I haven't seen Sienna in years. Don't worry, she'll make sure our day runs flawlessly.'

I ignore his assumption that we're having the wedding here.

Seth snaps his seatbelt into place and starts the engine.

'So, were you and she . . . like, an item?' I ask, feeling like I'm holding my breath. Not sure why this is bothering me so much. We both have exes; we both have pasts. I give an internal shudder as I think about Damian. I guess I just didn't expect to be up so close and personal with one of Seth's exes at our possible wedding venue.

His mouth twists as he puts the car in first and drives off down the avenue. 'We did have a bit of a thing back in the day, but—'

'A bit of a thing?' I interrupt. 'What? So she's your ex-girlfriend?' My heart plummets. I suspected as much, but it's not great to hear.

'Not really,' Seth replies. 'It was just light-hearted stuff. Nothing serious. We were young. It fizzled out after she left to go travelling.'

'So, if she hadn't gone travelling, you might still be together?' I can hear the jealous accusations flying out of my mouth and internally I'm yelling at myself to calm down and shut up. I know I'm blowing

the situation way out of proportion, but I'm tired, irritable, and that girl is so beautiful that she's managed to intimidate the hell out of me.

'I doubt it,' Seth replies. 'I was too focused on my career. She was all about having a good time. We were very different.'

Well, that's something at least. Although she's obviously settled into a career now.

As we cruise along the avenue, the setting sun plays hide-and-seek through the bare branches of the trees, blinding me every second or so. I pull down the sunshade and try to put Sienna Doyle out of my head.

I trust Seth, of course I do. But the question is, do I trust Sienna?

Chapter Seventeen

Now

The pub's already filling up when Laurence and I arrive after my counselling session, but we manage to nab a table in the beer garden, glad of the oversized parasol as the sun is really warming up now. I order a Caesar salad, and Laurence orders a vegan burger and fries. The food is being delivered to our table by a friendly waitress who flirts shamelessly with Laurence when we see a familiar figure walking towards us, a worried expression on her face.

'*Fran?*' Laurence gets to his feet.

'Hi, Francesca,' I say, hoping everything's okay.

'Hi, Alice.' She gives me an apologetic smile. 'Sorry to interrupt you guys. I've been trying to ring you, Loz.'

He pulls his phone from his pocket and grimaces. 'No signal.'

'Yeah, that's what I figured. That client of yours – Sarah W. – she's outside the flat and says she won't leave until she's seen you.'

Laurence swears under his breath. He turns to me with an apologetic expression. 'I'm going to have to go. She's a vulnerable client . . .'

'Of course. You go. At least we drove separately. Get them to put your burger in a doggy bag.'

'It's fine, I'll just have a few bites,' he replies, proceeding to demolish the whole thing in two mouthfuls. 'You can have my chips.'

'Ooh, chips!' Francesca says. 'I might stay and keep you company, Alice, if that's okay?'

'Of course,' I reply. 'Although I'm not sure I'll be the greatest company.'

'That's fine. We can just eat and relax.'

'Sorry you had to come out here to get me,' Laurence says to Fran.

She gives him a reassuring smile. 'It's only up the road. I wasn't sure what to do.'

'You did the right thing. Okay, I'm going to head off. You two enjoy your lunch.'

Laurence leaves and I can't help feeling a bit awkward. I haven't seen Francesca since the wedding and I'm not sure how much she knows about what happened. Added to that, my brain is like mush, having just laid my emotions bare.

She slides into Laurence's seat and starts tucking into his chips. I make a start on my salad, surprised at how hungry I am. As I eat, my mental energy starts to perk up a little. I sip my sparkling water and take a few calming breaths.

'Hope it all went well today with Laurence,' she says. I like the way she doesn't do a head-tilt and sound all pitying and concerned. Maybe that's because she's suffered from anxiety in the past and knows how to act around people who have it.

'Yeah, it was really helpful thanks. He's a good listener.'

'He is,' she agrees. 'Sorry about the wedding. How are you doing?'

'Pretty awful, but I'm hoping things will become clearer with time.'

'I'm sure they will,' she says. 'And you have lots of support,' she adds. 'Friends who care about you – me included!'

'Thanks, Fran. That means a lot. It's just . . . my whole life feels like it's fallen off a cliff. I was about to spend the rest of my life with someone, and now I don't recognise him. I don't even want to be in the same room as him.'

Fran stops eating and fixes me with her warm hazel eyes. 'I can't imagine what that's like.'

I shrug. 'It's . . . shit, basically.' I give a bitter laugh.

'Yeah. Sounds like it.'

'I mean, imagine if you woke up one morning and you didn't recognise Laurence, but all his friends and family said it *was* him. What would you do?'

She shakes her head and shudders. 'That actually sounds terrifying.'

I press my hand to my chest, trying to ease the anxious thump of my heart.

'You don't think . . .' She tails off. 'No, never mind.'

'No. Go on. Say what you were going to say.'

'I hope I'm not speaking out of turn, but you don't think that maybe this was a subconscious act? A kind of defence mechanism.'

'What do you mean?' I think I know where she's going with this, and I don't think I like it.

She sets down her cutlery for a moment and rests her chin on her hands. 'That maybe you didn't want to go through with the wedding. It could have been your brain's way of telling you not to marry him.'

I can hardly believe what she's just said.

Francesca flushes. 'You know what, forget I said that. I heard it out loud and it sounded really terrible. I'm sorry. I must still be a bit stressed from earlier, with Laurence's client.'

'No, it's fine. I'm glad you spoke your mind. I might not agree with what you said, but I don't want people tiptoeing around me. I appreciate you having lunch and spending time with me. I've been a bit reclusive since it happened.'

'I'm not surprised. It must have been such a shock.'

In my head, I can't help wondering if perhaps, on some level, Fran might be right. Was it my subconscious somehow sabotaging my relationship? Was there something about Seth that made me create this scenario to get me out of marrying him? But I never thought of myself as the sort of person to shy away from saying what needs to be said. I think about my dad and how I'm always trying and failing to please him. Did I do the same with Seth? Is he anything like my dad? I don't think so, but I can't be sure. Everything feels so fuzzy when I think about Seth.

'Are you okay, Alice?'

I realise Fran's been talking to me but I must have zoned out of the conversation for a minute. 'So sorry, I'm just not myself at the moment. You must think I'm really rude.'

'Not at all. I honestly don't know how you're coping with everything.'

'Like you said, I have lovely friends. They're the ones keeping me going,' I reply, realising it's true. Without my friends, I don't know what I'd be doing. Probably still hiding out in my bedroom.

After some lighter chit-chat, we finish up our lunch and head back to the car park. I'm so exhausted I think I might go back to bed when I get home. It feels wrong while the sun is shining and it's not even 1 p.m. yet, but it's been an emotionally draining morning.

I hug Fran goodbye.

'You know,' she says, 'if you ever need to switch off from everything, you should come by the shelter and take one of the dogs out. They're great therapy and they always love the chance for an extra walk. They're my lifeline whenever I feel stressed. Text me any time, okay?'

'I might just take you up on that,' I reply.

On the short drive back home, I have the windows down letting in fresh air to keep me alert. I think back to what Laurence said earlier about comparing *my* Seth's face with the imposter-Seth's face and trying to pinpoint the differences. I don't know why I didn't think of doing that before. Maybe if I can differentiate their features, then I can get people to see that they're two different men.

The imposter-Seth's face pops into my mind straightaway. I can catalogue his features quite easily. Now, I try to do the same with my Seth. He's . . . I frown and try to conjure up a mental image of my fiancé's face.

It's the strangest, most unsettling sensation . . . I can't seem to do it.

I know Seth is my fiancé and I know we have a life together, but when I think about him, *really* think about him, I can't bring his face to my mind.

This is stupid. How am I not able to do this?

Okay, I'll picture Seth's parents' faces instead . . .

But then I stop myself. I realise I don't want to. I don't want to think about what they look like, and I also don't want to think about what my Seth looks like either.

Because the terrifying thing is that I'm pretty certain *I can't remember*.

Chapter Eighteen

THEN

I flop down on to Laurence's sofa, pulling my legs up under me.

'How was your wedding venue tour?' he asks, bringing out two wine glasses topped up to the brim with Sauvignon Blanc.

'Don't even ask,' I grumble.

'Oh. Sounds ominous. So now you have to tell me,' Laurence replies, sitting next to me, his long legs stretched out on the coffee table.

'Ugh.' I take an indecent swig of my wine, trying not to think about today's tour with Sienna. Seth went home soon after to avoid the Sunday evening traffic, so the two of us didn't get much of a chance to talk. 'I'll tell you later,' I say, not wanting to rehash it all right now. 'Let's stick the film on first. I need to decompress. What are we watching? It better be a good one.' We always take turns choosing, and tonight is Laurence's turn.

'Don't you worry about that.' He flicks on the movie channel where the image of a blood-soaked zombie stares back at me from the screen.

'Good choice, Kennedy.' I nod my approval.

Hardly any of my friends like horror films, whereas I absolutely love them (despite the fact they terrify me). But I can't watch them on my own. Laurence is the only other person I know who loves them as much as I do, so whenever Francesca is out with her friends, he and I do a movie night. Francesca is grateful to me for watching them with Laurence as she can't even bear to be in the flat when they're on in case she accidentally sees something awful. I'm not sure how our movie nights will work once I'm married to Seth, but we'll cross that bridge when I come to it. Hopefully Laurence will win Seth over and Seth will realise that Laurence is just a friend.

'Pringles,' Laurence says, jumping up and heading over to the kitchen. He opens one of the units and pulls out two tubes – original for him, sour cream and onion for me. Once he's settled back on to the couch, we start the movie. Within seconds, I'm completely engrossed, today's worries evaporating into a post-apocalyptic zombie world. Laurence laughs mercilessly at me when I scream at the jump scares, and I throw an assortment of cushions at his head, then grab them back to hide behind.

Around halfway through the film, the door buzzer sounds, and Laurence pauses the TV while he goes to collect our pizzas from the delivery person. I top up our glasses and close my eyes for a moment, suddenly feeling tired and emotional.

We start tucking into our Veggie Feasts and potato wedges, eating them straight out of the boxes to save on washing up.

'Shall I press play?' I ask.

'Not yet. I want to hear about today. Didn't you like the hotel? I thought you had your heart set on it.'

'The hotel was fine; it was the wedding coordinator who messed things up.' I hold my pizza slice out to Laurence. He picks off the mushrooms and dumps them on to his slice while I remove his artichoke hearts and put them on to mine.

Laurence gives me a quizzical look and I go on to tell him about Sienna Doyle, the stunning wedding coordinator who just so happens to be Seth's ex-girlfriend. And how she spent the whole tour flirting with him while he reciprocated.

'Oh shit,' Laurence says, giving me a sympathetic look and topping up my wine.

'That about sums it up.' I take a huge bite of pizza and chew morosely. 'I mean, I know it wasn't Seth's fault she was there, but he didn't have to flirt back.'

'No. Sure. Maybe he was just being friendly. He would have been surprised to see her. It might have been awkward for him.'

'Trust me, the only person feeling awkward in that situation was me. If that had been one of my exes, he would have gone ballistic.'

'Haven't you had the "exes" chat yet?' Laurence asks.

'Of course. But Sienna was never mentioned until today.'

'Oh.'

I reach for a second pizza slice and we both chew in silence for a moment.

'Maybe you need to have another talk to Seth,' Laurence suggests. 'Get him to put your mind at rest.'

'Maybe . . . but I don't want him to think I'm jealous.'

'Fine, but if you don't say anything, then he won't realise he made you feel bad.'

I slump down into the sofa. 'I wouldn't even know how to bring it up without coming across all possessive and paranoid.'

'Alice, you're marrying the guy. If you can't talk to him . . .' Laurence raises an eyebrow.

I bristle at the suggestion that my relationship with Seth is anything other than perfect. 'Of course I can talk to him! It's just a weird situation, that's all.'

'And what about him not turning up to Elizabeth's anniversary dinner?'

'Who told you that?' I frown.

'I ran into Lizzie at the post office a couple of days ago.'

Internally, I curse living in a small town, even though I love it really. 'Elizabeth got annoyed with me when Seth didn't show up at

109

the dinner last week. I apologised. But it's not like we arranged it on purpose. He couldn't help his meeting running late, could he?'

'No, but it was a special occasion for them. If there was a possibility of him not making it, maybe he should have let you know.'

'Don't you give me a hard time about it too. I thought you'd be on my side.' I glower at him, hurt that he's siding with my sister.

He gives me a rueful grin. 'Sorry, you're right. I'm just worried about you, that's all.'

I sigh. 'No. I'm sorry for snapping. I think it must be pre-wedding jitters. I never thought I'd be one of those brides-to-be who gets all uptight and stressed. But, actually, it wasn't just me Elizabeth was moody with – she was annoyed with Graham too. They were trying to pretend they weren't fighting, but it was so obvious. Such an awkward atmosphere. Although I guess that could have been triggered by Seth's no-show.'

Laurence presses his lips together.

'What's that look for?' I ask.

'Nothing.'

I narrow my eyes and sip my wine.

'Okay, look,' Laurence says. 'I don't think they were arguing about Seth not coming to the dinner.'

'You don't think?'

'Okay, I know they weren't arguing about that.'

'So tell me.'

He sighs. 'Elizabeth's feeling a little insecure at the moment.' Laurence offers me a potato wedge, like a deep-fried carb hit is going to offset whatever he's about to tell me.

I shake my head at his offering. 'Insecure? In what way?'

'Graham told her he doesn't think you should marry Seth.'

I frown in confusion. 'He hasn't even met Seth.'

'No, I know, but just from what he's heard and seen. You know, Seth's no-shows – missing your engagement party, the anniversary. The fact that he hasn't made the effort to meet any of us yet.'

I'm taken aback by Laurence's revelation about Graham, and about them all bad-mouthing my fiancé behind his back. I feel an instant surge of protectiveness towards Seth. 'And is this how you feel too?'

'Me? No. I'm just telling you why Graham and Elizabeth got in a fight.'

'So she was sticking up for me and Seth?'

Laurence's neck mottles a deep red.

'What? Just tell me.'

He sucks air through his teeth. 'Well, Elizabeth seems to think . . . she's worried that Graham's overly concerned about your well-being. Basically, she thinks Graham still has feelings for you.'

'What? That's ridiculous. We split up years ago. He adores Elizabeth.'

'Well, I know that and you know that, but Lizzie doesn't seem to have got the memo.'

'Damn.'

'Damn indeed.'

I think back to my sister's outburst in the hotel loo last week. No wonder she was on the verge of tears if that's what she thinks. It's crazy that she's still holding on to this idea about me and Graham. We weren't even that close when we were going out, so there's no reason for her to think there could be any illicit feelings. I thought we'd moved past all this.

'Sorry,' Laurence says, interrupting my thoughts. 'Maybe I shouldn't have said anything.'

'No, I'm glad you did. I suppose I need to talk to Elizabeth. Again. Try to get it through her head that her husband only has eyes for her.'

'Probably, yes.'

'So, what do you think about the situation? Elizabeth's got this totally wrong, right?'

'I don't know anything about Graham's feelings.' Laurence shrugs. 'I just thought I'd better let you know what's going on so you can put your sister's mind at rest.'

111

'So much drama,' I sigh. 'What about you, Kennedy? How's things with work and Fran?'

'Yeah, fine. No drama here.'

'Lucky you,' I reply. I hold out my hand for a potato wedge and Laurence re-offers me the box.

'Are we ready for part two?' he asks, holding out the remote.

'Do it.'

Laurence presses play and I focus on the screen, but I've been yanked too far out of the moment by our unsettling conversation. I can't seem to immerse myself back into the horror of zombies taking over the world. Not when I have my own real-life problems to face – first, how to smooth things out with my sister and, second, how to get my relationship back on track with Seth. Neither of which I'm looking forward to tackling.

Chapter Nineteen

Now

I step out of the car into the warm London afternoon and the air is sucked from my lungs as I'm hit with a hailstorm of memories: Seth looking out of his window, waving down at me; the time my car broke down in the middle of the road just a few hundred yards from his flat; the two of us coming back to his place, tipsy after a night out; the list goes on. But overlaying each of these memories is a strange blur where I can't quite make out Seth's face.

The realisation I had on Saturday after Laurence's counselling session keeps flying back to me like a sucker punch – the fact that I no longer remember what my Seth looks like. I'm starting to comprehend that fake Seth could very well be my Seth. That all this time, I'm the one who's got it wrong. But, despite all the evidence mounting up to prove they're the same person, a kernel of doubt is still wriggling around in my gut. A voice in my ear still whispering that something's off.

I met up with Seth again yesterday, even though I didn't want to. Everything in me was screaming to stay away from him, but after Saturday's horrible realisation, I came to the conclusion that it might be helpful for us to talk again. To see if this time I might recognise him.

We met on neutral ground in a local park. As soon as I saw him there, sitting on that scuffed wooden bench, I wanted to turn around and go home again. I must have visibly recoiled because his smile disappeared the instant he saw my expression. Again, I was blindsided by his unfamiliarity. By the knowledge that this was not my fiancé. Needless to say, our meeting was short and unproductive. I barely said two words to him and came away feeling worse than ever. Which is why I've made the trip to London to see if I might discover what's really going on.

I don't know what I'm looking for exactly. Just . . . something.

I feed the parking meter and cross the road, and walk towards Seth's building as though in a dream. My throat is scratchy and my vision blurs as I reach the entrance and wave my key fob over the sensor. The door swings open with a click. Seth's building is a seventies yellow-brick block – ugly on the outside, but spacious and airy on the inside, with large rooms and huge windows that face the park. I press the lift button and wait in the empty lobby, wrinkling my nose against warring smells of cooked food and fake-pine air freshener.

I startle as the lift door slides open with a loud ping, pushing away the thought that I probably shouldn't be doing this. That I'm here without 'Seth's' knowledge. I reason that he gave me a key so that I could come and go as I please. But that was then. Back when everything was normal. Now, as I walk into the lift and press the button for the fifth floor, I feel like an intruder.

My stomach swoops as the lift lurches upwards. The last time I was here, we were excitedly planning our wedding. Now, I don't even know who Seth is, and my life is in tatters. The lift stops and I take a breath and step out, turning left towards his front door. I'm about to put the key in the lock, but a growing feeling of unease makes me pause. What if I've been right all this time and the real Seth is here in his flat? Restrained, hurt . . . or worse. My heart begins to pound and I tell myself not to be so stupid. So melodramatic. But I pull out my mobile phone, just in case I need to call for help quickly.

I decide to press the bell first. The pounding of my heartbeat in my ears mingles with the echo of the ringing bell. I wait for a moment, and then a moment more, still harbouring the improbable hope that my Seth will open the door with some perfectly reasonable explanation for it all. But I soon realise no one's coming to the door, so I unlock it and push it open.

I stare into the wide hallway. So familiar and yet so, so different now. Like a view to another life. Even though we were going to be living in Hampshire together, Seth had planned to keep hold of the flat to rent it out. Consequently, there are boxes, bags and cases stacked in the hall, waiting to be shifted. Waiting for our new life to begin.

I listen carefully, but there are no sounds from within. Gingerly, I step over the threshold and let the door close behind me, leaving it on the latch so I can get out quickly if needed. I feel a bit silly being this paranoid, this scared, but my life has flipped around so much that I don't feel as though I can trust anything or anyone fully right now.

I peer into the bedroom first. It's dark in there. My pulse pounds.

'Hello?' I call out. 'Seth?'

The air is warm and musty, but I can't smell anything untoward like a dead body, thank goodness. I walk into the bedroom and pull the cord to open the blinds, flooding the large space with light. I blink and glance around the empty room. The king-size bed has been stripped of bedding, the triple wardrobe is open but empty, the chest of drawers is cleared of clutter, the rug rolled up and leaning against the wall. I relax my shoulders. There's no one here. I'm not sure whether to feel relief or disappointment. The room feels so strange without its personality. I run my fingers over the chest of drawers, remembering how much I liked seeing my make-up and perfume sitting alongside his aftershave and razors. How happy I used to be that our lives were so entwined.

The bathroom is similarly empty. The kitchen has only been partially cleared out. The fridge is bare aside from a small unopened carton of orange juice, but the cupboards still contain a few packets and tins of food. Finally, I head into the living room. Apart from the furniture, it too is bare. No personal decoration, cushions, art, photos . . . nothing. No sign of Seth. Of the life he had here.

What now?

I was hoping so badly that I'd find something. If not my fiancé, then a clue at least. But this empty flat has yielded nothing, unless . . .

I stride back into the hall. Thankfully, Seth has labelled each packing box in black marker pen. The first three are bedding and clothes, but then I spy one that could be promising, marked 'Pictures etc'. I crouch beside it, peel back the brown parcel tape and open the box. Everything has been wrapped in paper. There are a couple of plant pots, some sporting trophies, candles, and other knick-knacks. I lift them all out until I come to what I'm looking for – the framed photos that used to sit in the lounge and bedroom. I hold my breath as I unwrap the first one. But then I almost drop it as the front door flies open.

I yelp and clasp the photo to my chest, looking up into the open doorway.

A middle-aged man stands there, his eyes narrowed, his belly straining under navy work overalls, his hands stained with white paint.

'What the hell?' I back up before realising that I recognise him. He scowls. 'Who are you?'

'I'm Seth's fiancée,' I reply.

'Well, I know that's not true,' he says.

'Excuse me?' I get to my feet, dropping the framed photograph back into the box.

He clears his throat and straightens up. 'I live in the flat opposite. He told me he was going on honeymoon. Asked me to keep an eye on the place.' He points a finger at me. 'So, how can you be his fiancée if he's on his honeymoon? If you leave now I won't call the coppers, all right? There's nothing of any value here anyway. He's moving out.'

'Yes, that's because he's moving in with me!' I snap. No need to tell him what's really going on. 'We've met before. You're Rob, right? I'm Alice.' I'm nervous that he won't remember me. That this whole situation is about to get even more complicated.

He squints. 'Alice?' He relaxes. 'Oh, right, it is you. Sorry, not wearing my glasses. Thought you were a burglar. We've had a few break-ins in the area recently.'

Well at least that's something – I recognise Seth's neighbour and he recognises me. 'The honeymoon's been delayed,' I reply. 'I've just popped back to pick up some things.'

He nods. 'Fine. I was just being a good neighbour, that's all.'

I nod. 'Thank you.'

'Okay, well, I'll be off then.' He turns to go.

'Hang on a minute.' I take a step towards him and open up one of the images of Seth that I got Daisy to forward to my phone.

'What's that?' he asks.

'Just humour me a minute and tell me if you recognise this person.' I hold out my phone and show him the photo of Seth sitting in Regent's Park.

'Bit difficult to see, love, without my glasses.' He peers down at the screen. 'Looks like Seth.' He gives me a bemused look.

My heart sinks at his confirmation that this is my fiancé. 'What about this one?' I show him another image of the two of us – a close-up, our heads tilted together.

'Well, that's the two of you together, isn't it? It's okay, you don't need to prove who you are. I recognise you now.' He nods and pats my arm.

I bite my lip, bitterly disappointed that Seth's neighbour believes that the man in the photos is Seth.

'Okay, well, I'll leave you in peace,' he says. 'Congratulations on the wedding.'

'Thanks,' I reply bleakly as he leaves, pulling the door closed behind him.

I put a hand to my chest to quiet my beating heart. I bet he'll tell Seth I've been here. I'll have to come clean now. I'll call him later . . . or maybe I won't.

I bend to pick up the framed photo from the box. Turning it over, I see that it's the one of Seth and his parents sitting in the garden of Brook Cottage. The man in the photo is not my Seth. I give a bitter smile as I realise this whole trip has been nothing but a wild goose chase. Half-heartedly, I tear the paper off the other photos, which are all of the fake Seth. Of course they are.

The pictures surround me – smiling, happy images of a man I don't know.

I finally understand that the problem must be with me. That there is no fake Seth. That all this time, I've been looking for an illusion. A delusion. A man who doesn't exist.

Chapter Twenty

Now

I stand beneath the wooden front porch and wipe my palms on my jeans, trying to get my breathing under control. This is my third meeting with Seth since the wedding. The first was when my parents brought him along to the flat unannounced, and the second was that brief meet-up in the park. Neither meeting went well, but after another counselling session with Laurence, he suggested I persevere. So here I am outside Brook Cottage, trying to raise enough courage to knock on the dove-grey painted wooden door.

I've come to the reluctant conclusion that the man I'm here to see today probably *is* the real Seth. My acceptance of the truth came in stages. First, when I realised I couldn't picture Seth in my head. That I have no recollection of what my Seth actually looks like. Surely, if I loved this man and was about to marry him, I should have been able to summon some kind of mental picture of him. But I couldn't. Second, when I went to his flat in London and was faced with photographic evidence that the man who lived there is the same man who showed up at the church. The man who everyone else believes is Seth Evans. And third, when Seth's neighbour confirmed it too.

Whatever weird conspiracy theories I had going on in my brain were just *that* – conspiracy theories. I think they were simply a way to explain the glitch in my brain that stopped me recognising my fiancé. The only problem with dismissing that theory is that I now have to accept the fact this stranger actually is the real Seth. That the fault lies with me. In my mind, and not with other people playing some kind of trick on me.

When I spoke to Laurence about it, he had a way of putting me at ease and not making me feel like a total freak for what happened on my wedding day. For what's *still* happening. Because I still don't recognise my fiancé. Not properly. I wonder if I ever will.

I knock on the door and listen for Seth's footsteps, hoping against hope that today might be the day when I experience a glimmer of recognition. My heart is in my mouth as the door opens. But it plummets again when I'm faced with the same handsome stranger standing before me, and not my familiar Seth – even though I now understand they're one and the same.

'Alice,' he says, his eyes warm. 'You came.'

My heart twangs with nerves. I open my mouth to reply, but nothing comes out so I give a short nod instead. I'm aware I must seem standoffish, hostile even, but I can't help this gut reaction I have every time I see the man. In fact, every cell in my body is screaming at me to turn around, get back in my car and drive away.

'After the park, I honestly wasn't sure you'd show up,' he says.

I'm a little offended by his comment, but I don't reply. There's nothing to say to such a statement. Especially as I realise he's got a point.

'Anyway, come in,' he says, taking a step back so I can move inside.

The interior is dark and cool. We walk through the narrow hallway to the bright living room at the rear. The painted white French windows open out on to a pretty country garden with a stream at the far end that looks like an impressionist painting. A garden I thought would be mine. *Ours.* I'm sad at how Brook Cottage is so familiar to me with its scent of fresh flowers and furniture polish, its warm wooden beams, heritage colours on the walls and comfy cream sofas. As I drink in my surroundings, I can almost imagine that nothing bad has happened. That all is as it should be. Until I look at Seth.

He gestures to one of the sofas and I gingerly take a seat. He sits opposite before immediately springing up again. 'Sorry, can I get you a drink?'

'Maybe a water?'

'Sure.' He disappears into the kitchen for a moment and I hear the whoosh of the tap from next door.

I wonder what I'm even doing here. What will it achieve? Am I supposed to have a sudden rush of memory? Will things become clearer? I doubt it.

Seth returns and, as he hands me the cool glass, I feel myself cringing back.

I catch his brief, hurt scowl before he rearranges his features into a more neutral expression. 'How are you?' he grunts, sitting down on the sofa opposite.

I'm grateful for the barrier the glass coffee table forms between us. I'm not sure why. I suddenly remember an argument we had in this very room a few months ago. I'd wanted Seth to come out that evening to meet my friends, but he'd said his time was too precious. That he'd come to Hampshire to see me, not a bunch of strangers. That we only had two days together each week so why would we want to waste time with other people? I'd tried to explain how important my friends were, and that I thought it would be good for them to meet, but Seth simply didn't get it.

The conversation deteriorated and Seth ended up telling me that if my friends were so important then why didn't I just go out with them instead. It was a ridiculous argument, but thankfully I managed to tease and cajole him back into a good mood. From then on, I made sure to put him first, and never pressed the issue of him wanting to spend all his time with only me. I was flattered that I meant so much to him. But looking back on it, I wonder if it was a mistake to capitulate so easily.

'Alice . . .' he prompts, one eyebrow slightly raised.

'Sorry, I was just . . . never mind. What did you say?'

'Just wondered how you are. How your week's been. I know you went to the flat.' He fixes me with a questioning stare.

I flush under his gaze. 'Your neighbour told you.'

'Rob sent me a text, yeah.' Seth is still staring at me as though he's trying to read my mind.

I shake my head. 'I'm sorry. I'll give you back your keys.'

'It's fine. Alice, I want us to make this work.' He leans forward. 'Did you go there to find answers?'

'I don't know. Maybe. I'm not sure.'

'And?'

I shrug. Silence hangs between us.

'So, what else has been happening?' he asks.

I wrench my mind back to the present, trying to recall this past week. I decide not to tell him about my counselling sessions with Laurence. Seth has never been Laurence's biggest fan. He can't understand why one of my best friends is a man. I've reassured Seth time and again that Laurence is like a brother to me and Daisy, but he just doesn't get it. He thinks Laurence must be after something more.

'I don't think I told you, but I had my MRI scan last Friday,' I say, pushing down the cuticle of my left forefinger with my thumbnail.

'That's good. Have you had the results yet? I wish I could have come with you. I want to support you in all this, Alice. I still don't know what's going on here. Do you really not recognise me?' He leans forward and I sense his gaze, but I don't look up. Since the non-wedding, he asks me this same question every time he sees me.

'The scan was clear,' I reply, ignoring his other question. 'Thankfully they didn't find any lesions on my brain.' I try not to think about the sheer terror I felt at the hospital yesterday. The cold sweats and racing heart.

Seth exhales. 'Well that's good. So it's not prosopagnosia.'

'They don't think so. No.'

'So, if it's not that, then what the hell is it? Do they have any other possible diagnoses?'

I turn my attention to the cuticle of my third finger. 'I wish I knew.'

'And you honestly don't?' he pushes.

'No. I already told you. Why would I lie about something like this? What would be the point?' I glance up to see his dark expression and immediately look back down.

'I have no idea,' he replies moodily, flopping back against the sofa cushions.

Something in his tone sparks a memory in me. Or maybe it's just the feeling of a memory. Something not entirely clear. Like I'm remembering the shape of a conversation through a blurred lens. I try to grab hold of it, but it slides away so quickly that I'm not even sure it was real.

Silence descends on the room again. A breeze swishes the cream muslin curtains and I notice the steady tick of the grandmother clock in the corner of the room – an heirloom from Seth's father's side of the family.

The silence soon becomes uncomfortable enough for me to break it. 'Are you still taking the Southampton job, or will you move back to London?' As soon as I ask the question, I realise it was the wrong thing to say. It's basically telling him that I don't want him here. That I'm doubtful things will get back to how they were. That I'm hoping he *will* return to London.

Seth doesn't answer immediately.

I wonder if I should try to retract the question. Smooth things over.

'I guess that depends on you,' he replies, hurt lacing his voice.

I don't know what to say. I feel like a bitch, but I can't help it. My emotions are visceral, bubbling over without warning. I'm dismayed by our thorough lack of connection. Aside from Seth's obvious good looks, I wonder what it was that I originally saw in him. Should I stick it out and keep trying to get to know him again? Try to regain what we had. Find the love. The connection. Hope that I grow to recognise him once more. Or should I just call it quits? All options feel like losing.

I glance up again to see Seth shaking his head, his gaze still fixed on me. I look back down at my nails, trying to shake off my anxiety.

'I'm not even sure going back to London would be possible,' Seth grunts. 'I already handed in my notice and took the new job at Southampton. I'd have to re-apply . . . but what are you saying, Alice? You *want* me to go back to London, is that it?'

'*No*. I don't know. It's really hot in here.' I pull at my shirt, then reach for my water and gulp the rest of it down before returning the empty glass to the coffee table with a loud clunk. I start picking at my nails once more, wondering how soon I can leave. I need to collect my thoughts. While I'm in the same vicinity as him, I can't seem to think straight.

'Alice, can you at least look up? Maybe if you looked at me rather than down at your fingers, we'd have more chance of you recognising me again, if that's even what's really going on here.'

He still doesn't believe me. He refuses to accept that I'm telling him the truth. I curl my fingers into fists and wrench my gaze upwards. His face is tanned, his eyes dark, cheekbones high, jaw square – all the disparate elements that make up a very handsome man. But is he really the man I fell in love with? Because all I see when I look at him is the face of a stranger.

A stranger who scares me.

Chapter Twenty-One

So far, so good.

But I don't want to get complacent.

It's not done yet. Not even half of it.

I pace the living room and contemplate my current situation. My life. What it has been, what it could be. No, I need to think positive. Not what it could be. What it will *be.*

I got lucky, but I need to take advantage of that luck and make this work for me. I need to ease this physical ache. This yearning for the life I was denied.

It's always other people who seem to get their hearts' desires. Always the undeserving ones. The spoilt ones. The charmed ones. Everything falls into their laps. Meanwhile, my life either stagnates or crumbles. People on the outside looking in might envy me. They might say I have everything a person could want. But they're not me. They don't know what I want.

They have no idea.

Chapter Twenty-Two

THEN

I'm so engrossed in my book – a creepy crime novel – that it takes me a moment to register the sound of the doorbell. I look up and frown. I'm not expecting anyone. It's almost nine on a Wednesday evening. Daisy's staying over at Martin's and Seth is in London. A cursory glance at my phone shows no new messages.

With a sigh, I uncurl myself from the sofa and retie my dressing gown over my pyjamas. I peer out of the window, through the bare branches of the sycamore tree, down to the street below and see a man standing there in the rain. He looks up, his face illuminated beneath the security lighting. As he catches my eye, he gives a little wave. My heart sinks. It's Graham, and he's alone.

At the front door, I press the buzzer and wait for him to come up.

Thirty seconds later the bell rings, making me jump, and I open the door to see my brother-in-law standing round-shouldered in the communal hallway, his fair hair damp from the December rain.

'Hey, Alice. Sorry to call round unannounced.' His gaze travels down to take in my dressing gown. His face falls. 'I didn't wake you up, did I?'

'Hi, Graham. No, that's okay, I was just reading.' My sister's fear that he still has feelings for me flashes through my brain. Surely not.

'Oh, that's a relief,' he replies. 'Sorry it's a bit late. I should've come round earlier. Too much work to get through before the holidays. Anyway, I'm rambling . . .'

'Come in.' I stand back to allow him into the flat and he follows me across the hall into the living room. 'Can I get you a drink?' I ask, hoping he says no.

'I'd love a tea. Have you got anything herbal?'

'Mint? Rooibos?'

'Either of those would be great.'

'Take a seat, I'll be back in a sec.' In the kitchen, I make us both a cup of rooibos, using the same teabag for both mugs as it's the last one and we have no mint tea either. I really must go shopping.

Returning to the living room, I see Graham sitting in my favourite spot on the sofa. 'Here you go . . .' I set his mug on the coffee table and take mine over to the dining table, where I sit on the chair furthest away. I don't want us to be having an intimate chat on our own. I'm sure there's nothing untoward going on here, but if Elizabeth is already having suspicions about Graham's feelings towards me, then I don't want to risk any awkward situations.

Graham picks up his mug, blows on his tea and puts it down again. He's still wearing his coat, and the seat where I was curled up moments ago is now damp with rainwater.

'Everything okay?' I ask.

'Oh, you know, the usual. We've got an Ofsted inspection coming up at school so it's absolute mayhem. The teachers are frazzled, the children are hyped up with Christmas around the corner.' He smiles to offset his mini rant.

'Sounds stressful,' I reply. 'But I'm sure you'll pull it off.'

'I hope so.' He shifts in his seat. 'How about you? Work good?'

'Not bad,' I reply. 'Busy, but I like it that way.'

'Good, good.' He clears his throat. 'I wanted to say that I'm sorry about the dinner last week. At the Manor House. I know it wasn't your fault that Seth didn't show up.'

I take offence at his use of the phrase 'didn't show up'. But I don't have the energy to pull him up on it. 'Seth was so sorry to have missed it,' I reply. 'But you really didn't have to come over in this awful weather to apologise. It's all water under the bridge.'

'Lizzie and I didn't mean to make you uncomfortable.'

'It's forgotten,' I say, anxious to get this conversation over with.

He picks up my paperback that's lying on the sofa. 'Any good?' he asks, turning it over and looking at the back cover.

'Well I'm on book five in the series, so yes.' I smile. 'I can lend you book one if you like?'

'That would be great.'

I reach behind me to the bookshelf and pull out two paperbacks. 'Here are the first two. They're pretty addictive.'

'Excellent, thanks.' He picks up his tea and blows on it again, takes a tentative sip and sets it down.

This is painful; I need him to get to the point. 'So, any other reason you wanted to come over tonight? Or was it just to say sorry?'

Twin spots of colour appear on his cheeks and he rubs at his upper arms. 'Well, there is another reason . . .'

Here we go.

'I hope you don't mind me asking, but . . . are you sure you want to marry Seth? It's just . . . I'm not sure he's good enough for you, Alice.'

I shouldn't be surprised at his question after my conversation with Laurence at the weekend, but it's still a bit of a shock. And it's also quite rude. 'Well, I wouldn't have said yes if I wasn't sure,' I reply. My words come out more snappishly than I'd intended, but, honestly, what does he expect?

The colour in his cheeks deepens further.

'Please tell me this isn't what you and Elizabeth were arguing about the other night.'

'She thinks I'm being paranoid about him.'

'Well, maybe she has a point. I mean, you haven't even met Seth, so how can you be passing judgements on him already?'

'Exactly!' Graham says, waggling his finger at me. 'You've been going out with him for months, you're getting married, for goodness' sake, and none of us has met him. Doesn't that tell you something?'

'Yes, it tells me that we all have incredibly busy lives and we need to make more time for each other.'

'Come on, Alice, it's a bit weird.'

I grit my teeth and dig my nails into my thighs. The annoying thing is that Graham's only saying out loud what I've been feeling for months. Why is Seth so resistant to meeting my family? Friends I can kind of understand – it might be a bit intimidating or whatever, but he hasn't even met my parents. Seth and I went out to dinner with his mum and dad in London a couple of months ago, before he proposed. I guess that was Seth wanting to get his parents' seal of approval before he popped the question. So if I could make the effort with his family, then why can't he make the effort with mine?

Christine and Geoff seemed like lovely people. Both doctors, both understandably proud of their only son. And, thankfully, very warm towards me. They also expressed an interest in meeting my family. In fact . . . that could be the way to get Seth down here to meet every-one – if I can get his parents down for a weekend, then he'll have to come along too.

'Look, Graham, I really appreciate you being worried about me, but I'm a grown woman. I can work things out for myself. I think it's more important for you and Elizabeth to be getting along than for you to be worrying about me and Seth.'

'Thanks, but I'll always look out for you, Alice, you know that.'

'Yes, but I don't need you to.'

'But—'

'No. I mean it. Go home and fix things with my sister. I don't want to be the reason you two are fighting.'

Knowing what Elizabeth thinks, I'm annoyed Graham has come here alone. When she hears about this visit, it will undoubtedly make matters ten time worse. Especially as I haven't had a chance to talk to her yet, to put her mind at ease. And now I'm going to have to tell her Graham was here. Because if I don't and it ends up coming out, then this will look like something it isn't.

'Does Elizabeth know you've come over tonight?'

He scratches the side of his head. 'No, I didn't want to bring it all up again. Thought it would be better if you and I smoothed things out between us. She doesn't agree with me regarding Seth, but it would have been wrong of me not to let you know my worries.'

I couldn't disagree with that last sentence more, but maybe he really is trying to be nice without an ulterior motive. I'll give him the benefit of the doubt.

'Okay, well, thanks,' I reply. 'But I think you should tell Elizabeth you popped round. Tell her you borrowed a couple of books. Best not to have any secrets, eh?'

'Oh . . . well . . . yes . . . of course.' His mouth is opening and closing like a fish.

Could Graham really still have feelings for me? I bloody hope not. He's married to my sister. This is awful. I decide to be light-hearted and act as though this is all absolutely normal. 'Thank you so much,' I gush, standing up and handing him the paperbacks. 'It's really good to know that you and Elizabeth are looking out for me. Seth's getting a job transfer to Southampton, so the long-distance thing won't be an issue after the wedding.'

'No, but it's not just the long-distance thing. It's more than that. You're different since you met him.'

'I'm in love,' I say with a breezy laugh.

His face clouds over. 'I just don't want you making a mistake and regretting it, that's all. I care about you, Alice.'

I refuse to be drawn into this conversation, and I especially don't want him to make any embarrassing declaration that he might still have feelings for me. He needs to leave before he says something we both regret.

I fake a yawn. 'Thanks so much again for coming over. I really feel like I have a brother now as well as a sister.' If that doesn't set things straight, then I don't know what will.

He gets to his feet, his tea barely touched. 'Okay, well, I just wanted to say my piece. Thanks for the books. I'll let you know how I get on with them.'

'Great. Say hi to Elizabeth from me.'

He nods and I let him walk ahead of me towards the front door.

'Good luck with Ofsted,' I say. 'I'm sure it'll go well.'

He raises a hand in acknowledgment and finally leaves. I close the door behind him with relief. I feel like I've escaped something. Graham is a good-hearted man and my sister adores him. I always thought he adored her too. But now I'm not so sure.

Chapter Twenty-Three

Now

After days of dodging my parents' calls and visits, I've finally given in to their summons and find myself at theirs for Sunday lunch. I've managed to avoid the previous two weekends, but I couldn't get out of it any longer. My sister and Graham have been messaging me too. Sending their love and support. But I'd rather no one made a fuss. Maybe if they all acted normally around me, I wouldn't feel like such a giant freak. That's not fair. I know it's only because they care.

Thankfully, Graham and Elizabeth couldn't make it today as it's Graham's grandmother's eightieth birthday party. I think it would have been too overwhelming with all four of them passing judgement and making 'helpful' suggestions.

I follow Mum into the garden with a tray of glasses and iced lemonade. She's immaculate as always in a strappy floral sundress, pale-pink raffia sandals and a straw sunhat. I feel underdressed by comparison in navy cargo pants and a white vest top. We're eating on the patio today as the weather still thinks we're having a European summer rather than the usual drizzly British affair.

Dad takes the jug off the tray and starts pouring, ice cubes clinking as they slide into each glass. 'What you need, Alice, is a bit of routine. You should get back to work.'

'I will. I'm just not quite ready yet.' I take a seat in the shadiest spot beneath the sun umbrella. Mum, Dad and Elizabeth are all sun worshippers, but I've always preferred shade. Mum sits next to Dad so they're both facing me and I realise they're colour-coordinated – Dad in a lavender short-sleeved shirt the same tone as Mum's dress. 'Anyway, I'm not due back until next week.'

'Doesn't matter when you're due back,' he replies, vigorously slicing into his Yorkshire pudding. 'What matters is that you start getting back to normal.'

His no-nonsense pep-talk irritates me, yet I can't help begrudgingly agreeing with what he's saying. I have had too much time on my hands. Too much space to brood and think. To wonder about what might have been. To fear the future and doubt myself. But the thought of going back to work makes my stomach lurch. What if I can't do my job any more? How will I be able to face my clients without wondering if they're aware of what happened to me? Ringwood is a small town. Everyone knows everyone's business, so it's not unreasonable to assume that everyone's been talking about it. About *me*.

'The sooner you get back to normal, the sooner you can put all this behind you,' Dad says, bulldozing on. 'What's happening with Seth? You went to see him yesterday, right?'

'Yes.'

'And . . . ?' he asks, putting a forkful of roast potatoes and green beans into his mouth.

I clench my teeth. 'And . . . I still don't recognise him, if that's what you're asking.' I haven't touched my food. Not sure why we're having a roast dinner on what feels like the hottest day of the year, but heaven forbid we break with tradition. I sip my lemonade and try to dredge up an appetite.

Dad nods. 'Okay, but now that we know your scan was clear, you need to spend more time with the man. Get to know him again. You fell in love once, you can do it again, no?'

'Um . . .' We've only just started the main course, but I don't think I can sit here any longer and listen to my father's advice-slash-lecture. The sun has moved around and is now shining directly into my eyes like an interrogation lamp. I shift my chair to the left, but I'm hot and sweaty, jittery and anxious.

'Just going to the loo,' I say, getting up. As I leave, I catch my father's exasperated glance at my mother. I walk across the baking hot terrace, back into the relative cool of the kitchen, along the carpeted hallway and into the downstairs loo where I sit on the toilet seat to gather my thoughts and try to make sense of my car-wreck of a relationship.

It's quiet and chilly in the cloakroom. My eyes still haven't adjusted from the brightness of the garden, but the gloomy interior is a welcome relief. Dad's insistence that I get on with my life is frustrating because of course that's what I want to do. I'd like nothing more than to snap my fingers and get back to how everything was before the wedding, but unfortunately my brain isn't complying. Do I swallow down my doubts and fears and just push on with my previous life? Or do I abandon it all until I figure out whether Seth is still the one?

But how can I get back with a man who I can't even bear to be in the same room as?

I let out a frustrated groan. Why is this happening to me? I just want to live my life! Although it's completely different, I can't help drawing comparisons to my relationship with Damian. That was another horrible situation where I wanted to jump ship. I think I must be cursed.

A tap on the cloakroom door makes me jump.

'Alice, darling, it's Mum.'

I sigh. At least it's not Dad trying to wrestle a decision out of me. 'Coming,' I squeak, standing and peering at myself in the mirror above the basin. My hair has gone frizzy in the humidity, and my skin is covered in a sheen of sweat. I splash my face and blot it with the hand towel before taking a breath and letting myself out of the loo.

Mum is standing at the bottom of the stairs, rubbing at an invisible stain on the banister. 'I was having a clear-out of my wardrobe and came across a couple of nice tops that might suit you,' she says. 'Come up and have a look.'

'What about Dad?' I ask, glancing back towards the garden.

'Oh, he'll be happy out there with his lunch for a while. Come on, it won't take long.'

I'm relieved at the change of subject. Mum and I have always bonded over clothes. I follow her up the stairs, across the landing and into my parents' dressing room, a pristine space of white wood, mirrors and plush grey carpet.

Mum pulls open one of the doors to reveal shelves of tops and sweaters. 'Now, where's that orange cami-top?' She frowns and runs her fingers down a stack of folded silk. 'Ah, here. Try this . . .' She hands me a gorgeous apricot-coloured top that I instantly know will suit me.

'That's so nice!'

She smiles and kisses my cheek, strokes one of my curls. 'I knew you'd like it. Let's see what it looks like on. Better than that grubby vest thing you're wearing, anyway.' She smiles to let me know she's not being mean, just honest. 'Tell me you didn't wear that to Seth's yesterday!'

'No, course not,' I reply, omitting to tell her about the old jeans and stained T-shirt I actually did wear. I peel off my vest top and let the apricot silk slide over my head.

'The colour looks perfect on you,' Mum says. 'I knew it would.' She sits on the large white-velvet ottoman and looks at my reflection in the floor-to-ceiling mirror. 'So, it didn't go very well yesterday?' she asks.

I tense up at her question, feeling the shutters come down on my briefly lifted mood.

'I'm only asking because I'm worried about you,' she continues. 'We both are.'

'Dad's just worried about how it looks to everybody else,' I mutter.

Mum frowns. 'Now that's not fair, Alice. Your father loves you.'

I inhale and will myself not to snap. Not to revert to angry teen-mode. 'I know he loves me, but I just . . . he doesn't want to hear the truth.'

'The *truth*? Of course he does.'

'No he doesn't, Mum. And the thing is, I don't feel anything for Seth. No, that's not true – when I'm around him I feel anxiety, stress . . . I don't even think I actually like him.'

Mum catches my eye in the mirror. She looks shocked and suddenly a lot older than her sixty-one years. 'But you were going to marry him. You were excited. Happy.'

I shrug and sit on the floor cross-legged, picking at the carpet which I know will drive my mother mad, but I can't help it.

'So what are you saying, Alice? You've changed your mind?'

A lump has formed in my throat and I'm finding it hard to speak. Once I say the words out loud then they become real. Am I ready to do that?

'Darling, you know you can tell me anything.' She walks over and sits next to me on the carpet, putting her arm around my shoulders and bringing me in close so I can smell her distinctive scent of Chloé perfume and Dove body lotion. 'Whatever's going on in that head of yours?' She kisses my hair.

'Oh, Mum, it's all gone wrong.' My voice breaks as my emotions rush to the surface. The back of my nose smarts and my eyes sting.

'It's okay, Ally-bear, just have a good cry.' My mother hasn't called me that in years.

This is not what I had planned for today. The idea was to get in and get out, go home and watch a movie or read. Basically block out all emotions and refuse to think about any of it. Instead, the tears are cascading down my sweaty cheeks and dripping off my chin.

'I don't want to marry him, Mum,' I sob. 'I don't think I even like him. I remember the old Seth, but I'm not even yearning after him or anything. And I know I'm probably not even making any sense right now.' I don't tell her that Seth scares me, because he hasn't actually done anything bad. It's just a feeling I get when I'm around him. And I don't want my parents worrying that he's been horrible to me in any way.

Mum strokes my hair and makes soothing noises. 'It'll be okay, Alice. Just have a good cry and you'll feel better. If you don't want to marry the man, then that's fine.'

'What about Dad?' I gulp.

'He'll be all right. He's just worried about you, that's all. If you don't want to marry Seth, that's your decision. Not mine or Dad's. We'll stand behind you, whatever you decide.'

'Thanks, Mum,' I say, sitting up and swiping at my tears with the back of my hand. Even though she's reassured me that Dad will accept my decision, I'm not sure she's right. He's already made it clear he wants us to fix things.

Mum stands and pulls a couple of tissues from a box on her dressing table. 'Here.'

I take them and dab at my face as even more tears start to fall. Now I've started, I can't seem to stop.

'Were you having doubts before the wedding?' she asks tentatively.

I stop and think for a moment. 'I don't think so, no. That's the weird thing about it. Yes, we had our disagreements, but doesn't everyone? I was excited to marry him. Couldn't wait for our wedding. But now, when I look at him or talk to him, I just know that he's not the man for me. Not at all.'

'Well then,' Mum replies. 'That's all you need to know. If he's not the man for you, then of course you're not going to get married. I just want you girls to be happy. That's the most important thing.'

'I think I ruined this top,' I say, looking down at the newly stained silk.

'Better a ruined top than a ruined life,' she replies, pulling me closer for another hug.

I murmur my agreement into her hair. But the trouble is, right now, I feel as though my *life* might be ruined too.

Chapter Twenty-Four

THEN

'You ready?' my sister asks with a twinkly smile as I open the flat door to her.

'Hello. Yes, let me just get my suitcase and phone,' I reply, stupidly nervous.

'I can't wait for this,' Daisy declares, wheeling her purple metallic case across the hall.

We lock up the flat and the three of us make our way downstairs and out into the chilly late-afternoon sunshine. The winter months have fallen away and spring is finally here. We're going off on my hen weekend and I have no idea what's happening. I asked Elizabeth not to plan anything too full on. Just something relaxing that we can all enjoy.

After last year's weirdness between me, Elizabeth and Graham, everything's settled down and Graham now seems to accept that I'll be marrying Seth. Graham hasn't called round on his own after that weird night in December, and, as far as I'm aware, Elizabeth hasn't since accused Graham of still having feelings for me. Thank goodness.

Mum is sitting in the front of Elizabeth's Peugeot and Francesca waves from the back. Elizabeth, Daisy and I load our cases into the car boot, spending a couple of minutes panicking that they won't fit. Eventually, we manage to cram everything in. Elizabeth gets into the driver's seat and Daisy and I slide into the back next to Francesca where we all squeal like kids.

'Where are we going?' I demand.

'Wait and see,' my sister replies.

'Surprises make me nervous,' I reply.

'You don't have to come,' she says, winking at me in the rear-view mirror.

'Fine.' I lean back in the car and fold my arms across my chest, pretending to be annoyed for all of two seconds.

'I made a playlist,' Elizabeth says, fiddling with her phone. After a moment Beyoncé's 'Single Ladies' pounds through the car speakers at full volume. The car pulls away and we all start singing, including Mum who doesn't know the words, but she's giving it a good go.

The drive takes us through the forest and there's already a build-up of Friday traffic, but nothing dampens our collective mood. Elizabeth's soundtrack is cheesily wedding-themed and we're now being treated to Bruno Mars' 'Marry You'.

'Can you at least tell me who else will be there?' I ask. 'I know Miriam's coming later this evening.'

'Just her and Charlotte,' Elizabeth calls from the front.

'Who?' I ask, with a horrible sinking feeling.

'Charlotte, your work colleague. Actually, she messaged me on Facebook and invited herself last minute so I couldn't really say no. That's okay, right?'

I don't want to make Elizabeth feel bad, but that is really not okay. It's bad enough I have to put up with her at work, let alone on my precious time off with friends and family.

'Not Charlotte with the infinite hairdos?' Daisy asks.

I've moaned about Charlotte enough times that Daisy knows exactly my feelings towards her. This would never have happened if Daisy had been my maid of honour.

'Should I not have let her come?' Elizabeth asks, turning down the music, worry sending her voice an octave higher than usual.

'No, it's fine,' I say. 'As long as I don't have to share a room with the girl.'

'She wanted her own room, so you're safe,' Elizabeth replies.

'Phew.' I wipe my brow.

'You're sharing a room with Francesca,' Elizabeth says.

'Yay!' I turn to Laurence's girlfriend and give her arm a squeeze. 'You don't snore, do you?'

'I don't think so,' she replies, looking a little nervous.

'I don't understand why Charlotte asked to come,' I say. 'I thought she couldn't stand me. Maybe she'll be different out of the office . . .'

'It's a shame Seth's mother couldn't join us,' my mum says.

'She couldn't get the time off,' I reply.

As we drive further into the forest, my excitement grows when I think I recognise where we're going. 'Grove Park Spa!' I exclaim as we pass through the impressive wrought-iron gates. 'I've always wanted to come here.'

'Ta-da!' my sister cries. 'Two nights of relaxation, spa treatments, food, drink and the best company.'

'I've never been to a spa before,' Francesca says. 'Not sure about all the massaging and stuff.'

'Oh, you'll love it,' Daisy says. 'You won't want to leave.'

'I'm so excited!' I squeal. Even the thought of Charlotte Emerson can't dampen my mood.

◆ ◆ ◆

After a late-afternoon massage and mani-pedi followed by a sauna and swim, the five of us gather in the hotel bar, wearing our fanciest cocktail attire. I was worried that Mum might have been out of her element, but she looks chic, relaxed and she's sipping cocktails with the rest of us.

It's just after 8 p.m. when Miriam walks into the bar with Charlotte by her side. Miriam does a subtle eye roll in her direction, followed by a huge smile for me and a warm hug.

'Happy Hen Weekend!' she cries, followed by a whispered, 'I didn't know she was coming too.'

'Neither did I,' I mouth back.

Charlotte is perfectly put together in a black cocktail dress, her chestnut hair arranged in a gordian knot at the nape of her neck.

'Love the hair, Charlotte,' Daisy says.

I dare not catch Daisy's eye in case I laugh. But then I immediately feel like a bitch. I've never been a mean girl and I'm not about to start now. It's just that Charlotte has a way of getting under my skin.

'Hi, Alice,' Charlotte says, leaning in to give me a brief kiss on the cheek. 'Sorry we're late, but Miriam and I didn't feel we should leave work early too. Didn't think it would have been fair to leave Paul in the lurch with you gone all afternoon.'

'It's fine, I took a half day's leave,' I reply. 'There was no lurch-leaving.'

'No, of course.' She pats my arm then glances around, raising her voice a notch. 'It's nice here, isn't it? But you should definitely try Milbury Hall in Dorset next time. My boyfriend surprised me for my thirtieth last year with a three-day spa-break there. It was absolutely amazing. We had the Ashiatsu Barefoot Massage.' She stares at us all, gauging our reactions.

Everyone looks blank.

'You must have heard of it,' she says. 'Where they use hanging parallel poles, working with gravity to walk on your back. Amazing for stress release. It's the absolute best thing.'

'Fancy doing that tomorrow, Alice?' Miriam asks dryly.

'Oh, no, sorry, they don't do it here,' Charlotte says with a head tilt. 'That's why I said we should go to Milbury next time.'

'Sounds like a plan,' Daisy replies.

'I'm so sorry,' my sister mouths at me.

'Coincidentally,' Daisy continues, 'we're all drinking Painkillers. What are you having, Charlotte?'

'Aperol Spritz please.' She turns to me. 'It's a bit soon for the hen party, isn't it, Alice? I thought you weren't getting married for a couple of months.'

'We wanted a nice gap between the two,' Elizabeth replies.

'Where are you having the wedding?' Charlotte asks.

'We're having the service at Ellingham Church, and then the reception at the Manor House Hotel,' I reply. 'Just outside Ringwood at—'

'Oh yes, I know it,' Charlotte interrupts and then goes on to detail a particularly sub-par meal she once had there with her boyfriend.

It would seem that Charlotte is not any different out of the office. In fact, she may indeed be worse. I tune her out and concentrate on my cocktail.

After my disagreement with Seth last year about holding our wedding reception at the Manor House, I eventually capitulated. After all, it's the venue I originally had my heart set on so why should I let his ex, Sienna bloody Doyle, put me off my wedding plans? I'm sure she'll do a good job as our wedding coordinator, if only to show Seth how amazing she is. I've pushed down my reservations about her being there because I don't want to turn Seth off me by becoming this demanding, jealous, stress-filled bride-to-be. I want to be Zen, relaxed, desirable, confident and everything in between.

So, the church is booked, the reception is arranged, and the invitations have been sent out. Our wedding date is June 10th, just under two months away. Sadly, it now looks as though I'll also have to invite Charlotte, but you can't win them all.

The rest of the evening passes in a blur of drink, good food and lots of laughter. Mum and Francesca do a great job of keeping Charlotte away from my end of the table so, after a rocky start, I barely notice she's here.

We're all pretty tired after our treatments followed by the alcohol and rich food, so opt for a reasonably early night. We'll let our hair down tomorrow evening when a few more of my friends will be arriving.

I just hope Charlotte isn't going to annoy everyone too much. How can one person spread so much discomfort? If she ends up making partner at work instead of me, I don't know what I'll do.

Chapter Twenty-Five

Now

I'm back at Brook Cottage and this time I'm even more nervous. Because now I'm here to break up with Seth.

It's a warm evening and the cottage is looking at its best with bees and butterflies lazily circling the lupins, hollyhocks and roses in the front garden. The trees are whispering beneath a powder-blue sky, and there's a blackbird perched on the stone chimney pot singing its heart out.

It's strange to think that this was supposed to have been our home together. So many times, I've pictured our lives playing out inside these four walls – love, hopes, dreams, socialising, family, children, maybe a dog and a couple of cats. And now that dream has been popped as easily as a rainbow soap bubble.

The door opens and Seth stands there in a white shirt and jeans. His cologne wafts towards me, mingling with the scent of summer flowers, and I'm hit with a flash of familiarity that leaves me reeling for a moment. But the feeling vanishes before I'm able to acknowledge it properly.

'Alice, are you okay?' Seth's forehead creases.

I'm standing here with my mouth hanging slightly open. I clamp it shut before replying. 'Uh, yes, sorry. I was miles away.' I don't want to admit the truth – that I just had a weird déjà vu-type memory of him.

'Come in,' he says. 'I made us some food. Your favourite, actually – my cashew stir-fry with noodles.'

I realise that *is* my favourite, but it's also tied up with these sudden complicated feelings that I can't explain. 'You didn't need to do that,' I say. 'It might not be a good idea for us to sit and have a meal together.'

'Why not?' He shrugs. 'It's prepared now. All I need to do is throw the ingredients into a wok. Five minutes and we can eat. I'm hungry, I don't know about you.'

I'm aware that I haven't eaten anything since lunchtime, six hours ago, although that's not the point. The point is, that if we sit down to eat, Seth might get the wrong idea about why I'm here. I pause. 'Okay, thank you,' I say, unable to think of an excuse why I can't stay for dinner without blurting that I'm here to end things, which would be far too harsh and abrupt.

I follow him through to the pretty country kitchen, acknowledging to myself that this will probably be the last time I set foot inside his beautiful home. That realisation gives me a complicated sense of relief and sadness.

Freshly sliced vegetables are already laid out in a colourful array on the wooden chopping board. Seth nods to an opened bottle of white on the side. 'Help yourself,' he says, turning on the centre gas-ring of the range that dominates the tiny kitchen. He drizzles olive oil into the huge black wok and reaches into the cupboard for a bottle of sweet chilli sauce.

I've come here to break up with this man, so it doesn't feel right to be drinking wine and watching him cook like everything is hunky-dory. 'No, that's okay,' I reply. 'I'll just have a glass of water.'

'Half a glass of wine won't kill you,' he says, splashing a generous half into both glasses.

I hear the subtle slur in his voice and am suddenly and sharply aware that Seth is drunk. I think I might need to get to the point of my visit before he knocks back any more alcohol.

He hands me a glass and clinks his against mine. 'Here's to us sorting things out,' he says loudly.

I'm unable to echo his toast.

'Alice?' he pushes. 'To sorting things out, right?'

'The thing is . . .' I begin, putting my wine glass back on the counter.

'No,' he declares, cutting me off. 'None of that. We'll eat first, talk later. Nothing good comes of talking on an empty stomach.'

I now sincerely wish I hadn't come here this evening. I should have met him earlier in the day in a neutral place like a café or a park. Somewhere without alcohol and without memories.

Seth tips the sliced onion into the wok, where it hisses and spits in the oil. Then he adds the cashews, and finally slides the rest of the veggies in. He's uncoordinated, and around 10 per cent of the ingredients miss the wok and end up either on the hob or the flagstone floor.

'Shit.' Seth flails, trying to save the flying vegetables, but ends up dropping the chopping board on to the floor with a dull clatter. I bend to pick it up, but he waves me away. 'It's fine, it's fine, I've got it.'

I take a step back and inhale, wondering if I should just go home immediately and attempt to initiate our break-up another time. But the thought of leaving our relationship open-ended is worse than the thought of having this difficult conversation right now.

I decide to power through and just do it.

'Seth . . .'

'Hang on, the onions are burning, I need to turn the hob down.'

The kitchen is already too warm from the heat of the range, and the vegetables are sizzling so loudly I can barely hear myself think. 'Seth, can you turn it off, I need to talk to you.'

'It won't take a minute. I just have to add the noodles and chilli sauce.' His previously pristine shirt is currently being spattered with cooking oil. He wipes at the stains ineffectually.

'*Please*, just turn it off and listen to me!' I cry.

'Fine! But if I turn it off now, dinner will end up soggy.' He pushes his dark hair back from his face and clenches his jaw.

I want to scream that I don't care about the bloody stir-fry, but I need to keep calm. Finally, he does as I ask and turns off the hob.

I exhale.

'What is it, Alice?' He turns to look at me, his cheeks red, sweat beading his forehead.

'I think you know,' I reply, pulling at the neck of my top to try to cool down. I shift my gaze away from his face as it still gives me anxiety to look at him. Makes me light-headed. Makes me need to catch my breath.

He slurps his wine. I still haven't touched mine.

'I'm sorry,' I reply, pulling at my fingers and staring at the stains on Seth's shirt. 'But I think it's best if we just end things now. To save any more heartache. It's just . . . it's not working. I don't feel like I know you. I really am sorry.'

His face seems to crumple. His body sags and he leans back against the counter. 'Alice, please,' he whispers. 'I love you.'

His expression makes me sad, but not sad enough to change my mind. It's as though I'm watching a really good actor on TV. Someone who makes me empathise with them, but I know it's not real. I don't know what else to say to him. I'd been vainly hoping that he might be relieved too. That me ending things would let him off the hook. Instead, he really does seem to be upset.

'Alice, you can't make such a huge decision yet. You're not yourself.' His eyes are filling with tears.

'I'm sorry,' I repeat for what seems like the hundredth time.

'Don't do this to me. I left my job for you. I moved here. For you. And now you're telling me it's over, that you don't know me. It's bullshit!' He wipes the tears from his cheeks and reaches out to take my hand.

I take a step back, keeping my hands by my sides. 'I wish I knew what to say, Seth. But I can't fake feelings. Something's happened that's changed things. It's not what I wanted or planned. But it is what it is.'

Hope flares in his eyes. 'If this isn't what you wanted or planned, then change it! You can get to *know* me. Pretend we've just met. You fell in love with me once, you can fall in love again.'

I shake my head. 'If it was that simple I would. But it's not,' I say, my voice sounding too loud in this small space. How can I explain to Seth that us being in the same room makes me uneasy, anxious, sick? He would never understand. *I* don't understand. *No*; the best thing for us is a clean break so we can both move on with our lives.

'You can get help,' he cries. 'I've been saying that ever since it happened. I know some good doctors in that field.' He picks up his phone from the counter. 'Let me send you their details. Or I can make you an appointment. Something has happened to you, Alice. Ever since the wedding, you've been a different person. You can't make this kind of decision about us until we've done everything we can to try to fix it.'

The thought of months of appointments, therapy and more brain scans makes me feel ill. But worse than that is the thought of spending months in the company of this man. It might sound harsh, but right now, I would rather just end things with Seth and carry on with the rest of my life. I can't allow his arguments to sway me. I have to stay firm in my decision. 'I'm sorry, Seth, but I've made up my mind.'

His expression darkens. 'You might not recognise me, Alice, but let me tell you something . . . I don't recognise you either! It's like someone else has taken over your brain. Where's the sweet, fun, confident woman I was about to marry? Because you're not it.'

I shake my head at his words. 'Do you think I chose this?'

'I don't know.' He drags his fingers through his hair. 'I can't stop wondering if you might have made this whole thing up to get out of marrying me! Although I've no idea what I did to make you change your mind.'

'Do you honestly believe I would do this on purpose?' I reply. 'Everything's a mess! My whole life has been turned upside down. But instead of worrying about *me*, you're more concerned about yourself. About how this affects *you*. I know it's hard for you too, but I thought that as the person who was going to be my husband, you might have been just a little bit more supportive about what I'm going through, instead of accusing me of making things up.'

'That's not fair,' he says. 'Of course I'm worried about you! I'm just finding this whole thing hard to wrap my head around. You have to admit it's not a normal situation.'

I can't see this conversation heading anywhere good. Seth wants me to change my mind, but I'm 100 per cent set on ending things. I take his London keys from my pocket and place them on the countertop. 'I'm going to leave now, Seth.' I turn to go.

'Don't.' He reaches out his hand again and I recoil, banging my hip on the door handle and swearing under my breath. I'm hot and stressed and I need to get out of here.

He raises his hands in surrender. 'Fine, go. But just know that you've broken my heart, Alice Porter.'

I choke out another, 'I'm sorry,' before stumbling back through the dimly lit hall and out into the sun-drenched evening where I'm now gasping for breath. I thought I would feel pure relief after ending things, but instead there's an ache in my chest and a coldness spreading through my body that even the sun isn't able to warm.

If I still don't want that man in there, then why do I feel so sad?

I walk blindly through the front garden back to my car where I slide into the driver's seat, shut the door and take a few moments to pull myself together. Glancing back at the cottage, I see a shape at the upstairs window. Seth has obviously gone up there to watch me leave. Despite my trembling fingers, I start up the car and pull away, driving shakily along the narrow winding country lanes.

There's a silver car behind me, the dying sun glinting off its shiny paintwork. I need to be more careful, or the driver will think I'm under the influence. I turn on the radio, searching for music rather than the annoyingly chirpy adverts I keep landing on. Finally I find a nineties channel and hum along to a song I vaguely recognise from my childhood.

The music helps soothe me, but it doesn't drown out Seth's parting words – that I've broken his heart – which keep spinning round and around in my head. I glance in my rear-view mirror to see that the silver car has dropped back.

I take a breath and focus on the road ahead, trying not to read anything into the fact that I suddenly remember there was a silver car parked along the lane outside Seth's house when I left. There are hundreds of silver cars. Thousands. Even if it was the same car, that doesn't mean anything. Why then do my thoughts keep boomeranging back to Damian? I don't even know what car he drives these days. I don't even know if it was him I saw a couple of weeks back. I'm being stupid.

My eyes flick back up to the mirror. I swallow. The car is still there, more sinister now that my imagination is in full flow. I press down a little harder on the accelerator. I can't be sure, but it feels like the silver car is matching my speed. I'm forced to slow as I approach the junction that will take me back on to the main road towards Ringwood. My heart rate speeds up as the car tightens the gap between us, drawing closer. The sun is so bright, I can't see through its windscreen. I wonder if the driver can see me inside my car. I wonder if it's him.

Cars and lorries thunder along the main road, preventing me from pulling out. Sweat breaks out on my upper lip as I check my car doors are all locked now that the silver car is right behind mine. I tell myself that I'm just stressed after breaking up with Seth. That my emotions are making me paranoid. But even though I tell myself this, it doesn't stop the fear rolling through me.

Finally, a tiny gap in the traffic opens and I clumsily pull out, making an approaching BMW brake hard. The guy sounds his horn and flashes his lights at me. I flinch and speed up, wiping a sweaty palm on my top and waving in an apology that hasn't been accepted if the red-faced man's facial expressions are anything to go by. His BMW draws aggressively close for a moment before eventually dropping back.

I exhale and check my mirrors for the silver car. I don't see it, but that doesn't mean it isn't back there somewhere. Even though I continue to check my mirrors obsessively all the way home, thankfully I don't spot it again. But still a residual fear clings to me for the rest of the evening, mingling with the relief and sadness of having ended my relationship with Seth.

Chapter Twenty-Six

THEN

We all meet downstairs in the orangery for a late breakfast.

'I feel like we're in an Edwardian play,' Mum says, lifting her bone-china teacup and looking around, 'what with all the hot-house plants and wicker furniture.'

'And these mosaic floor tiles are gorgeous,' I add.

'I know, right?' Elizabeth laughs. 'After breakfast, we should gather our parasols and take a stroll in the morning air,' she proclaims, getting into the spirit of things.

'Actually, I think this is more of a Victorian design than Edwardian,' Charlotte says.

'Did you sleep well, Alice?' Daisy asks, purposely ignoring Charlotte.

'Really well, thanks. Fran and I chatted for about ten minutes, but I must have nodded off.'

'I think you fell asleep mid-sentence,' Francesca says with a giggle.

'Sorry about that! I'm not used to so much rest and relaxation. I think my body is going into shut-down mode. So, what's the plan for today?'

'I saw a tennis court round the back,' Charlotte says. 'Who's up for a game?'

'Maybe later,' Miriam replies. 'I'm too hungover for sports right now. But I'm definitely up for a walk around the grounds. Anyone fancy it?'

'Me,' Elizabeth replies. 'I booked lunch for one fifteen, and then some of us have treatments at three.'

'Then chilling by the pool after?' Daisy asks.

'Definitely,' I reply.

'I'll have a knockabout with you on the court, Charlotte,' Mum says, kindly.

'Oh, thanks.' Charlotte purses her lips. 'But I was thinking more of a proper game. I used to play semi-professionally when I was younger and I don't get much of an opportunity to play these days.'

'Oh dear,' Mum replies. 'I'm not really at that level. Maybe I'll join the walk instead.'

I squeeze Mum's hand.

'Anyone else fancy a game?' Charlotte asks, her head swivelling, her gaze encompassing the group.

But no one responds to her tennis challenge, so we finish breakfast and arrange to meet in the lobby in half an hour for a walk.

The morning passes in a wonderful haze of friendship, laughter, stunning scenery and gentle sunshine. Then, after a delicious lunch, we head back to our rooms for an indulgent nap before arranging to meet down at the spa after our treatments. I've opted for an aromatherapy massage and, as I head out of the locker room in my robe and slippers, I already feel pleasantly woozy from my nap. In fact, I can barely keep my eyes open.

'Alice. Alice . . . Miss Porter.'

I gasp and try to open my eyes, A feeling of dread shrouds me, followed by heat and panic.

'Are you okay? I think you drifted off there.'

I blink and grimace at the sour taste in my mouth, trying to work out what's going on. It comes back to me in fragments.

The last thing I remember was the massage therapist leading me into one of the treatment rooms. Soft music and sounds of the ocean. The air was perfumed with something rich and expensive. I've bought candles and diffusers before, but never managed to recreate that perfect 'spa' scent. I remember lying on the bed with my head facing down through the hole. The therapist's voice coming at me from a long way away, muffled as though she was talking to me through a wall. My eyes drooping and finally closing.

I remember thinking that it was such a wasted opportunity to fall asleep and not be present to enjoy the soft pummelling of my skin, the delicious scents and feelings of deep relaxation, but I just couldn't help myself. I felt like I was falling off a cliff into nothingness. But as I fell, I looked up. And I saw that Seth was up there on the cliff . . . watching me fall.

And now I'm awake.

I feel slightly embarrassed and ridiculous.

'Sorry,' I croak. 'I think I fell asleep.'

'You were pretty out of it,' the therapist says. 'Hopefully, you'll still feel the benefit of the massage. I'll leave you to wake up properly and get back into your robe. I'll be back in a few minutes, okay?'

'Thanks.'

I hear the door open and feel the whisper of fresh air over my skin, followed by the dull thud of the door closing again.

My throat is parched, and I feel groggy and nauseous. I sit up, relieved to see my water bottle on the chair. I slip my robe back on, slide into my slippers and take a few long swigs. I'm desperate to get some fresh air into my lungs. To cool off and try to feel normal again.

Annoyingly, despite a cool shower, a walk outside, and lots of water, I still feel weirdly out of it for the rest of the afternoon. Perhaps I had too much alcohol last night and that, combined with the detoxifying massage, has wiped me out. Whatever the reason, it's frustrating and feels like such a waste. We all meet by the pool and relax on the loungers, but my head is throbbing and my throat still dry, despite drinking what feels like gallons of water. And I can't shake a deep feeling of dread. One that's strangely tied up with that terrible image of Seth standing up on the clifftop, a dark shape receding as I fell.

I hope and pray that my head will clear by the time the evening comes, but it's still as woolly as it was earlier. I'm having to brush off all the concern from everyone as to whether I'm feeling okay. I'm trying to act my way through it. To be as present as I'm able to be. I nip back to my room and wash down a couple of paracetamol, but they have no effect whatsoever. It seems like I'm locked into this state of mind.

◆ ◆ ◆

By 10 p.m. everyone except me is very drunk. Even Mum is tipsier than I've ever seen her before. After the meal, she kisses my forehead and says she's going up to bed to leave us all to it. I wish I could go up too, but Elizabeth has organised this whole weekend for me so I need to try to power through. To pretend I'm enjoying myself. Maybe I'm just overwhelmed by everything. After all, this is my hen night. I'm getting married in a couple of months. Moving into Brook Cottage with Seth. That's quite a big deal.

My school friends Janey, Madeline and Danica arrived some time earlier and I have a vague recollection of hugging them, trying to act happy and normal, instead of this strange heavy-headed sensation that's stuck with me ever since my massage. I wonder if maybe I was allergic to one of the essential oils and it's affected my mind.

'Are you listening, Alice?'

I look across the table in the hotel bar to see a woman with shiny dark hair frowning across at me. I realise it's Charlotte, but her hair

157

is loose for once and she looks so different. Like an alternate-reality version of herself.

'*Sorry, Charlotte, what were you saying?*'

I realise she looks upset, and I sigh internally. I don't have the mental capacity to deal with her drama right now. I glance around, but everyone else is at the bar.

'*I just wanted to ask you,*' *she says,* '*why you asked Miriam to be a bridesmaid and not me. I mean, I know it's your choice, but she's only the office manager and you and I have known each other for longer. I was actually really hurt when she told me yesterday that you'd asked her. I thought you and I were friends.*' *Her lower lip juts out and she blinks, trying to hold my gaze.*

I'm actually so taken aback by her words that my head begins to clear, fizzing away at the edges like spray cleaner on a smeary windscreen.

'*Alice? Did you hear what I said?*' *Charlotte tucks a strand of hair behind her ear and gives me an earnest look. Her eyes are wide with hurt, and she's chewing her lower lip.*

'*Um, yes.*' *I half nod, half shake my head, and take a breath.* '*To be honest, Charlotte, I thought you hated me.*'

She screws up her face. '*What? Why would you think that?*'

I scrutinise her expression and realise she's serious. '*Because . . . I guess you come across that way at work. Like I annoy you. You make snide comments and talk about me to Paul.*' *I wonder if I've gone too far, telling her all this. But maybe it's better to get everything out into the open.*

'*That's just banter,*' *she says, wrinkling her nose.*

If that's the case, then her version of banter between friends is very different to mine. '*Oh,*' *I reply.*

'*You know, two friends having a laugh,*' *she continues.* '*It's work. It's competitive, but that shouldn't ruin our friendship.*'

'*But we don't see each other socially.*'

'What do you call this?' She throws her arms wide to encompass our evening.

I refrain from telling her she invited herself.

'So, yeah,' she says. 'I just wanted you to know, you hurt my feelings.'

'Well, I'm sorry,' I say. 'That wasn't my intention. But I'm glad you're here now.'

'Really?' she asks. 'You're glad I'm here?'

'Of course,' I reply. 'Wouldn't have said so otherwise.' She doesn't look convinced so I stand up and hold out my arms. 'Let's hug it out.'

She comes around the table and we have an awkward hug. In a weird way, despite how annoying she can be, I am glad Charlotte came. Maybe this will clear the air between us and the office environment will feel less hostile. Now I know that her comments are just 'banter', I can stop being so on edge.

I realise I'm actually grateful to Elizabeth for inviting her. Charlotte might not be my favourite person in the world, but maybe now at least we can have a better working relationship. As long as she doesn't push the point about wanting to be a bridesmaid. I'm glad we've called a truce, but I don't think I could cope with her being up there front and centre on the most important day of my life.

Chapter Twenty-Seven

Now

My pulse races as I walk hesitantly to the front door. I haven't seen Miriam since my wedding day and, while I'm pretty confident she'll be supportive of me, you never can tell for sure.

She's been messaging me ever since it happened, regularly checking in on how I am, even though I never replied. But then she wrote a couple of days ago asking if we could meet up. I know I can't ignore my friends forever, but I've been dreading the inevitable pitying looks and awkward questions from everyone. It wouldn't be so bad if I had answers to give them. But I don't.

Since my official break-up with Seth two days ago, I've been dragging myself around the flat like someone who's broken-hearted. But that can't be right because I don't love Seth Evans. Not this version of him anyway. Maybe it's not my heart that's broken. Maybe it's my whole self.

I finally messaged Miriam back and said she was welcome to pop round today after work, and now here she is.

I open my front door, preparing to put on a happy, don't-worry-everything's-okay act. But as soon as I see Miriam, I know I don't have to put on any kind of show. My lovely friend flings her arms around me and gives me the biggest hug.

Don't cry, don't cry, don't cry, I tell myself. Too late.

'I've been so worried about you!' she says, stepping back and giving me a glare that melts into a tear-filled frown when she sees my face.

'I'm sorry,' I gulp. 'I just didn't feel up to talking to anyone. I was so embarrassed and sad and—'

She holds up a hand. 'Stop. You don't have to explain.'

'Anyway,' I say, attempting to sound normal, 'come in.'

She hands me a gift bag that contains a bottle of gin, tonic water, a fresh lemon and a packet of posh crisps.

'You didn't need to do that,' I say.

'Yes I did,' she replies. 'It's for me as much as for you. I hope you've got ice.'

'Thanks. I think so, yes.' We head to the kitchen where I prepare our drinks on autopilot. 'Daisy's at Martin's place, so it's just us here.'

'Is she staying there at the moment?'

'On and off,' I reply, tipping the last four ice cubes into our drinks before refilling the tray. 'Martin's supposed to be moving in here soon, but I'm not sure when. I think I wrecked their plans.' I dump the crisps into a bowl and we head into the lounge where we both sit on the sofa.

'Look,' Miriam says, 'I just want you to know, you don't have to tell me anything about what happened with Seth. I wanted to see you because you're my friend and I'm here for you.'

'You're going to make me cry again,' I say with an emotional half-cough, half-laugh.

'Well I don't want that,' she says with a frown, sipping her G & T. 'Mm, that's good.'

'I actually ended things with Seth a couple of days ago,' I blurt out.

161

Miriam doesn't reply straight away. She blinks her cat eyes slowly and sips her drink. 'I'm sorry,' she finally says. 'Are you okay?'

I sigh. 'Partly relieved, partly devastated.'

'I get that.'

I love the way Miriam doesn't ask a hundred questions. She's calm and supportive without judging or digging for more information.

'I just don't feel the same way about him any more,' I add. 'But now I feel a bit all over the place. With Martin moving in here soon, I have to move out and find somewhere else . . . Not that Daisy's kicking me out or anything. She said I can stay as long as I like. But I know that's not fair on her.'

'Parents?' she asks.

I shake my head. 'They'd have me back but it would drive me crazy. No, I need my own space. I'm going to look for a little one-bedder to rent.'

'Sounds good.'

'Unless . . .' I glance at Miriam. 'Don't suppose you're looking to move out of your parents' place and want to get a flat together?'

She shakes her head. 'If I were, you'd be the first person I'd ask. But I'm saving for a deposit. Trying to get on that elusive ladder.'

'Don't blame you. I should probably do the same. We were going to move into Seth's parents' cottage, but now . . .' My stomach feels as though it's dropping away.

'You'll be okay,' Miriam says. 'Having your own little cosy flat will be lovely.'

'You're right.' I nod, feeling a little more cheered by her words. I glance down at the sofa as my phone pings. It's a WhatsApp from Laurence:

Just to let you know, I did some digging and Damian definitely still lives in Wales, so no need to worry about him x

I exhale and close my eyes briefly before banging out a quick reply:
Thank you 😊 xx

'Everything okay?' Miriam asks.

'Yeah, all good. Just Laurence confirming something for me.'

'Oh, okay, cool.'

'Anyway, how's work?' I ask, unwilling to get into a discussion about Damian. I'd be happy to never have to think about him again. I only hope that Laurence's discovery is accurate. Just because Damian lives in Wales doesn't mean he can't come back for a visit. My skin grows hot then cold at the thought.

'Work is definitely not as enjoyable without you there,' Miriam replies.

I'm happy Miriam's here to take my mind off my ex. Even if talking about work makes me feel strange. The office seems like worlds away. A foreign land I haven't visited in years. 'And *Charlotte*?' I ask.

'Awful. Worse, if anything.' Miriam looks glummer than I've ever seen her.

'*Why?* I thought she'd got over herself. She's been kind of okay since the hen weekend. Almost human. What's happened?'

Miriam blows out a noisy breath. 'Since . . . the wedding' – she hesitates over those two words – 'Charlotte's gone right back to her old self. Rude, snooty, sucking up to Paul even more than before. Revelling in the fact you're not there. And . . .'

'And *what*?' I ask, not sure if I want to hear the answer.

'I didn't want to add to your worries, but the main reason I wanted to come over is to let you know . . . I think your career plans might be in danger.'

My first instinct is to dismiss Miriam's worries. Work and office politics are the last things on my mind right now after everything

I've been through. But, even so, I can't help my chest constricting at her words. 'In danger? How?'

'Sorry, I know that sounds over-dramatic, but she's definitely gunning for the partnership position.'

'That's nothing new,' I reply, trying to quell my alarm. 'She's always been insecure and jealous. She's wanted to make partner ever since she joined.'

'Yes, but since the wedding, she's been using really below-the-belt tactics to edge you out of the running.'

'Let me guess,' I say. 'Talking about me behind my back?'

'Afraid so. I've heard her bad-mouthing you to Paul more than a few times. Really unsubtle stuff about your state of mind. Digging the knife in and outright lying.'

I grit my teeth. My already raw emotions are now hardening into a fury that Charlotte's been using my distress for her own ends. It makes me wonder if she's simply turning my absence to her advantage, or whether this is what she's been planning all along. My loss has certainly become her gain. But how much of that was premeditated? I take a sip of my drink, and then another, as Miriam continues listing Charlotte's transgressions.

'She's been attacking the quality of your work and criticising how you handle your clients. Which is all absolute bollocks, as we both know she's useless with clients. I've tried to big you up to Paul, but he doesn't listen to me. To him, I'm just a glorified admin assistant.'

'Well that's not true!' I say. 'The office would fall apart without you there.'

'Thanks, but don't worry about *me*, I think you need to get back in the office to remind Paul Faraday how incredible you are at your job. Charlotte knows damn well you're more likely to be made partner. So she's totally revelling in this new-found opportunity while you're away. You need to come back pronto.'

My heartbeats are thrumming in my chest. Reverberating through my body. My nerve endings tingle and my head swims as I picture my career going down the toilet. I've been so caught up in my personal life that I haven't given work a moment's thought over the past two weeks. I take another gulp of my drink as I try to take everything in.

I wasn't due to return to the office until Monday, but I think I might need to go back tomorrow. I haven't felt emotionally ready to face it yet, but I can't let Charlotte get away with this. I have to get in there and stand my ground. Show Paul that I'm the better candidate. Make him see that Charlotte's been talking out of her arse. I'm not prepared to throw away years of work. To sit at home crying while she swoops in and takes what's mine.

I can't lose my career as well as my relationship. Otherwise what will I have left?

Nothing.

Chapter Twenty-Eight

I can't believe it!

I absolutely. Cannot. Believe it.

As I walk away down the road, I'm filled to the brim with nervous energy. Birds are chirping in the trees and the sky is a jubilant blue. The warm summer air is thick with the promise of a perfect future.

Part one of my plan is actually complete. Which means part two can now go ahead. Although I'll have to orchestrate this next part just as carefully. I can't afford to get sloppy now. Not while everything is going so well.

Only in my wildest dreams did I think this could happen. The sickness in my stomach is receding. The never-ending darkness is lightening because the stars are finally aligning. It's like an actual miracle is occurring. All the gods have heard my prayers and have decided to answer with a resounding YES.

Things are falling into place better than I could have ever expected. Now, I simply have to hold my nerve and see things through to the end.

Chapter Twenty-Nine

Now

I press my right hand to my belly. It feels like an actual, physical punch to the gut.

I've come back to work after Miriam's warning. But it's too late. *I'm* too late.

Charlotte has just told me her 'exciting' news while Paul is on his mobile pretending he hasn't seen me come in. I bet he's faking his phone call while he works out what he's going to say to me to explain his actions.

'Paul literally asked me yesterday after work,' Charlotte says, her eyes bright, *triumphant*. 'And of course I said yes. How could I not? It's such a validation of all the hard work I've put in over the years.'

It's a good job I'm already sitting at my desk, because I don't think my legs would have kept me upright. 'Congratulations,' I say blankly, my mind spooling forward, thinking about how even more unbearable she's going to be once she's an actual partner here.

'But how are *you*?' she asks, her head tilted, her features arranged into an insincere expression of concern. 'Are you sure you're all right to be back at work? I'm sure Paul and I can grant you some compassionate leave, if you need it. I was telling him that my friend's sister had a breakdown and it took her months to get back on track. You just take all the time you need. Although obviously we'd have to talk about timescales.'

I lock eyes with Miriam who's standing by the printer and looks just about ready to come over and throttle her.

'I didn't have a breakdown, Charlotte,' I say calmly. 'I split from my fiancé.'

'Oh.' She frowns. 'It's just, at the church it looked like . . . I don't know, like you had some kind of episode.'

Miriam strides over. 'Hey, Charlotte, it's probably not appropriate to grill work colleagues about their personal and health issues.'

Charlotte's colour rises. 'I was just showing concern. And anyway, Alice is a friend as well as a colleague.'

'Thanks for the concern,' I reply. 'But there's no need. I'm fine.'

'Well, good,' Charlotte says a little huffily. 'Now that I'm being made partner, I want to make sure all our employees are fit, happy and healthy.'

'Jeez, she's not a racehorse,' Miriam says.

'Alice, you're back,' Paul says, walking over to my desk like he's only just spotted me. 'We weren't expecting you until Monday.'

'No, well, I was going a bit stir-crazy at home. Needed to get back into the office. You know I've never been very good at holidays.'

He nods and re-adjusts his glasses. 'I'm sorry about the wedding. That must have been hard.'

I nod, wondering which version of events he heard. Seth cheating? Me cheating? Me having a breakdown? Alien abduction?

'Must have been a bit of a blow,' he adds.

Almost as much of a blow as finding out the last five years of my working life count for nothing, I want to reply.

'Shall we chat in the conference room?' he asks me.

'Sure,' I reply, feeling my blood stir.

'Maybe I should come too,' Charlotte says, nodding officiously.

'No, that's fine,' Paul replies to my relief. 'Alice and I have things to discuss.'

Charlotte purses her lips, nods and slinks back to her desk.

Miriam gives me a look of solidarity as I follow Paul across the office. This was not how I was expecting to spend my first day back. I thought I'd be catching up on emails and checking up on clients. Not hearing excuses as to why and how my work nemesis has stolen my promotion.

Paul and I sit at the large conference table at right angles to one another. He takes off his glasses and gives them a quick clean with a cloth from his pocket before replacing them on the bridge of his nose. He clears his throat. 'That's not how I wanted you to find out about the partnership,' he says. 'I wasn't expecting you back until Monday so I was going to brief Charlotte to stay quiet and let me tell you about it.'

I take a breath. 'To be honest, Paul, it doesn't really matter who told me; it's still a kick in the teeth.'

He presses his lips together. 'I know you're disappointed, but I have to think of the business.'

'When have I ever *not* thought of the business?'

'I know,' he says, 'but with your breakdown, I couldn't risk—'

'Um, who said anything about a breakdown?' I snap, fed up with all the conclusions everyone's jumping to.

'Well . . .' he holds his hands out. 'The wedding. I was there, and Charlotte said—'

'Oh, well, if Charlotte said something detrimental about me then it must be true. I mean it's not as if she'd have any ulterior motive for denigrating me, is it?' I roll my eyes, knowing that this isn't going to do anything to help my cause. Paul doesn't do well with 'scenes' or drama of any kind. I should just try to stay calm and professional. But the problem is, I'm at the end of my rope; I couldn't stay calm right now if my life depended on it.

'I still really value you as an accountant,' he says weakly.

I nod and get to my feet. 'Thanks. Good to know how much you value me. Well, I think I'll skip today and come back on Monday as planned.'

'Oh. Yes, of course.' He stands awkwardly. 'I didn't ask, how are you doing, Alice? After the wedding and everything.'

I give him a look of utter disbelief. 'Oh, just peachy, Paul. Thanks for asking.' I leave the conference room, grab my bag, and mouth to Miriam that I'll message her later. As I walk down the stairs and out into the relentlessly bright sunshine, I feel like the weather is mocking me. We spend so many days complaining about cold, wet Britain, but now when there are these endless days of sunshine, all I feel like doing is hiding away in my room.

My phone rings and I rummage in my bag trying to fish it out. By the time I have it, the call has gone to voicemail. I walk in the direction of home and wait for a minute before playing the message:

'Hey, Porter, just calling to see how you are. We haven't caught up since last week. Wondered what you're doing this evening. Fran's organised a fundraiser at the pub tonight for the animal shelter and wondered if you wanted to come along. She's setting things up early, but I could swing by and call for you at sevenish if you're up for it. Let me know.'

I curl my lip and feel my shoulders slump. There's no way I'll feel up to going out and being sociable tonight. Then again, do I really want to stay home and wallow? I can already feel myself sinking. I don't want to be this miserable person, but I don't know how to shake myself out of it. I'm dreading a whole day at home alone.

I return Laurence's call and he answers straight away. 'Did you get my message?'

'Yeah, but I was wondering if you're free to meet up now?'

'What, *right* now?'

'Yes, if you're not busy.'

'Okay, sure, shall I come to yours?'

'That would be great.' I exhale and feel marginally better knowing I won't be alone all day with my thoughts.

'I'll bring coffees,' he adds.

'And a Danish?' I ask cheekily.

'Definitely a Danish.'

I walk the rest of the way with a slightly lighter step, trying to absorb the shock of this morning. But I'm just so frustrated and angry with the unfairness of it all. If Charlotte were a better accountant than me, or even an equal, it wouldn't sting so much. But the fact is, she's all show and no real substance. Oh well, I suppose Paul will just have to find out the hard way.

As I approach my road, a figure catches my eye. A man walking away with a distinctive swagger. His broad shoulders and dark hair reminding me of someone . . .

Damian.

I freeze for a moment, blinking and staring at the receding figure. Could it really be him? I think back to a couple of weeks ago when I thought I saw him outside Hibiscus. I dismissed it then, but what if it really is him? What if he glances back and sees me?

I press myself into the open porch of a doorway, my heart pounding, my breaths tight. After a moment, I peer out to see him disappear around a corner. Was it him? Or just someone with the same physique and hair colour? Laurence said Damian's living in Wales now. But what if he's visiting or, even worse, what if he's moved back to Ringwood? Even if he has, it's been years; I'm sure he's moved on from me.

Sweat trickles down my back. How can this man be having such an effect on me after all this time? It's not right. Why am I even hiding? It's broad daylight. If Damian is hanging around my home, I need to know. I've already had a shitty day; I'm not going to let my ex make it worse. With a spurt of angry courage, I leave my hiding place and hurry after him, my emotions whirling.

Heading past my apartment entrance, I pause before turning left down the road where he went. Do I really want to do this? Yes. Yes, I do. Even if it's only to find out whether or not it's really him.

I turn the corner and glance down the quiet residential street to see nothing but parked cars, trees, and rows of semi-detached houses. The only people in sight are a woman in a suit, and a female jogger with a springer spaniel. No men at all. I cross over and run my gaze along the pavement. Maybe he got into one of the cars or went into one of the houses. What if he's watching me right now? My heart judders. No, I can't do this.

My moment of courage has evaporated. I turn away and quickly head back towards home, casting anxious glances over my shoulder, palms sweating, heart racing, hoping to God it wasn't him.

Chapter Thirty

Now

Letting myself into the flat, I close the door behind me and pause for a moment to get my breath back. Now that I'm safely home, I realise I probably overreacted back there. I doubt that was Damian and even if it were, he could simply be back visiting friends – nothing to do with me at all. I have enough to worry about in my life without adding hallucinations of my ex-boyfriend to the mix. I'm going to put the whole incident down to stress. The Seth situation hasn't helped my mental state, and my emotions were already on the surface after such a rough morning at work. Ugh, work.

I can't believe it was only an hour or so ago that I left here to go to the office with so much determination and purpose. If only I'd replied to Miriam's texts last week, she might have warned me about Charlotte earlier and I could have returned to work before Paul made his decision to make her partner. I could have swayed him.

Too late now.

I quickly change out of my work clothes and throw on some chambray shorts and a white crochet top that Daisy bought me for my birthday. It's cute. She's got good taste. But I don't even know why I care what I look like. It's not as though I have anyone to impress. As I dress, I realise my hands are still shaking. I clasp them together decisively to put a stop to it.

The doorbell goes and I feel nothing but pure relief as I press the buzzer and open the flat door.

Laurence appears up the stairs, bearing a cardboard tray of coffees and an enticing brown paper bag. He takes one look at my sad expression and ushers me into the lounge.

'Okay, what's happened?' He passes me my coffee and a delicious-looking apricot Danish that would normally elicit a grin, but I can't even muster a half-smile. I put them both on the side table for now and thank him for coming over.

'You don't have to thank me. I'll always be here for you and Daisy. No question.'

'Same,' I reply.

'I should think so,' he replies. 'Now, am I going to have to wrestle it out of you, or are you going to tell me what's so bad that your apricot Danish and hazelnut latte aren't being devoured immediately?'

I try to respond to his quip, but my mind and body are clouded by the whole Damian thing which I'm trying my best to forget.

'Alice?' he prompts softly. I know he's worried when he calls me by my first name.

I throw up my hands and tell him about my horribly disappointing morning at the office. And once I've got through that, I also tell him that I've now officially ended things with Seth.

'I'm sorry to offload all this on you, on top of everything else you've been helping me with. I don't want to be one of those friends who moans about everything.'

'Porter, we've known each other since school, and this is the first time you've been really badly upset. Even back when Damian treated you like crap, you kept most of it to yourself. I'm here for you, okay?'

I bite my lip at his mention of my ex and nod. I decide not to tell him about my possible sighting of Damian as I think I'd rather erase the whole incident from my mind. 'It's just . . . everything is sliding out of control. It feels like there are all these massive holes appearing everywhere in my life. Just weeks ago I had a fiancé, a great place to live, a successful career. Now, everything's breaking apart. And I can't . . . I can't stop feeling miserable and stressed all the time.'

'Cut yourself some slack, Porter. You're having a shit time; you're allowed to feel rubbish.'

I nod and burst into tears, angry with myself for crying yet *again*.

Laurence puts down his coffee and slides closer, putting his arm around me, letting me cry.

'Thank you,' I sniff. 'I don't know what I'd do without you.'

'The feeling's mutual.'

I bump him with my shoulder and we sit in companiable silence for a while. I pick up my coffee and take a few sips.

'Hasn't it gone cold by now?' Laurence asks.

'Lukewarm.' I grimace.

He grins and then frowns.

'What is it?' I ask.

He gives his head a shake. 'Nothing.'

I give him a look. 'I've literally just poured my heart out to you, Kennedy. You don't get to say "nothing".'

'It's not the right time.'

I'm unnerved by his serious expression. 'What's going on?'

'I . . .' Laurence stares down at his lap and then up again. Fixes me with a strange, intense gaze.

'You *what?*' I notice how the cornflower blue of his eyes stands out against his dark lashes.

175

'I just want you to know that you mean a lot to me, Alice. In case you didn't know.'

'Same,' I reply.

'No,' he says. 'Not the same.'

I look away and set down my coffee. Heat floods my throat and face as I try to work out if he's saying what I think he's saying.

'Alice, I love you.' Laurence's voice is deep and clear. It fills up the room. Fills up my mind. It unbalances me.

For a moment, I wonder if he's joking around. But when I look at him, I realise he's serious. He looks anxious. Scared even.

I open my mouth to say something, but I can't formulate the words. This is all too much to take in.

'It's always been you, Alice.'

I exhale and my pulse begins to race. I'm totally shocked by his declaration. Blindsided. All I can think about is how Seth told me he didn't believe that Laurence and I could just be friends. That there's no such thing as a purely platonic friendship between a straight man and woman. That there's always going to be an element of sexual tension. I dismissed Seth's words with a curl of my lip, but now here's Laurence to prove me wrong.

His throat bobs. 'When I heard you were going to marry Seth, I felt like the air was being sucked out of my lungs. I always thought that somehow we'd end up together. That we were meant to be. I know how corny that sounds . . .'

I stand on wobbly legs and walk over to the lounge window, looking out at the cars driving past. At the people going about their day, oblivious to my turmoil. I feel so weird about this. Laurence is my best friend and now he's telling me about this huge secret that he's been carrying around. A confession that changes everything. How did I never suspect? Never see it? 'Why didn't you say anything before?' I ask, turning back to face him. Looking at him in a whole new way that's quite unnerving.

He rubs his stubbled jaw with two fingers. 'I guess . . . I didn't want to risk losing our friendship. You know, I counsel all these clients to be true to their feelings. To be honest with themselves and work through their issues in order to live their best lives. But I haven't taken my own advice. I'm a hypocrite. The truth is, for years I've been too scared to tell you how I feel.'

'*Years?*' I suddenly remember that Laurence has a long-term girlfriend. Someone who loves him. Who's talked about marrying him one day. She's also my friend. What's going to happen now? My stomach tightens at the thought of the potential fallout from this. 'What about Francesca?' I ask.

'I know.' He shakes his head. 'She doesn't deserve this. She's lovely, and sweet and hasn't done anything wrong. I love her, I do. I'm just not *in* love with her.'

I don't reply. Unable to think of anything good to say.

'We met at uni,' Laurence continues, 'and our relationship started out as fun. But, over the years, it's become more habit than anything else. And, ever since your engagement, it's become so clear to me that she and I aren't right for each other. I'm going to end things with her whatever happens . . . with us.'

Laurence comes over and takes both my hands in his. I can't ignore the current that sparks along my skin. But is it caused by shock, or is it something more? He gazes into my eyes and I'm terrified that he might be about to kiss me.

'I know I shouldn't say this,' he says softly, 'but I was so thankful that you never went through with the wedding. That you're no longer with Seth. It was like a sign. A second chance.'

I blink and try to get hold of my emotions. Try to work out what all this means. How it will change things. Because how can I be myself around him now? I can't lose my friend. I need him too much right now. If I lost Laurence on top of everything else, I don't know what I'd do.

'I'm sorry, Laurence. I can't do this.' I take my hands away from his, and I break our gaze.

The colour drains from his face. He hugs himself and then lets his arms drop to his sides. He nods. 'It's fine. I understand.'

'No. It's just. I can't. It's too much. I need your friendship right now. More than anything else.'

'You're right. I'm sorry. I shouldn't have said anything.' He rubs his arm. 'I'm an idiot. I should go, right?'

I nod. 'Maybe. Yes. I think that's best.'

Although, as I'm saying it, I realise that I absolutely *don't* want him to go.

I want him to stay.

Chapter Thirty-One

THEN

'I can't believe I'm getting married tomorrow!' I gaze around the table at my friends, grateful that Daisy, Martin, Laurence and Francesca are here with me on my last ever night at the flat. We've ordered a Chinese takeaway and have spread all the cartons out on the table so we can have a pick and mix. 'Don't let me eat any more. I have to fit into my dress. I don't want to be bloated.' I gaze at my empty plate regretfully. 'Maybe just one more spring roll.'

The windows are all wide open as we're having a bit of a heatwave this week. At least that means sunshine tomorrow – every bride's dream. Well, either that or snow, like Elizabeth's wedding.

'How are you feeling?' Daisy asks, spooning more rice on to her plate.

'Weird,' I reply with a nervous smile. 'Excited, but also kind of terrified.'

'I'm not surprised,' she replies. 'I wonder how Seth's doing.'

'He's staying at the cottage with his parents tonight,' I reply, imagining him there having a lovely, relaxed evening. I bet they're having dinner in the garden. His parents will have made some lavish Mediterranean salad, or maybe they'll be having a posh barbecue. I suddenly have an irrational fear that they'll have invited their neighbours round, including Sienna Doyle's parents, and she'll just happen to be staying there

tonight, so she'll show up too. And Seth will realise he's made a horrible mistake getting engaged to me and decide he really loves Sienna.

'Have you spoken to him today?' Francesca asks.

'What?' She jolts me out of my worst-case-scenario daydream. 'Oh, yes, we had a quick WhatsApp chat earlier, but decided not to talk in case it's bad luck or something.'

'He must feel odd staying with his parents,' Fran says. 'Like he's regressed back to his childhood days.'

'I know,' I reply. 'Mum asked if I wanted to stay round at their place tonight, but that would have made me feel stranger than I do right now. I want things to feel as normal as possible, if that makes sense. Although, nothing about this evening feels normal,' I admit.

'You're the first one of us to tie the knot,' Francesca says. 'It's bound to feel weird. Apart from your sister of course.'

'It all seems to have happened so quickly,' Laurence says. 'You and Seth only met a year ago.'

'I guess when you know, you know,' Daisy says, glancing at Martin who's been very quiet this evening.

I hope those two are okay. They've been going through a bit of a rocky patch recently. I'll have to arrange a proper catch-up with Daisy once I get back from my honeymoon.

'I'm stuffed,' Laurence says, patting his belly like it's huge and not the six-pack he seems to have developed over the past couple of years. 'Maybe we should make a move, Fran. Let Alice get an early night.'

I breathe in deeply, trying to settle my nerves. My fingers are actually trembling. I have this feeling like I'm on a very fast train that won't slow down. It's racing past all the stations so quickly that the signs blur.

'Are you okay, Alice?' Fran is gazing at me, her eyes full of concern.

'Yeah, fine.' I stretch my arms out in front of me. 'I think I will get an early night. Although I don't know how on earth I'm going to sleep.'

'Alcohol?' Daisy suggests waving the wine bottle at me.

'I am not showing up to my wedding with a hangover.'

180

'Fair enough.' She grins and pours herself half a glass.

Everyone starts clearing the table, telling me I'm not allowed to help, that I have to sit and relax. But I wish they'd let me join in. I'm so jittery, I feel like I need to do something productive to calm down.

Once everything is cleaned and put away, I say my goodbyes to everyone except Daisy who's staying here tonight. It's funny to think that Martin will be moving in here. This will be their place instead of mine. I wonder how I'll feel coming over to visit.

'Everything okay?' Daisy asks, returning to the lounge where I'm sitting on the sofa staring into space. 'You've been quiet all evening.'

Tears sting my eyes. I manage to keep them at bay. But only just. I clear my throat. 'I'm fine, just feeling a bit overwhelmed.'

'Of course,' she replies, coming to sit next to me. 'As long as you're overwhelmed and happy.'

'I am,' I say more decisively than I feel.

'Good. It's the end of an era, Alice. We've lived together for . . .' She frowns.

'Nine years,' I say.

'Blimey.'

'I know. It'll be strange not calling you my flatmate any more,' I say, leaning back against the sofa that won't be my sofa for much longer.

'Yep. We'll just be run-of-the-mill friends instead,' she says with a smile.

'Never run-of-the-mill.'

'And we're both going to be living with boys. Can you believe it?' Daisy's eyes widen.

'We must be mad,' I reply.

Suddenly we dissolve into laughter that soon turns to tears – mainly mine. 'Don't let me cry,' I say. 'My face will be all blotchy tomorrow.'

'Go and splash it with cold water, quick!' Daisy instructs.

I hurry to the bathroom, half crying, half laughing and turn on the tap, cupping my hands under the stream of water and bringing it up to my face.

'I'm going to make you a coconut milk hot chocolate!' Daisy calls out. It's our go-to comfort drink. The one we always crave when either of us is sad or anxious. 'Get into your PJs!'

'Yes, Mum,' I call back. I dry my face and pull myself together. Tomorrow is the day I've been looking forward to for months. It's all been perfectly planned. There's no reason for me to be nervous.

Back in the lounge, Daisy is waiting with two mugs of the good stuff. She's even gone the extra mile and topped our hot chocolates with squirty cream and mini marshmallows.

'Not sure this is the best idea after all that food,' I say. 'But I'm willing to give it a go.'

'That's my girl,' Daisy says. 'I've also got these amazing herbal drops from the chemist that will help calm your nerves. Do you want me to squeeze a couple into your drink?'

I squint at the small glass vial in her hand. 'They won't knock me out, will they? I want to be clear-headed tomorrow.'

'No, nothing like that. They're not strong. They'll just take the edge off your nerves.'

I realise my left hand is still shaking. 'Okay, yes please. Whack a couple of drops in there.' I hold out my mug and watch her use the dropper – once, twice.

I start sipping my milky drink.

Within minutes, I already feel pleasantly relaxed and ready for bed, a warm sense of well-being blooming in my chest. 'Thanks, Daisy. For everything. You've been a great flatmate. The best.' I drain the last drops of my drink.

'Right back at ya,' she says with a fond smile.

I stand woozily and give her a hug before toddling off to bed. All my earlier worries and doubts have been banished into a hazy fog as I give myself up to a deep and dreamless sleep.

Chapter Thirty-Two

Now

'Alice Porter?' The twenty-something-year-old letting agent is dressed in a pale-grey suit, his hair newly cut, his woodsy aftershave a bit too liberally applied.

I cough to clear my throat. 'Yes, hi, you must be Tom.' I shake his hand before turning my face to the side to suck down some fresh air. 'This is my friend, Daisy. She's here for moral support.'

'Great, no problem,' he says in a professional, friendly-yet-businesslike manner.

It's Saturday afternoon and Daisy has offered to come along to check out a potential one-bedroom flat to rent – a character conversion in the heart of town. The details aren't up on Rightmove yet, so I haven't seen photos, but the letting agent assured me it's exactly what I'm looking for. Gazing at the overgrown front garden and hearing the thumping house music emanating from the downstairs flat, I highly doubt it.

I probably should have cancelled the appointment. I'm not at all in the right frame of mind to make such an important decision. Not with the maelstrom of emotions whizzing around my body – the wedding disaster, Seth, work, Charlotte, moving out of my apartment . . . everything in my life is so up in the air. Why is it, though, that all I can think about is *Laurence*?

The letting agent unlocks the front door and shows us into a dingy hall that smells of old soup. Daisy gives me a horrified stare that makes me want to laugh. The wine-coloured carpet is shiny in places and covered in fluff. I've already decided this place is a definite no. But I suppose we're going to have to go through the charade of looking around and pretending to consider it.

As we trudge up the stairs, Tom is elaborating on the benefits of living in Ringwood. I don't have the heart to tell him I know because I already live here. Instead, I tune him out and wonder whether I should tell Daisy about Laurence's declaration. What will she think of it? Seeing as how it's always been the three of us, will she be as weirded out as I was? Or might she think it's a good idea? I highly doubt she'll be pleased. Maybe I shouldn't say anything, but I need to talk it through with *someone*, and as the person I would normally talk to is Laurence, then Daisy is my next-best option.

The inside of the rental flat is small, dark and unwelcoming. The music from downstairs filters up through the floorboards, filling the rooms with a muffled bassline and repetitive keyboard riff. The nicest thing about the place is the view from the bedroom that looks out on to some tall trees at the end of a pretty garden belonging to the downstairs flat.

'Lovely aspect, isn't it?' Tom says.

'Mm,' I reply, staring out at the greenery, my mind still stuck on Laurence. On his earnest face as he told me how he felt. My belly has started fluttering, but I can't tell if the flutters are caused by excited anticipation at what might be, or delayed shock.

Daisy's hand on my arm jolts me back to my surroundings. 'Ready to go?' she asks.

'Oh. Yes, sorry, I was miles away.'

She gives me a bemused smile.

'What do you think?' Tom asks, hope in his eyes.

'I'm afraid it's not quite right,' I reply. 'But thank you for showing us round.'

'Oh.' His face falls. 'Is it the music?'

'That doesn't help, but no. It's just not for me. If you could send details of any other one-bedroom flats in the area, that would be great.'

'Sure.'

Daisy and I leave the flat and I'm happy to be back out in the fresh air. I hope there are better places out there to rent. Otherwise, I might well find myself back at my parents'.

'There's something different about you,' Daisy says, staring at me.

I feel my cheeks warm under her gaze.

'Different?'

'Yes. There's a definite vibe going on.' She points at me with her forefinger, waving it around.

I shake my head. 'No. No vibe.' I change the subject. 'Do you think I'm being too picky about the flat?' I ask as we head back towards our own gorgeous apartment. An apartment that I'm now beginning to realise we've been *very* lucky to have. I'm not sure I'll ever find anywhere half as nice.

'Absolutely not,' she replies. 'That place was a dive. You can't live there.'

I'm grateful to her for being honest when it's in her best interest to have me find somewhere and move out. 'Thanks, Dais. I promise I'll do everything I can to find somewhere soon. I know you and Martin were looking forward to having the flat to yourselves.'

'Honestly, Alice, I promise there's no rush.'

'And you know he can absolutely move in now. I don't mind.'

'I know you don't, but I don't want to make it weird for you. You've been through such a traumatic time. He's fine where he is for now.'

'It's not weird for me. I like Martin.'

She nods and looks down at the pavement.

'Everything okay, Daisy?'

'Yeah,' she replies glumly. 'If you want the truth, I told Martin he could move into our flat now, but he said he's happy to wait. I think he's dragging his heels.'

'No, he's probably just busy.'

'Too busy for *me*,' she replies.

'What are we like?' I shake my head.

'Pathetic,' she replies. 'We should have a girls' holiday or something. Cheer ourselves up.'

'Sounds like heaven, but I've literally just had two weeks off work, and I'm not sure it would go down too well if I took any more time off. Plus, I'm skint, apart from my deposit money.'

'Next year,' she replies.

'Definitely.'

We walk in silence for a moment or two, lost in our own thoughts.

'How are you doing since you ended things with Seth?' she asks.

'Okay, kind of,' I reply, as we turn into our street. 'I think I made the right call. I feel better, knowing I don't have to see him any more.'

'Really?' Daisy still doesn't get why I ended things with Seth. I know it must seem strange to have been so in love with someone one minute and then ending things the next. But it was an odd, unexplainable situation. I wonder if I'll ever get to the bottom of it.

I also can't help wondering if maybe Laurence would be a better fit for me than Seth was. We're already so close. We know almost everything about each other so there would be no nasty surprises. But do we have that all-important chemistry? Do I actually fancy Laurence? I can honestly say I've never thought about him like that before. I'm not the kind of person whose eyes stray to other people while I'm in a relationship. When I was with Seth, I was all in. *Until I wasn't.* I don't love Seth any more, but could I love Laurence?

'Something happened yesterday,' I say, my heart starting to pound as I realise I'm about to tell Daisy.

'With Seth?' she asks.

'With Laurence,' I reply, my heart skipping a beat as I say his name.

Daisy frowns as I open the door. *'Laurence?'*

I wonder if perhaps I shouldn't tell her. Maybe Laurence would prefer to keep this to ourselves to avoid any extra awkwardness. But I feel like it's one of those things that isn't going to stay quiet. Especially as I already can't stop thinking about it. About *him*.

We walk up the stairs, go into our apartment, kick off our shoes and sink on to the sofa. 'That flat was depressing,' I say with a shudder.

'I know. I think I could smell damp. But what were you saying about Laurence?'

'He came over yesterday.'

'*When?* Daisy's eyes narrow. 'He was at Fran's fundraising thing last night. Why weren't *you* there?'

'Didn't feel up to socialising.'

'Fair enough.' She reaches for a cushion and wedges it behind her back. 'Anyway, you saw Laurence . . .'

'He came over in the morning because I was a bit upset about work.'

'What happened at work?'

'Ugh, it's a whole thing, but I'll tell you later.' I shake away the memory of Charlotte's smug face. The dramas in my life are coming so thick and fast that it's getting hard to keep up. 'So,' I continue, 'Laurence came over with a coffee to cheer me up and he told me something a bit unexpected.'

'He's getting married?' Daisy cries. 'Fran's pregnant? They're not splitting up, are they?' Daisy does her usual thing of jumping in to answer her own questions.

I give her a *come-on-now* look and she mimes zipping her mouth closed.

'Actually, he and Fran *might* be splitting up,' I reply.

'No! *Why?* They seemed fine last night. Happy, even.'

Here goes. I take a breath. 'Laurence told me . . . he told me he has feelings for me.'

Daisy's mouth falls open and she's utterly silent.

'He said he's felt something for me for years but hasn't acted on it.' Heat floods my cheeks as I say, 'He told me he loves me.'

Daisy's face is stony. I can't tell if it's shock or if she's really upset.

'Are you going to say something?' I ask.

She shrugs. 'I mean, what is there to say?'

Oh no. She's not happy at all.

'Do you feel the same way?' she asks coldly.

'Honestly, I don't know.'

'I knew there was something different about you today,' she says through gritted teeth.

'Are you angry?' I ask.

'Not angry,' she replies, swallowing. 'I just feel a bit stupid. I thought the three of us were best friends. This close trio of mates who've had each other's backs through thick and thin. When, all along, it was only because Laurence fancied you. I guess I must have been there as some kind of . . . buffer, or third wheel, or whatever.'

'*What?* Don't be daft! Of course not. I didn't have a clue about this until yesterday. I thought the same as you – that we were the three amigos like we were back at school. We *were* best friends. We still are. There was never anything romantic on my part.'

'So you don't feel the same?' I see her hopes rise. Daisy's relief is obvious as her shoulders relax and her eyes soften.

I look down into my lap. 'I honestly don't know. It was a shock.'

She tenses again. 'If you two get together, it will be like I've lost both my friends,' she says.

'That would never happen,' I reply. 'We'll always be friends.' But I think about the consequences if anything *were* to happen between me and Laurence; it would cause such a scandal in our friendship circle. It's already creating toxic ripples. Daisy is hurt, and I can't say I blame her. I'd probably feel the same if Laurence had feelings for Daisy instead of me. I already feel sick for Francesca. Laurence said he was going to end things with her regardless of what happens between me and him, but they've been together for years.

'Poor Francesca,' Daisy says, echoing my thoughts. 'She's going to be gutted.'

I can't disagree.

My thoughts and emotions are spinning this way and that. His feelings towards me could either turn out to be a blessing or they could screw everything up monumentally. But, the more I think about it, the more I realise that this could actually be incredible. Laurence declaring his love could be the turning point in my life.

The moment where everything starts coming together. Instead of falling apart.

Chapter Thirty-Three

Now

The doorbell rings, and Daisy and I both turn our heads at the same time.

'Are you expecting anyone?' she asks.

'No.' I get up off the sofa, hoping it isn't Laurence. It would be beyond awkward for the three of us to be in a room together right now, just after I've told Daisy about his revelation. Her reaction wasn't exactly a positive one.

I think Daisy has the same suspicions as to who it might be, because she scowls and stands up too. 'I'll get it,' she says, marching out of the living room and pulling the door closed behind her. If that's Laurence, this is going to be incredibly uncomfortable.

I peer through the window, but it's impossible to see who's down there now the sycamore tree is in full leaf, blocking the view. I'm too keyed-up to sit back down, so I fiddle with the hem of my top while I wait. Hopefully, it's just a delivery. I'd even prefer it to be Charlotte or my dad than Laurence.

The buzzer goes and, after what feels like an eternal wait, the front door opens.

'Is she here?' It's a woman's voice, muffled by the lounge door. So, not Laurence then. I exhale, relieved beyond belief, and then I jump out of my skin as the door opens with force.

Shit. It's Francesca.

She's wearing a long cotton skirt, beaded flip-flops, and a loose vest top with a jade pendant. Her face is drawn and her eyes are red-rimmed and glistening with tears.

My heart squeezes under her pitiful gaze.

'How could you?' she cries. But it's a sad cry rather than an angry one.

Daisy follows her into the room. She's shaking her head and looking down at the carpet.

I guess Laurence must have told Francesca. *This is a nightmare.* I need to say something, but my brain has seized up. I don't know how to begin. 'Francesca, I—'

'There's nothing you can say.' She cuts me off. 'Laurence told me you didn't know how he felt, but you must have had an idea.' She sniffs and taps her foot repeatedly. 'He's supposed to be your best friend, isn't he? And in my experience, you tell your best friends everything.'

'I swear. I didn't know until yesterday.' It sounds like a lie even to *my* ears.

'I don't believe you,' she replies, turning to Daisy. 'Did you know about this too? Were you all in on it? *Poor little Francesca in love with Laurence when he's in love with Alice. Isn't it a shame. We all feel so sorry for her.*'

'No,' Daisy replies, holding up her hands. 'I promise you, I literally only just found out this afternoon. Look, come and sit down, Fran.' She puts an arm around Francesca and leads her over to the sofa like she's an invalid.

Francesca gives in to Daisy's ministrations. She seems to shrink into the sofa.

191

I still don't know what to say. I'm heartbroken for the girl. She obviously loves Laurence and she probably thought, like the rest of us, that they'd end up together, get married, start a family.

'It's just so out of the blue,' she says, almost to herself, rubbing at her bare arms. 'If I'd had an inkling. If he'd been distant, or moody, or been pulling away from me. But there were no signs at all. He's been the perfect boyfriend. I can't even get my head around it.'

I'm still motionless in the middle of the living room. I don't feel as though I can sit down yet. I'm too wired. Too shocked by this whole thing. And it's all made worse by the fact that the more I think about it, the more I realise I have deeper feelings for Laurence than I first thought. Which is something I'm going to have to keep to myself for a while because this whole thing needs to be calmed down, not stirred up.

I'm startled by the sound of the front door opening and turn to see Laurence burst in, his eyes wild, his fair hair messy, and his jaw more stubbled than usual. He sees me, but his eyes go straight to Francesca.

'I've been running round all over the place looking for you!' he cries.

'Well, you found me,' she says with quiet venom.

'How did you get in?' Daisy asks him.

'The door was open,' Laurence replies, not taking his eyes off Francesca. 'Come back to the flat. We need to talk.'

'I've got absolutely nothing to say to you,' Francesca replies, sinking deeper into the sofa.

Daisy gets to her feet and the two of us head for the door, both of the same mind that these two need some privacy to talk.

'Where are you going, Alice?' Francesca calls out to me. 'Is it all getting a bit too real for you?'

192

I turn to see her straightening up. Her small chin jutting forward.

'Fran,' Laurence says, walking over to her, 'it's not Alice's fault. She didn't know how I felt.'

I cringe as Laurence sticks up for me, wanting to shrivel up into a little ball and roll away.

'I don't even know what I'm doing here,' Francesca says, shaking her head, her voice catching. 'I should leave.' She stands shakily, still hugging herself before giving a bitter laugh. 'Not that I know where to go. I don't suppose I have a home any more.'

'Of course you have a home,' Laurence replies. 'Come back to the flat with me. We can talk. You can stay there. I'll move out.'

'Like I can afford to live there on my own,' she says, her voice cracking.

I'm mortified to be witnessing the intricacies of their break-up.

'Don't worry about that,' Laurence tries to reassure her. 'I'll sort it.'

'I don't want you to sort it. I don't want *anything* from you,' she cries.

I'm suddenly distracted by thudding footsteps on the stairs beyond the open front door. I turn to see a dark-haired man stride across our hall and into the lounge, a murderous expression slashed across his face.

Chapter Thirty-Four

THEN

I wake up surprisingly refreshed. Those herbal drops Daisy gave me last night must have done the trick. My first thought as I open my eyes is I'm getting married today. My second thought is to acknowledge the sunlight filtering through the gaps in the curtains. The forecasters were right – it's going to be a beautiful day.

'Knock, knock.' The door to my bedroom edges open and I see my mother standing in the doorway dressed in white capri pants and a short-sleeved green blouse, a cup of tea in one hand and a garment carrier in the other.

'Morning, Mum.' I stretch and sit up, arranging the pillow behind my head.

'Morning, darling. Excited?'

'Yes, but it doesn't feel quite real. Is that tea for me?'

'It is.' She comes over and sets the mug on my bedside table.

'Thanks.'

'I remember my wedding morning,' she says. 'I was so nervous I could barely speak.'

'Really?'

'Of course. Your father was such a handsome, charismatic man. He still is.'

I grin at Mum. 'You really love him, don't you?'

'Of course I do. I know he can be a bit . . . demanding . . .'

I roll my eyes at the understatement and she gives me a chiding look.

'But he loves all of us with a passion. And he wants the best for you girls.'

I nod, but I know that Mum is often blinded by her love for Dad. I sometimes think she puts his well-being ahead of ours. The thought makes me clench my jaw. I need to change my train of thought. I think Mum senses this too.

I swallow. 'You . . . you do like Seth, don't you? You and Dad.'

'We do,' she replies with a smile. 'Even Elizabeth gave her seal of approval.'

'Okay, good.' I let out a breath and feel relieved that they're still happy about the marriage. Our families finally met just after the hen weekend when Seth's parents came to stay in Brook Cottage. My parents invited them and Seth to dinner, and everyone seemed to get on well. But that was a while ago, and it was the one and only time they met. I still couldn't pin Seth down to meet my friends, so they'll all be seeing one another for the first time today.

'Can I make you some toast?' Mum asks, smoothing my hair away from my eyes.

'No, it's fine. I'll get up in a minute.' I take a sip of tea. Mum is the only person who makes my tea exactly how I like it – strong with the smallest dash of milk. 'Is Dad here?'

'In the lounge,' she replies. 'And Elizabeth's on her way over. Can I put this somewhere?' She holds out the garment carrier.

'There's a hook on the back of the door.'

'Great.' She hangs up her mother-of-the-bride dress carefully. 'Can I do anything else for you?'

'No, go sit with Dad. I'll be out in a few minutes. Is Daisy up yet?'

'Yes, she let us in half an hour ago. I'll leave you to it. Don't take too long, it's almost eight thirty.' Mum leaves my bedroom, pulling the door closed behind her.

I wasn't lying when I said I was excited, but I'm also nervous and my stomach feels weak and watery. Like Mum said, I guess that's normal for a bride on her wedding morning. I close my eyes and draw in a long deep breath through my nose, then blow it out slowly through my mouth. I should probably do a few of these breaths, but I'm too antsy to concentrate. I open my eyes and take another sip of tea instead.

There's so much to do – shower, breakfast, hair, make-up, wedding dress. It all feels quite overwhelming. I almost wish I could sink back under the covers and do nothing all day. I give myself a shake. Come on, Alice, move your arse. You're getting married today!

I put my tea back down, fling back the covers and get up, my feet sinking luxuriously into the white fluffy rug by my bed. I'm suddenly hyper-aware of the fact that my special day is stretched out ahead of me like a row of polished diamonds. I need to savour every glittering moment.

By the time I've showered and thrown on a robe, Elizabeth, Miriam and Fran have arrived too, and, as I leave the bathroom, I'm met with squeals and hugs from all of them, including Daisy. Dad has been keeping out of the way in the living room, his nose buried in the newspaper he brought along, a mug of coffee by his side. Mum is gliding around the kitchen, making drinks for everyone and doing time-checks to make sure we're on schedule.

The morning is spent beautifying ourselves. Elizabeth is great at make-up, so she does mine, and I marvel at her light touch that has transformed me. Miriam jokes that we should have got Charlotte in to do my hair in one of her elaborate chignon-knot-braid thingies. I'm actually wearing my hair loose, with just a few of the front strands caught back off my face with diamanté clips.

Part of me feels a bit mean that I didn't ask Charlotte to be a bridesmaid too. But I don't think I could have borne her constant one-upmanship, even though I know it comes from a place of insecurity. I just need calm, positive people around me today.

My bridesmaids are stunning in their chiffon burgundy dresses, all tailored and styled individually to suit each of them. Mum looks glamorous in a dove-grey fitted dress with a short-sleeved lace bodice and matching short lace jacket. Satin court shoes and an elegant mesh fascinator finish off her outfit.

Finally, Mum and Elizabeth help me into the wedding gown of my dreams, its beaded lace bodice clinging to my curves and then flaring out into a floor-length silk organza skirt floating over layers of tulle.

'You look absolutely beautiful, darling.' Mum's eyes are bright with emotion, and I dig my thumbnails into my fingertips to stop my own tears.

'Thanks, Mum,' I manage to reply. 'You look stunning too.'

She takes my hand and squeezes it. 'You girls all look gorgeous.'

We have a group hug, careful not to crease dresses, smudge make-up or ruin hairstyles.

'Let's take photos in the lounge!' Daisy declares.

I notice my father's eyes widen slightly as Mum enters the living room. He puts down his newspaper and gets to his feet. He's also changed into his wedding attire – a charcoal suit and burgundy silk tie that makes him seem even more imposing than usual.

'You look lovely, Jane,' he says to Mum, nodding his approval.

'You look very handsome,' she replies. 'That colour tie suits you.'

I walk in behind Mum, with everyone else following.

When Dad sees me, he clears his throat and I swear he's a little choked up. 'Very nice,' he says. 'Very nice.'

Two very nices. I'm honoured. 'Thanks, Dad,' I reply. I'm being snarky in my head to stop the emotion that's bubbling up from my core, threatening to turn into real tears, and I can't have that. Not now my make-up's done. But it's hard to stay composed. My friends and family are all here for me. To support me and watch me get married. It's getting very real now. I'm conscious that I need to savour every moment. Document every second to relive later.

Daisy fetches my bouquet from the fridge, along with Dad's matching white rose and fern buttonhole. She sets up the timer on her camera phone and we spend the next few minutes posing for photos. They start out serious, but soon degenerate into silly poses and more candid shots.

'The cars are here!' Fran calls from the other end of the room where she's been intermittently peering out of the window.

My nerves are starting to kick in now.

Chapter Thirty-Five

Now

'*Seth?*' I'm so confused by my still-unrecognisable ex-fiancé's arrival at the flat in the midst of all this drama with Laurence and Francesca. 'What are you doing here?'

'I messaged him,' Francesca says, her voice small but defiant. 'I got his number from Elizabeth.'

I stare at Seth, who seems to take up half the living room. 'But why would you do that?' I ask, turning back to her, my heart hammering so loudly I can barely think.

Seth replies. 'Because Fran thought I deserved to know the real reason you called off the wedding.' He scowls before crossing the room to reach Laurence. 'This piece of shit, here. He's the reason you didn't go through with it, isn't he?'

'*What?* No.' I don't like the look of where this is heading. I'm dismayed as the two of them face off in the centre of the room, Laurence tall, blond and nervous, Seth dark, stocky and murderous.

Seth's jaw tightens and his fingers flex. 'Francesca kindly told me that Laurence is more than just your friend.'

'That's not true,' I reply.

'Why would she lie?' Seth's eyes narrow.

'Take it easy, mate,' Laurence says, raising his hands in a placatory manner that's having absolutely no effect.

'Don't tell me to take it easy,' Seth replies. 'And I'm not your mate.'

'Hey, let's talk about this calmly,' Daisy says, but neither of them is listening.

'So, is it true?' Seth asks Laurence. 'Are you seeing Alice?'

'No!' he replies.

'Okay, let me phrase it differently. Do you have feelings for Alice?'

I'm wracking my brains for something to say that might defuse the situation, but my mind is frozen.

'It's complicated,' Laurence replies.

'No it's not. Simple yes or no will do.' Seth's body is as tense as a bow string. He's wholly focused on Laurence and I'm terrified he's about to do something incredibly stupid.

Daisy glares at me as though this is my fault, and I feel as though somehow it is.

Laurence gives me a helpless look and then turns his gaze to Francesca. 'I don't understand why you messaged Seth,' he says.

'Because he deserves to know what's going on here,' she replies quietly. 'Seth thinks Alice had some kind of breakdown on their wedding day, but now I find out that you two are more than just friends. Something's not right.'

'I asked you a question,' Seth says to Laurence. 'Do you have feelings for the girl I was going to marry?'

Laurence shakes his head and then looks Seth dead in the eyes. 'I'm going to be honest with you.' He pauses, squares his shoulders and says, 'I'm in love with her, okay?'

The next few seconds are such a blur, I barely take them in. Seth's right arm pulls back and he lets it fly straight into Laurence's face. He follows up with a left fist to his stomach.

Daisy and I scream, but Francesca doesn't make a sound. She presses her hands to her face.

Laurence doubles over, then sinks to his knees, his face dripping blood, his breaths coming in wheezing gasps.

'Seth!' I cry. 'What the hell?'

Daisy and I rush over to Laurence who's tentatively touching his face to see if anything's damaged.

'We need to get you to the hospital,' I say. 'Can you straighten up?'

'I think so.' Laurence's voice is thick, like he has a heavy cold. 'I think my nose might be broken. Maybe a couple of ribs too.'

'I'll get an ice pack from the freezer.' Daisy throws me a furious glance before she heads off to the kitchen. I wish she wasn't so angry at me.

Seth looks down as I crouch next to Laurence. 'Just tell me,' he snarls, his eyes glittering with rage. 'Is this bastard the reason you broke up with me? Was that charade in the church so you two could run off into the sunset? Be honest, Alice.'

'Of course not!' I cry. 'Do you think I'd put myself through something that humiliating and upsetting on purpose?'

'People have done stranger things,' Francesca says.

'Thank you,' Seth replies to her. He examines his knuckles, carefully opening his fingers and wincing at the self-inflicted pain.

'There's absolutely nothing going on between me and Laurence,' I add, trying to keep my voice calm, but I can't hide the emotional wobble. '*Nothing*. And if I'd had feelings for Laurence before the wedding, I would have told you. But I didn't.'

Laurence tries to stem the flow of blood from his nose with the side of his hand, but it's still gushing.

'I don't believe you,' Seth replies.

'Seth, you and I aren't even together any more. I'm sorry I hurt you, but I'm telling you, hand on heart, that Laurence has nothing to do with what happened between us. I only found out how Laurence feels yesterday. That's God's honest truth. I still can't believe you punched him.'

'He's lucky that's all I did.'

Daisy returns with an ice pack wrapped in a tea towel. 'Hold that on your nose.'

'I might need another tea towel for the blood,' Laurence says thickly.

'Here.' She hands him a wodge of kitchen roll. 'Lean forward a bit and pinch your nose just above your nostrils if it's not too painful. My car's at Martin's – can someone else drive him to the hospital?'

'Don't look at me,' Seth says. 'Anyway, he doesn't need the hospital. He'll be fine.'

Francesca shakes her head. 'I'm leaving.'

'Don't go, Fran,' Laurence cries. 'We need to talk.'

'I've got nothing to say to you,' she replies, and starts walking away.

'Do you need a lift?' Seth asks her.

Francesca pauses. 'Oh . . . okay, thanks. I was going to get some fresh air. Clear my head. But maybe, yes, a lift would be great. This has all been . . .' Her voice breaks. 'A nightmare.'

'Come on,' he says.

'So that's it?' I call after him. 'You come here, punch Laurence and leave?'

'Pretty much,' he replies, pausing. 'Oh, and yes, his nose is definitely broken. No damaged ribs though. He'll be fine. Just keep putting the ice packs on it.'

Seth leaves with Francesca and my limbs suddenly feel as weak as spaghetti.

'I'll drive you to the hospital,' I tell Laurence, who's managed to stagger to his feet. I don't mention how shaky I feel too.

'The carpet's ruined,' Daisy says, glaring at the blood. 'Looks like there's been a murder in here.'

'I'll sort it out when I get back,' I say.

'The carpet or the rest of it?' she replies.

'Give her a break, Dais,' Laurence says.

Daisy storms out of the room and slams the door behind her.

'I should see if she's okay,' I say.

'Give her some space,' Laurence replies. 'She's pissed off with me, not you.'

'What a mess,' I say. 'And I'm not talking about your face.'

Laurence tries to smile at that, but the pain is too much for him and he gasps. 'You okay to drive?'

I nod. 'Come on, let's get you fixed up.'

It's weird, but for the first time in my life, I'm nervous in his presence. Our relationship has already changed from simple friendship . . . to something else.

Chapter Thirty-Six

Today was a masterclass in drama.

I think my talents have been wasted. I should have gone into acting. Even if I say so myself, I'm SO convincing. Without a doubt, I could have starred in movies and won all the Oscars. I can imagine the stunned surprise on my face as my name is called out, the proud and tender kiss from my significant other before I walk up on to the stage to tumultuous applause.

But even if all that were a possibility, I would still rather be right here, right now with the promise of everything I've ever wanted just a hop, skip and a jump away . . .

Chapter Thirty-Seven

Now

I slip on my coat and head out of the office to get myself a sandwich. Despite being the middle of July, the weather has finally turned and it's a chilly, drizzly day. I keep my head bowed against the wind, and hurry along the pavement.

Work has now become a chore to be endured, rather than a career I love. As a new partner at Faraday's, Charlotte is even more insufferable than before, and Paul avoids eye contact as much as possible, embarrassed at having broken his career promises to me. The only bright spot is Miriam, who's been predictably lovely and supportive after my work dreams crumbled.

The other gloomy outcome in my life is that I couldn't find a decent flat in my price bracket, so I decided to move in with my parents for a while. I know I'm lucky to have the option of a few rent-free months to get back on track, but I can't help feeling like I've regressed a decade. Mum is clucking around me like I'm eight years old. And Dad keeps offering me stern pep talks and nuggets of wisdom that are supposed to fire me up, but only make me feel even more inadequate.

Immediately after the whole Seth–Laurence debacle, my friendship with Daisy just didn't feel the same. She was spending nearly all of her time at Martin's and kept fobbing me off every time I asked her to come round or meet for a drink. So I informed her a couple of weeks ago that I was moving back to my parents' house, and that she and Martin should move in properly, like they were supposed to after the wedding. I think me leaving has helped our friendship a bit, but we're still not fully back on track.

I reach Bites & Beans and join the queue of soggy customers staring up at the specials board. Once I reach the counter, I'm still trying to decide between a mozzarella-and-tomato wrap, or a straightforward ploughman's crusty roll.

'Hi, Alice,' Danica's sister Tabitha says from behind the counter, with a smile. 'What can I get you?'

I plump for the comfort option. 'Hey, Tabitha, ploughman's roll and a packet of ready-salted crisps to take away please.'

'Good choice,' the person next to me says.

I freeze. My pulse starts to race. I know that voice. That person. I've been trying to forget him for years.

Damian.

My left hand starts to shake uncontrollably. I think back to those moments over the past few weeks when I thought I saw him, but dismissed it as my imagination. As stress. I drag up the courage to turn to look at him. He's changed a little. Lost some weight in his face. But he still has those same dark eyes that seem to see into my soul and shrivel up my spirit. He still has that condescending smile. The one that turns my stomach to water.

'What are you doing here?' I manage to stutter out.

'Just visiting a friend.' He lingers on the word 'friend' like there's a double meaning. Like the friend he's referring to is me.

I want to ask him if he's been following me, but I can't quite choke out the words.

'That's £3.90,' Tabitha says with a cheerful smile, oblivious to the turmoil twisting through me.

I'm brought back to my present surroundings with a jolt and somehow manage to swipe my card and put 50p in the tips jar.

'Generous,' Damian says with a smirk in his voice.

Tabitha looks from me to Damian with undisguised curiosity.

I can't do this. 'Actually, Tabitha, I've just remembered something. Don't worry about the roll.' I turn to leave, knocking shoulders with a woman queuing behind me.

'Don't mind me,' she snaps.

I shake my head, unable to even say sorry. My heart is clattering, my breaths are coming in short little gasps and my eyes are blurry as I make my way blindly through the café and back out into the freezing rain that's falling heavier by the second. I feel as though I've been transported back to that time when I was under Damian's thumb. When I was scared to go out, to say the wrong thing, to even look at him the wrong way. Why has he come back? Why now?

I start walking, not caring in which direction, not caring that I have no umbrella to shield me from the downpour. I just have to get away from him. I need to clear my head. I'm not that timid person any longer. I'm not. I've made a great new life for myself. I . . . I realise I was thinking about my fiancé and my successful career, but I don't have those things any longer. My engagement has ended and my career has stalled. I technically don't even have a place to live.

As I hurry from the café, I cast a glance over my shoulder, checking to see if Damian is following me. I can't see him. I quicken my pace, anyway, wanting to put as much distance between us as possible. I should go back to work, but I can't face any of them right now. Miriam will ask me what's wrong, and I can't give her yet another sob story. Everything is such a mess and I'm already soaked right through to my skin. I should go home and get changed.

I stop where I am in the middle of the pavement as the lunch-time crowd rushes past, huddled under umbrellas, raincoats pulled tight, hoods obscuring their faces.

'You forgot this.'

I jump and almost trip backwards into the road as one of the figures stops in front of me.

It's Damian holding out a brown paper bag. 'Your lunch.'

'Keep it,' I say, regaining my balance. I'm shivering with cold, my teeth chattering.

'I've missed you, Alice.' His voice sends another jolt of anxiety to my gut.

'What are you doing here?' I cry. 'Have you been following me?'

His eyes widen and he holds up his hands. 'Woah, calm down, little one.'

My skin crawls at the use of his pet name for me. Back when we first got together, I loved it, but after a while he would say it in a mocking way, like I was this helpless, useless creature. 'Have you?' I push.

'Have I what?'

'Been following me?'

'You're being paranoid.'

'What car do you drive?' I ask, thinking back to last month when I thought I saw a silver car following me. I stare at him, repulsed by the lazy smile that spreads across his features.

'Relax, Alice. It's a free country. I can come back to Ringwood if I like. You don't own the place.'

I grit my teeth. Now that I've got over the shock of seeing him face to face, now that he's here in front of me and I know I wasn't going crazy, imagining things, I need answers. 'Why are you here, Damian?'

'Told you. I'm visiting—'

'Yeah, a friend, you already said. I mean why have you been following me? Why are you here now talking to me? We broke up. I told you I never wanted to see you again.'

'I thought you'd be pleased to see me now you've split up with your fiancé.'

'How do you know about that?' I ask, my heart lurching.

'Everyone knows. You had a breakdown on your wedding day. He obviously wasn't the right man for you. I could've predicted it. You're fragile, little one. You need a tender hand.'

His words make me shudder. Make my gorge rise. I remember this is how he used to be – making out I was helpless, that I couldn't do or be anything without him. But I'm not that person any more. I'm not about to put up with his crap all over again.

'Piss off, Damian.'

He puts a hand to his heart as though wounded. 'That's not very nice. Why don't we go somewhere warm and dry. Talk about things. Make up.'

'I'm not going anywhere with you. You need to leave me alone, or I'll—'

'You'll what?' He gives me another slow smile. 'You won't do anything, little one. You haven't got it in you. Look, I'll come clean, okay? I'm here because I miss you. I heard about your wedding day and I realised it was an opportunity to make amends. We loved each other once. I want a second chance.'

'You're out of your mind.' Despite the icy rain, I'm suddenly hot with anger. 'I don't want to see you again. Ever. Don't talk to me, don't call me, don't follow me or threaten me. If you come anywhere near me again, I'll call the police, get a restraining order, whatever it takes to keep you out of my life.'

Damian's features darken. 'You think you're too good for me now, is that it? Now you've been engaged to a rich London doctor.' He lets the brown paper bag containing my lunch fall on to the wet

209

ground and he takes hold of my hand, starts to drag me along the pavement. 'Come with me. We're going to talk about this properly.'

'Let go!' I try to free my hand, but he's holding on too tight. I plant my feet and refuse to budge. If he wants me to move, he'll have to drag me along the ground. My arm is almost wrenched out of its socket, but he's forced to either let go or stop walking. He chooses the latter and turns to face me, leaning in close.

'Don't worry, little one,' he croons with malice in his voice. 'I'll break it out of you.'

I bring my knee up as hard as I can between his legs. He lets go of my hand and I drive the heel of my palm into his solar plexus.

'I'm not the same person!' I cry with more courage than I feel. 'You don't scare me any more, Damian.' Leaving him gasping on the pavement, I stagger away and break into a run towards the closest safe place I know.

Moments later, panting, soaking, crying, I stand in the still-pouring rain and press the buzzer to Laurence's flat.

I haven't seen Laurence since that terrible afternoon three weeks ago when Seth punched him and we had to drive to the hospital. Since then, Laurence has texted me a couple of times, asking to meet up. But I've refused, unable to face it. Aside from worrying about everyone else's opinions, I haven't felt in a strong enough head space to make any kind of relationship decisions. Not yet.

I feel bad landing on his doorstep like this, in such distress, but he's the only person I want to see right now. I only hope he's home.

Seconds later, the door opens and I almost collapse with relief as Laurence stands there, hitting me with his devastatingly familiar smile, his light-blue eyes crinkling.

'Bloody hell, Porter, you're drenched.' His voice is deep and soft with a hint of humour as he takes in my bedraggled state. But then he sees my face and his expression creases with concern. 'What's happened?'

'Sorry to show up like this out of the blue,' I say, trying not to sound as hysterical as I feel.

'No, no, that's fine. Come in.'

I follow him up the stairs into his flat where I instantly feel ten times safer. 'What about Francesca?' I ask, looking past him into the living room in case she might be around.

'She's not here,' he replies with a shake of his head.

I wonder if that means she's not here at the moment, or she's not here permanently. Laurence enlightens me. 'She moved out the same day we broke up. She's renting a room from a girl from work, and she won't return my calls. I've missed you, Porter. I've missed our friendship.'

I nod, not trusting myself to say anything else without sobbing. Now that I'm safe, every last drop of adrenaline has fled and I feel as though I might dissolve into a puddle on the floor.

'Are you going to tell me what's wrong?' he presses.

'Damian.' I give a violent shiver.

'What?' Laurence's expression darkens. 'Has he been in touch?'

'Worse.' My voice is hoarse, ragged. 'I wasn't imagining it before. He's been following me. He just . . . he was just . . .'

'Hey.' Laurence pulls me into a hug.

'I'm getting your top all wet,' I sob.

He hugs me tighter. 'Let's get you into some dry clothes. Then you can tell me what's happened.'

I nod as he lets me go.

I take a quick hot shower and change into a pair of Laurence's joggers and a sweatshirt that he hands me through a crack in the bathroom door.

'Tea?' he asks, as I emerge feeling a little more together.

'Please.' I head over to the breakfast bar and sit heavily on one of the stools. I've finally stopped shaking, but I now feel hollow and strange.

Laurence doesn't pressure me straight away to tell him what happened; he busies himself making the tea.

I love how we can be together without talking and it never feels awkward. I finally blurt it all out, hardly believing that I actually stood up to Damian. That I kneed him in the balls! I realise I've been wanting to do that for a long time.

'Bloody hell, Alice!' Laurence's eyes widen and then narrow as he takes it all in. He straightens up. 'Stay here. I'm going to see if he's still hanging around.' He takes a step towards the door.

'No!' The thought of Laurence confronting Damian makes me feel ill. I want nothing more to do with the man.

Laurence frowns. 'But he might be—'

'Please just stay. I . . . I can't cope with any more drama. And anyway, I told him I won't put up with his shit any more. I left him doubled-up on the pavement.'

Laurence's shoulders drop. 'Fine. But we should at least report him to the police.'

'I don't know,' I reply, my heart gradually slowing. 'I can't face doing any of that right now.'

'Are you sure?'

'Please. I just can't.'

'Okay, I guess. Well done for standing up to him though. What a prick.' He brings my tea round to the lounge area where we sit next to one another.

I cradle my tea, letting the warmth seep into my fingers, which are already cold again despite the hot shower. I realise I should probably be getting back to work, but I just can't do it. The thought of trying to act normally after what's just happened is impossible. I'll text Miriam in a bit, let her know I won't be back today.

'Anyway,' I say, glancing up at Laurence, 'how have you been? How's your nose?' I instantly regret asking the question as my mind

212

is abruptly transported back to that terrible afternoon when Seth punched him and we had to drive to the hospital.

'The nose isn't too bad,' Laurence replies, tweaking it. 'Almost back to normal now.'

I notice it's still a little swollen, but most people would never know the difference. Seth was right; the A & E doctor confirmed that Laurence's nose was broken. Thankfully, it wasn't bent too much out of shape. And his ribs were all fine, no fractures or breaks.

'I'm sorry you've had such a horrible experience,' Laurence says, sipping his tea. 'But I'm really glad you came round. I've missed you . . . and Daisy, of course. It's been lonely without you guys.' He gives a sad laugh.

Laurence is talking about our friendship rather than his declaration of love. Is he going to mention that at all, I wonder, or will we just act like it never happened? Move on.

'I really screwed up, didn't I?' He puts his drink down on the coffee table and gazes at me with an unreadable expression.

I don't reply. My heart is beating so fast and so loud, I can't believe he doesn't mention it. I'm not sure what's happening to me. My emotions are flying all over the place.

'Look, Alice,' he says, taking a breath. 'If it's easier for you, let's just pretend I never said anything about *us*. Go back to how things were before.'

My skin is still cool but my blood is suddenly hot, my nerve endings tingling, lighting up like little firecrackers. I lick my lips and swallow. 'What if I don't want to go back to how things were before?' I ask.

Laurence pauses before leaning towards me. And suddenly we're kissing, his hands on me, finding the skin beneath my sweatshirt, my fingers tangling in his hair.

A voice in the back of my head is telling me that this probably isn't the best decision to be making right now. But, as Laurence carries me into the bedroom, all rational thought flies away.

Chapter Thirty-Eight

THEN

The car journey to the church is a blur. Cruising through the busy town centre, I feel like a movie star as passers-by try to catch a glimpse of me, the bride, inside the limo. I'm sitting with my parents and sister, while my bridesmaids are in the other car.

When we finally turn down the winding drive lined with thick green hedgerows, the birds so loud I can hear them singing over the sound of the car engine, my heart begins to pound.

'Nearly there,' Elizabeth says, reaching across Mum to give my hand a squeeze.

At the end of the lane, the little stone church finally comes into view, its familiar brown gate and blue lamppost a comforting reminder that some things never change.

We exit the cars and I'm ushered from the bright sunshine into the cool church entrance, where I stand with my bridesmaids while my parents check that everything is as it should be.

'You look stunning,' Francesca says, her hazel eyes radiating warmth and calm.

'Thanks,' I manage to stammer. 'I don't think I've ever been this nervous and excited in my life.'

'Here.' Daisy takes a bottle of water from her bag, unscrews the top and passes it to me.

'Oh, you lifesaver. Thanks, Daisy.' I take it and sip the cool liquid slowly.

I pass it back and she goes to join Elizabeth, who starts fussing around her and Miriam like a mother hen with her chicks.

'Just take a few breaths,' Fran says. 'You'll be fine.'

She chats to me for a few minutes, soothing words to calm me. But I'm so keyed up that I can barely focus on what she's saying.

Laurence comes over and interrupts her pep talk. 'Wow, you don't scrub up too bad, Porter,' he says, elbowing me gently in the ribs.

'Not too bad yourself, Kennedy. And it's soon to be Porter-Evans, actually,' I remind him. Laurence's jokey attitude is just what I need to ground me right now.

'Fran, you look amazing,' Laurence says, turning to his girlfriend and kissing her carefully on the cheek so he doesn't smudge her lipstick.

She blushes and gives him a half-hug. 'Thanks. It's not the usual dog-walking outfit.'

I love how Fran and Laurence have been together for years but he still has the power to make her feel great. I hope Seth and I will have that kind of enduring relationship.

Elizabeth calls Fran over, continuing to make last-minute adjustments to all my bridesmaids, smoothing dresses and tucking in stray bits of hair. Laurence gives me a hug and tells me to enjoy the day. He says a bunch of other stuff too but, like with Francesca a minute ago, and everyone else's well-wishes, I'm finding it hard to focus on anything other than my beating heart and the fact that Seth is inside the church waiting for me.

Suddenly, there are whispered instructions and a flurry of extra activity. Mum hugs me before heading back into the church, and Dad comes to stand by my side.

This is it. I'm about to get married.

Chapter Thirty-Nine

Now

'Where've you been?' Laurence asks, as I come into the flat carrying my gold pineapple table lamp.

'Just went to pick this up from Daisy's. I'd forgotten about it. Remember? It was in the lounge. I thought it would go great in here.' Laurence's flat is lovely – clean, light and spacious – but it's got no soul. No character. It needs a bit of spicing up.

He gives the lamp a critical once-over. 'I don't know,' he says. 'It's a bit . . . kitsch for in here.'

'Exactly.' I smile. 'This place is far too serious. It could do with a shot of whimsy.'

'Uh, it really couldn't.' Laurence grins and takes the lamp out of my hands, placing it on the floor behind the sofa and wrapping his arms around me. 'I missed you this morning,' he says. 'Thought we were going to have breakfast together.' He kisses me and I give myself over to his lips and tongue, his hands pulling me closer.

After the day when we reconnected in his flat, and then slept together for the first time, I was shocked when Laurence immediately suggested that I move in with him. He had no hesitation. No doubts at all. Unlike me.

I was cautious at first. Scared to rush headlong into another relationship after the spectacular failure of my previous two. But, after another week of living in my parents' house, I finally succumbed to Laurence's pleas. We'd been spending every evening together anyway, so it seemed daft to keep commuting back to my parents' house just to sleep. Talking of my parents, Dad is not at all happy with my decision to move in with Laurence. I don't think Mum's overly pleased either, but at least she's keeping her opinions to herself.

Laurence and I finally break our kiss, coming up for air, and he gazes at me. 'I can't believe we're actually together,' he says. 'It's like all my Christmases have come at once.'

I smile lazily back. 'Same here, plus Easters and birthdays.'

'Why the hell did I wait so long to tell you how I felt?' he asks. 'Just think of all that time we wasted.'

'I know. But maybe it wouldn't have worked if we'd got together any earlier,' I muse. 'Maybe we needed to have those other relationships to be able to appreciate what we have now.'

'That's why I love you,' Laurence says. 'Because you talk so much sense.'

'I try my best.'

'And because you're gorgeous,' he adds with a laugh, pulling me in for another kiss. He breaks it off abruptly and holds my arms. 'But seriously, message if you're going to go out without telling me. I was worried when you didn't answer my texts.'

I ease myself from his grip and plonk myself down on to the sofa, wishing he'd drop the subject. 'You were still asleep, and I was wide awake, so I thought I'd nip over to fetch the lamp. Daisy talked me into staying for a quick breakfast and I didn't see your texts. Anyway, I'm back now.'

He folds his arms across his chest and frowns. 'Yes, but that's not the point. I was worried.'

'Okay, well, sorry, I guess.'

'Oh, you *guess*?' His expression is light-hearted, but there's a firmness behind his words.

'No, you know what I mean.' I fix him with my most winning smile. 'I'm sorry you were worried.'

'Okay, so next time you'll wait till I get up, right?'

'Sure. Or I'll text you so you don't worry.'

He sits next to me and kisses my right eyebrow and then my left. 'Thank you.'

I lean back against the cushions as Laurence gets up and moves over to the kitchen to make coffee. These little flashes of his possessiveness cause sparks of worry in my chest. He's not like this all the time, and whenever I call him out on it he laughs it off, so I hope this is just new-relationship nerves and that he'll settle down once he's reassured I'm all in. When he realises I'm not going anywhere.

Because this controlling version of Laurence is not the man I fell in love with.

This version of him is nothing like the laid-back best friend I've had for years.

No.

This Laurence feels different.

Chapter Forty

Now

I slot two slices of bread in the toaster and wander listlessly around Laurence's living room. I still think of it as *his* living room – *his* flat – despite having moved in three months ago. Mainly because there's hardly any of my stuff here, aside from my clothes and toiletries and a grand total of three knick-knacks – my white fluffy rug that lies by my side of the bed, my pineapple lamp in the lounge (Laurence begrudgingly said it could stay) and the huge wavy-armed cheese plant I've had since uni.

Laurence has suffered these three interlopers with bad grace. He liked his flat exactly the way it was. I always knew that about him, so I'm not sure why I was surprised and a little disappointed that he was reluctant for me to put my stamp on it. He's lived here for years, so I've been thinking that maybe next year we could look for a new place. A home that we can decorate together.

I haven't mentioned the idea of moving just yet. I'm waiting for the right moment. Although, the more time goes by, the more I'm inclined to think that he won't be keen on the idea. Especially as the spare room has been set up as the office where he sees his clients. I can certainly understand that it would be quite a hassle to move his place of business. Anyway, Laurence tried to explain that the rest of the apartment had to exude the same level of calm as his office, in case any of his clients happened to glance in. I teased him when he said that: 'Yes, heaven forbid they catch sight of a cheese plant.' I grinned. 'That could set them back months.'

He hadn't seen the funny side and told me not to joke about his clients' mental health. I hadn't meant it in that way. I'd just been trying to lighten the mood.

On Friday evening, Laurence left to go on a four-day cycling trip to South Wales with Martin. Those two have become close buddies since Martin moved in with Daisy. The four of us spend quite a lot of time together now. Daisy is slowly coming around to the idea of me and Laurence being an item, but she hasn't completely embraced it yet. I still catch her frowning at us when she thinks I'm not looking.

Normally, if I have a Sunday to myself with nothing planned, my favourite thing to do is to rearrange the furniture, or redecorate. Maybe go to a car-boot sale and search for interesting home decor – plants or crockery, perhaps a quirky piece of art. But with Laurence's aversion to changing anything in the flat, I'll have to restrain myself.

I'm bored.

Daisy's got a shift at the pharmacy today and Miriam has gone to a family lunch. Even my parents are away this weekend – Dad got some VIP tickets through work to a rugby game in France. They've flown over there with Elizabeth and Graham. Laurence and I were also invited, and I thought it would have been a great opportunity for Laurence to bond with my family in his new role as 'boyfriend' rather than 'friend'. But, of course, we couldn't go because of the cycling trip. I'm starting to think I should have gone without him.

I'm momentarily saved from my boredom by the door buzzer.

When I glance in the monitor to see who it is, I instantly wish I could return to my previous state of dullness.

It's Francesca.

Should I ignore it? Pretend I'm not in? It buzzes again, making me jump, setting my heart racing. Maybe she's here to see Laurence. But somehow I don't think so. I don't imagine it's any coincidence that she's arrived while he's away. At the third buzz, I realise she's not giving up.

I press the button, allowing her into the building, wondering why she might have come to see me after all this time. We haven't met since that day she arrived at the flat accusing me and Laurence of having an affair. She was wrong back then. But what about *now*? What defence can I offer?

I did message her a few times after Laurence and I got together. I asked if we could meet, wanting to apologise, but she never replied. I don't really blame her. So, Francesca visiting today should be a good thing. A chance for that all-important closure I was seeking. Instead, I'm a bag of nerves.

I glance at myself in the long hall mirror. My curls are tied back off my face which is free of make-up. I'm wearing leggings, a sweatshirt and a pair of chunky socks. I startle at the tap on the door, inhale and stretch out my fingers, then wipe away a bead of sweat from my top lip. I'm so unprepared for this.

Come on, Alice. Just get it over with.

I open the door and try to muster a smile, but all I manage is a tight-lipped grimace.

'Hello, Alice,' she says with no emotion.

'Hi.' I choke on the word, cough and pat my chest. 'Sorry, hi. Come in.' It feels wrong to be welcoming Francesca into what used to be her home. I feel like *I'm* the intruder. This would have been so much easier if we were on neutral ground. I clear my throat. 'Laurence isn't here. He's away for a few days.'

'I know,' she replies. 'I came to see *you*.'

A heaviness settles in my chest. 'Shall we go into the lounge?' I gesture for her to go first.

'Sure.' She steps into the hall, her gaze sweeping the area. 'It's funny how weird it feels to be back,' she says, almost to herself. 'But so normal at the same time.'

I follow her down the hall to the living room where her gaze takes in the new additions.

'Can I get you a drink?'

She shakes her head. 'No thanks.'

I want to ask her to sit down, but it feels so presumptuous. This was her home. I don't want to play host. I decide to remain standing for now, hoping she won't stay long.

'Francesca, I'm glad you came,' I say. 'I've been wanting to speak to you for ages. To apologise for how everything went down. I . . . I hope you're doing okay.' I'm babbling, my hands clasped in front of me while she stands there letting me ramble on. 'I wanted you to know that none of this was planned. Back then, I honestly had no idea about Laurence's feelings. I thought the two of you were solid. He was a friend. Nothing more, I promise you.'

'And now?' she asks.

I have the good grace to look down as my face heats up. I pick at my fingernails and think about what I should say next. The truth is, there's nothing I can say to make this any better. Her boyfriend was in love with me and now we're together.

'You know what,' she says. 'It's fine. You actually did me a favour.'

I'm blindsided by her words. I'd felt certain she would cry, or shout, or show *some* emotion. But here she is, standing before me, cool as a winter's day. Perhaps she's putting it on to let me think she's okay. To keep her dignity. Well, that's fine with me. But I wouldn't mind if she wanted to yell at me. I want her to be genuinely okay. To be over Laurence. To meet someone else and live happily ever after. But if she's still upset, then I wouldn't blame her if she wanted to let me know that.

I like Francesca. She's a sweet girl. She's never been anything but lovely to me, and she didn't deserve what happened.

'The thing is,' she says, 'there's something you should know.'

I don't like the way she said that. Like she's about to drop a bombshell. There's a creeping sensation in the pit of my stomach. I think I might need to sit down. I sink down on to the sofa and gesture to Francesca to do the same. She perches on one of the kitchen stools so that I'm looking up at her.

She's dressed smarter than usual in black jeans and a forest-green silk top that complements her hazel eyes and caramel hair. I feel scruffy in comparison, which is strange because she's usually the more casual dresser.

She seems reluctant to elaborate. 'What's up?' I say in a tone lighter than I'm feeling.

She pauses for a moment. 'I know this is going to come as a bit of a shock, but I think Laurence might have had something to do with what happened to you on your wedding day,' she says.

The air between us starts to vibrate with a deep, dark, negative energy.

With a jolt, I realise that Francesca has not come here to be calm and reasonable.

She's come here to cause trouble.

Chapter Forty-One

Now

Francesca has come here to cause a scene. She's angry with me. She's trying to come across as poised and sensible, but she's dropped this wild accusation that almost makes me want to laugh out loud it's so outlandish.

I take a deep, steadying breath and try not to rise to the bait or get drawn into a disagreement. I don't mind her being upset with me, but I'm not about to start playing stupid games. It takes every ounce of self-control not to ask what she's talking about.

'You know he studied psychology, right?' she says.

I give a slight nod.

'Well, he also has a Cognitive Behavioural Hypnotherapy diploma. Did you know that?'

I didn't know that, but I'm not going to admit it. 'What does that have to do with what happened at my wedding?' I ask, a sick feeling starting to creep up my gullet.

'Think about it,' she replies.

I'm trying to make sense of what she's saying, but my mind is fuzzy and slow.

'Laurence didn't want you to marry Seth,' she continues. 'He was in love with you. But you were in love with Seth. He couldn't have admitted to you how he felt. He didn't stand a chance. Instead, he used the power of suggestion to make you fall out of love with your groom.'

'I'm sorry, *what*?' I say with a disbelieving laugh. 'That just sounds ridiculous.'

'I know,' she agrees. 'It does. Which is why it's so brilliant. No one would ever guess what he'd done. No one would believe it.'

'Exactly,' I reply. 'And I'm afraid *I* don't believe it either.'

She shakes her head. 'Think about it . . . you were all set to marry Seth and then on your wedding day you suddenly didn't recognise him. What else could have caused that? The doctors were stumped. The brain scans came up clear . . .'

'Even if what you're saying is possible,' I reply. 'Laurence would never in a million years do anything like that. You forget, I've known him since we were kids. He might have studied hypnotherapy, but that doesn't mean anything. He's an ethical person. He's a *good* person.' Something else occurs to me. 'Do you actually have any evidence for any of this? It sounds like it's just a mad theory you've come up with.'

She bows her head for a moment before looking back up, hint of apology, and maybe some defiance, in her eyes. 'I've still got a key.'

'A *key*? You mean to the flat?'

'I came back here once while you were at work and Laurence was out.'

'What the hell? You broke in while we were out?' I straighten up and lean forward. 'You can't do that. You're not on the rental agreement any more.'

'Just hear me out, Alice. I did it with good intentions.'

'I don't believe this,' I mutter, shaking my head. The thought of her being here while we were out, going through our stuff. It gives me the creeps. She might have been hurt by Laurence, but this has crossed the line. It's stalkerish behaviour. 'I think you should go, Francesca. I know it's hard, but you need to move on with your life and let Laurence do the same.'

'Will you please just listen to me first? I know what I did was wrong and I won't do anything like that again, but just hear what I have to say. Please.'

'Fine. But then you have to leave.'

'I will, I promise.' She shifts on her stool and continues. 'So, when I was here, I went into Laurence's office. Checked out his emails and search history. At first, I admit, it was just to be nosy, to find some kind of clue about when you two started seeing one another. I didn't believe that you hadn't had an affair.'

'That is *not* okay,' I say, my agitation growing with every second. 'And I already told you that we weren't seeing each other.'

'Yeah, I know. But I wasn't about to take your word for it. Or his.'

'That's fair, I suppose,' I reply grudgingly. 'But it still doesn't excuse you breaking in here. You went on his laptop?'

She nods. 'I know his password. It's "Volition91", capital "V".'

I shake my head at this. Why would she tell me his password? I make a mental note to get him to change it asap.

'Anyway,' Francesca continues. 'I didn't find anything about you two having an affair, but I did notice that he'd been looking at hypnotherapy websites in the months before your wedding. Not just the regular sites, but the dodgy ones. The forums where people ask questions about what it's possible to achieve. He was especially interested in studies relating to editing patients' memories. How to do it. How to make them forget. How to make them go off someone. It got me thinking . . .'

I really don't like what she's saying. It's making me feel odd. 'I'd like you to leave now,' I say. My voice sounds as though it's coming from far away. I think I must be in shock, or something.

'I know it's upsetting to hear this, Alice. But I couldn't have lived with myself if I didn't say anything. I've been sitting on this news for a while, but when I heard Laurence was out of town, I had to come over and let you know. I think you need to be careful. I think Laurence might actually be dangerous.'

Sweat starts to gather under my armpits and between my breasts. This whole visit is freaking me the hell out, even if what she's saying is all a load of bullshit. My head is swimming and I really feel as though I might be about to throw up. 'Can you please stop talking and leave?' I repeat, weakly.

She slides off the stool, a genuine look of concern in her eyes. 'I realise this must be a shock. Can I get you anything? A glass of water? A cup of tea?'

'No. Just go, please.'

'Don't you even want to talk about this? If I were you, I'd have so many questions. I can show you the websites if you like . . .'

'Just go!'

'You need to be careful,' she says. 'Like I said before, if he's done this, then he's dangerous. He might have been a good friend to you, Alice, but he wasn't always the best boyfriend. You'll find that out.'

I can't focus on what she's saying. I feel like I'm underwater. Even my vision is blurred. 'Key,' I manage to say.

'Sorry?' she asks.

'Your key to the flat; can you leave it please?'

'Oh, yeah, sure. Sorry about that.' She places it on the kitchen counter with a click. 'I'll let myself out,' she adds, pausing for a moment. 'But if you want to talk, just message me, okay? I'm not happy with what you did, but you don't deserve what he's done to you.'

I don't reply.

Eventually, she leaves the living room. I don't even watch her go. I can't seem to get up off the sofa. Her preposterous words are swirling around my head, like a kaleidoscope of horror. I need to get control of myself. I place my hands either side of me on the sofa and take a few breaths. This girl, this ex of Laurence's, has simply come round to unsettle me. To take her revenge, that's all. She's obviously lying. Stirring things because she's upset. Jealous.

The front door closes and I sink back against the sofa, a tear squeezing out from the corner of my eye. I knew seeing Francesca would be awkward and uncomfortable, but I never thought it would be quite so traumatic. So . . . *disturbing*.

Her accusations are vile. That my best-friend-turned-boyfriend would mess with my mind to get what he wanted. That he would purposely ruin my life to enhance his own. Those would be the actions of a psychopath.

Why, then, is there this tiny seed of doubt burrowing its way through my mind?

I try to think logically about everything. Laurence was my friend for years. He's known me with boyfriends and without. Why wouldn't he have simply made a move on me back when I was single? Why wait until I was about to get married? It doesn't make any sense.

Although . . . he did admit that, while he'd been in love with me for years, it wasn't until I told him about Seth's proposal that he realised how much he loved me. That he was terrified he'd left it too late to tell me. Could that have been the trigger to make him act? I can't believe I'm actually entertaining Francesca's crazy accusation.

I stand shakily and start pacing the living room, examining her theory. After Laurence ended things with Francesca, he moved in on me so quickly. He didn't wait for the dust to settle after she moved out. Within three weeks we'd slept together, and then a week later I moved in. But that was my choice as much as his, wasn't it? I mean, I put up some resistance, but not much.

And, since then, if I'm totally honest with myself, things haven't been quite as wonderful as I was expecting. Laurence has shown small signs of becoming . . . not necessarily controlling, but not as easy-going as I'd expected. Not as relaxed. Not the same fun, kind person as when we were just friends.

But do those things mean he's capable of manipulating my mind in order to sabotage my life? I shudder and find that my feet are taking me out of the lounge. I'm heading along the hallway towards Laurence's office. I turn the handle and open the door. It makes a swishing sound as it brushes over the grey carpet.

Laurence's office is the larger of the two bedrooms. It's spotless. An impressive wooden desk occupies the wall to the right of the window, behind which sits a black leather swivel chair. In front of the desk are two chairs – one a simple straight-backed wooden seat, the other a more comfortable-looking armchair. Laurence says he likes to give his clients a choice of seating. An arc lamp hangs gracefully over the left side of his desk. The opposite wall has been given over to a floor-to-ceiling bookcase. Behind Laurence's desk, his many qualifications have been framed and hung on the wall. I walk over and peer at the wording on all of them. There are no hypnotherapy certificates hanging here, but that doesn't necessarily mean anything.

Sitting in Laurence's chair, I marvel at how comfortable it is. At how it seems to hug my body. Straight ahead of me, a framed photograph of me and Laurence sits proudly on the desk next to his laptop. The picture was taken at a music festival a few years ago. A group of us went for the weekend, but this photo is of just us two smiling into the camera, his arm slung around my shoulder. I wonder if it's a recent addition to his desk. And whether it replaced a photo of Francesca. I wonder what she thought of it when she broke into the flat with her key and saw it.

I open Laurence's silver laptop. His lock screen is also a photograph of me. Before today I would have been touched by his devotion, but right now I feel embarrassed thinking of Francesca seeing all these reminders that I'm his girlfriend now.

The password box sits in the centre of the screen, and I type in 'Volition91' with a capital 'V'.

It tells me that the password is incorrect, those bold red letters mocking me. Hopefully, Francesca made the whole thing up. I type it in again, but the same red denial flashes up. I'm not trying it again. I close the laptop with trembling fingers and leave Laurence's office.

I return to the living room and pick up my own laptop from the side table next to the sofa. I take it over to the breakfast bar and sit on the stool next to the one Francesca was perched on minutes ago.

I almost feel stupid as I open it up and type 'hypnosis' into the search bar. But I don't feel quite as stupid when I start clicking on some of the websites to see if what Francesca suggested is actually possible. Some of it reads like the plot of a sci-fi novel.

One man asked a therapist to totally erase the memory of his girlfriend as the thought of her caused him so much anguish. The therapist refused on ethical grounds, citing that, '*most information stored in the mind is cross-linked to other pieces of information. If you delete one category of information then other cross-linked information becomes incomplete and confusing.*'

My throat constricts as I wonder if that might have been done to *me*.

Another therapist says: '*Hypnotising yourself to forget someone is a bad idea. To make someone forget something for a longer period would require a deeper state of hypnosis and more than one session. The side effects would be an issue. It is much smarter to use hypnosis to help you deal with trauma than bury it.'*

Another study on induced amnesia shows that: *'Brain functions can be disrupted for short periods of time, so that the ability to fix memories is temporarily switched off, leading to memory loss like amnesia.'*

There are also positive stories about people overcoming phobias and giving up vices. Tales of giving birth with no pain, of helping to eliminate night terrors and ongoing worries. But I'm horrified to read a news article about a man who used hypnosis to rob convenience stores by putting his victims into a trance. Another where someone induced victims to willingly hand over their wallets and phones. So many terrible stories of people committing criminal acts using hypnosis, of trying to manipulate innocent people. But there's nothing that specifically details what happened to *me*.

Could what Francesca told me actually be possible? Would my best friend have really attempted such a terrible thing, knowing that it could damage my mind?

I think about the Laurence from before. The one who always had my back. I have a seriously hard time imagining him doing anything so sick and twisted as messing with my memories for his own benefit, risking my mental health.

But this new Laurence . . . the one who loves me so deeply . . . the one who doesn't want me going anywhere without telling him . . . the one who broke the heart of the girl he was with for years . . . the one who's trained to delve into people's minds . . . the one who spent hours in the lead-up to my wedding talking to me one-on-one . . . the one who later admitted it drove him crazy to see me with Seth . . .

That Laurence, I realise with a sick feeling of dread, I can almost imagine doing something exactly like this.

Chapter Forty-Two

Now

I've spent every waking moment swinging between absolute denial of Francesca's claim, to doubting my boyfriend. I'm still unsure if the type of hypnosis Francesca was talking about is even possible and, even if it were, can I really imagine Laurence doing it?

I'm also paranoid that if he has been manipulating my mind, then what if my memories and mental state are now irreparably damaged? I know I haven't been myself since the wedding, or even in the weeks leading up to it. I've had this underlying buzz of anxiety for months now. I've been overly tearful, melancholic, stressed. I should probably make an appointment to see a specialist, but the thought of what they might discover terrifies me.

Laurence returned from his cycling trip half an hour ago, excitedly recounting the highs and lows of the route. He's in the shower right now while I'm taking a lasagne out of the oven. I've already burnt my fingers twice because I'm so preoccupied with how I'm going to raise the subject of Francesca's visit. Right now, I honestly wish she'd never come. That she'd left me to my blissful ignorance.

'Something smells amazing,' Laurence says, walking into the living room. He's wearing joggers and a T-shirt – the same ones he lent me on the day we first got together. He wraps his arms around me. His skin is warm, his hair damp, and he smells of mint shampoo and grapefruit shower gel.

'I made lasagne,' I say, wondering if he can hear the strangeness in my voice.

'I'm so hungry. Is it ready now?' He kisses my neck, working his way up to my mouth.

I try to kiss him back, but my mind is full of everything Francesca told me. Of the websites I've been trawling since she left. I pull away. 'Come and sit down. I'll bring it over.'

'Amazing.' He sits at the dark-grey circular table while I take a sharp knife from the drawer to chop up a cucumber and tomato salad.

'Do you want wine?' I ask.

'Not on a work night,' he replies.

'That's never stopped you before,' I say with a half-smile.

'Trying to stay healthy. Shall we just have water?' he says, eyeing the chilled bottle of Sauvignon Blanc in my hands.

'You can. I'm having wine,' I reply, thinking about the conversation that lies ahead.

Laurence frowns, but doesn't say anything.

I pour myself a generous glass and take two large sips before dishing up the lasagne and adding a side of oven chips.

'So, you heard the highlights of *my* weekend,' he says, sipping his water. 'How was yours?'

I take a breath and bring our plates to the table, nipping back for my wine glass and the bowl of salad. Once I'm seated, I wonder whether I should wait until after we've eaten to tell him about Francesca's visit, or to just dive straight in. I still haven't answered his question.

'Mm, this looks great. Thanks, Alice.' He serves us both, then picks up his cutlery and starts eating.

I take another sip of my drink and drizzle some vinaigrette on my salad.

'So . . . your weekend?' He looks at me across the table and I examine his face for clues. But all I see is the Laurence I've always known – tousled blond hair, aquamarine eyes, stubbled jaw and a cheeky smile. Francesca has to be wrong about this.

But what if she's right?

'Francesca came over yesterday,' I say.

Laurence freezes, his fork hovering in front of his mouth for a moment. He sets it down, wipes his mouth and sits back in his seat. 'Fran came *here*? Why? Did she want to speak to me?'

'No. She wanted to speak to *me*.' I push away my plate, giving up any kind of pretence that I'm hungry. The smell of food is actually making my stomach turn.

'I'm so sorry,' Laurence says, his eyebrows drawing together. 'Was she upset? Did she try to make you feel guilty?' He sighs. 'I'll speak to her, get her to see that our break-up was nothing to do with you. I would have ended things anyway. We weren't right for each other—'

'It wasn't about that.' I cut him off.

'Oh? So why was she here?'

I pause and then go on to tell him about her accusation. That she thinks Laurence used hypnotherapy to get me to forget Seth's face.

'Are you joking?' He gives a disbelieving laugh. 'You're joking, right?'

'No.' I don't laugh back, or smile. I'm watching his face for any sign that what Francesca said could be true. It hits me now with a sick clarity that if I could even consider him capable of this, then our relationship is probably doomed.

'You're not telling me you believe this nonsense?'

'No, but—'

'Everything that comes before the word "but" is bullshit,' he says.

'*But*,' I continue, 'it would explain what happened to me at my wedding.'

He shakes his head slowly. 'You had an episode. A breakdown of some sort. If you want my opinion, I think you were subconsciously looking for a reason to get out of the marriage. I think you knew Seth wasn't right for you, but you felt trapped in the situation. This was your mind giving you a way to get out of it without having to make a conscious decision to end things.'

It's ironic that he's saying exactly what Francesca said to me a few months ago. Maybe they discussed it between them back then. 'No,' I reply. 'That's the thing; I was looking forward to marrying him. I was excited. I was in love . . . until he turned around at the altar and I saw his face. Please just tell me the truth, Laurence. Did you do something to make me forget him? To turn me off him somehow? I need to know so that I can make sense of it all. In some twisted kind of way, it would almost be a relief to know there's a reason why all of it happened. It's been driving me mad, the not knowing.'

'*Driving you mad?*' Laurence repeats, his head cocked. 'So you still have feelings for Seth?'

'*What?* No.'

He stares at me. 'I don't believe you.'

'Don't do that thing where you try to deflect,' I say. 'We're not talking about me and Seth, I'm asking you if there's any truth to what Francesca said.'

'Even if I wanted to,' Laurence replies, 'I don't have the power to make you forget someone. It's impossible to do something like that. You'd have to be highly suggestible – I'm talking top-tier suggestible – and we would have had to have weeks of sessions. Even then . . . no way. I still think that on some subconscious level, you wanted a reason to escape the relationship. You told me you can't even stand to be near the guy!'

'Maybe I can't stand the guy because my mind has been manipulated.'

'No.' Laurence shakes his head. 'Look,' he continues, 'I'll admit I was jealous. I thought you didn't see me as successful enough to go out with. That you wanted to spend time with me, but that I wasn't "husband material".'

'That's rubbish,' I scoff. 'I told you before, I had no clue you even liked me in that way. Anyway, there's something else Francesca told me . . .'

'Here we go.' He rolls his eyes. 'So, what else did she tell you?'

I swallow down my frustration at his attitude. Laurence was never like this with me in the past. He was always so warm and supportive. Such a good friend. Now that we're in a relationship, everything seems to have changed. And not for the better. He's bolshy, defensive, controlling. He's like a different person altogether. I feel like, when it comes to relationships, I'm cursed.

I keep talking, suddenly desperate to unload everything that's accelerating through my mind like a runaway train. 'She said that the search history on your laptop before the wedding was all about using hypnotherapy to make someone forget another person.'

Laurence's mouth drops open. 'That's a lie. And anyway, how the hell would she know what's in my search history? She's obviously clutching at straws now to break us up.' His eyes are darting left and right, I can see his brain working.

'She told me she still had a key to the apartment, and that she let herself in while we were out. She said she looked at your laptop.'

'She did *what*?' Laurence scrapes back his chair and gets to his feet. His face is white.

My heart hammers at his reaction. 'She told me your password was "Volition91".'

'That's just out of order!' He walks over to the kitchen counter where his phone is charging and unplugs it. 'I'm calling her.'

'Is that actually your password?' I ask, standing up, my hands resting on the tabletop for support.

'It used to be. I change my password every month.'

So that explains why I couldn't get in. I'm not going to tell Laurence that I also tried to get into his laptop. He's angry enough already.

'How the hell did she find out my password?' he snaps.

I ask the obvious. 'Is it written down somewhere?'

The colour rises in his cheeks. 'I'm such an idiot,' he mutters, holding his phone to his ear. His expression darkens as the call goes through:

'Francesca? . . . What the hell do you think you're doing telling Alice all these lies about me? . . . No, I'm not going to . . .' He huffs while she talks at him. 'Can you just listen to me for a minute . . . Well, what do you expect? You broke into the flat and went through my computer! . . . No, absolutely not! Don't even . . .'

Laurence glares at his phone in frustration, then slams it down on the counter. He takes in a heaving breath and runs both hands through his hair with a deep growl of frustration. Of anger. 'She hung up on me!'

'Well, I'm not surprised. You were yelling at her down the phone.' I straighten up and turn to look at him properly.

'I can't believe she broke in here and went through my stuff!' he cries.

I feel like he's missing the point of all this. 'I'm more bothered about what she found, than about her breaking in,' I reply. 'I want to get to the bottom of this. I want to know if she's telling the truth.'

'Don't tell me you actually *believe* her.'

I don't reply, but right now I actually *am* starting to believe her. Laurence's reaction has been shifty and angry. He hasn't exactly proved her wrong.

'She broke into our home!'

'Is she right about your search history?' I ask, chewing my thumbnail.

'What? No, of course not. Why would I look up all that stuff? I don't even practise hypnotherapy.'

'But you studied it, right?'

'I did a course a few years ago.'

I shake my head. 'You never told me about that.'

'There's lots of work stuff I don't tell you. Just like there's probably lots of work stuff you don't tell me. You've gained other accounting qualifications, haven't you?'

'Yes, but—'

'Exactly. I can't even believe she's managed to make you doubt me like this.'

I pause. There's something I want to ask him, even though I know that if I say it, it could ruin our relationship forever. But this is too important a thing to ignore. In fact, if Laurence is innocent, then he should be happy to answer. If not . . . well, I don't even want to think about that. So I open my mouth and ask the question. 'Would you mind if we look at your search history?'

Laurence's expression goes blank and he shakes his head, his nostrils flaring ever so slightly. 'I can't actually believe you're asking me to prove myself.'

'It's not like that,' I reply.

'It's exactly like that. If we don't have trust, we don't have anything.' His eyes start to glisten and he blinks furiously.

'So you won't show me?' My mind is scrambling to make sense of his reluctance, of his emotion, of *everything*.

He gives a bitter laugh. 'You shouldn't need to see it to know I'm telling the truth.'

A lump of disappointment drops into my gut. I walk over to the kitchen counter to collect my phone. 'I think it's best if I go back to my parents'. Just while I straighten things out in my mind.' I pick up my mobile and turn to leave, but he's standing in the narrow gap between the kitchen counter and the breakfast bar, blocking my way.

'Don't do this, Alice. Don't let Francesca's jealousy ruin what we've got.'

'Then show me your search history. It's simple.'

'I would, but there's stuff on there that I can't show anyone. Not even you. Things relating to my clients. I could be barred from practising if anyone sees their private information. Surely you understand that? The very fact that Francesca's been in my computer is a gross violation.'

'I'm not interested in any of your clients' private information. I just want to see if there's anything in your search history about hypnosis. Surely you can understand that I need to know.'

He shakes his head. 'You do realise she could have planted things in my search history to incriminate me.'

'What? From months ago? How would she do that? *Why?* What would be the point?'

'This is a no-win situation for me,' he says.

'For *you*? Forget client confidentiality, if you used hypnosis on me, then not only is it unethical, but I'm pretty sure it's illegal. I could report you!'

His lips tighten. 'I didn't do anything. I can't believe you're acting this way, Alice. You might have been fooled by Francesca, but I'm not going to let you ruin my career as well. Can't you see I love you? I've always loved you. If you can't see that . . . If you could even think of reporting me for something that I haven't even done . . .'

'Then what?'

'I can't let you go.' He takes hold of my upper arms and stares at me.

My heart is pounding and my skin tingles. Right this second, it feels as though I'm looking into the eyes of a stranger, and I'm genuinely terrified for my safety.

Chapter Forty-Three

Now

Laurence and I both startle at the sound of the front door opening.

'What the hell?' he says, frowning.

The distraction enables me to free my right arm, but he still has a tight hold of the left.

Seconds later, Francesca strides into the living room, out of breath, her hair tied back off her face.

'Francesca?' Laurence says, confused. 'What are you doing here? How did you get in?'

'I had another spare key,' she replies. 'You still haven't changed the locks, have you?'

'You can't just barge in here, Fran,' Laurence replies. 'I'm sorry, but you don't live here any more.'

'Let her go, Laurence.' Francesca glances from him to me. 'Are you okay, Alice?' she asks, her brow creasing in concern.

'I'm . . . yes. I . . .' I'm suddenly aware that I'm trembling. I don't know how to answer her. Am I okay? I don't think I am. I'm breathless. My heart is still pounding from our argument. I realise that I'm relieved she showed up. That, for a moment, I was actually quite scared of Laurence.

'It's over,' Fran says to him. 'You need to admit what you did to her.'

'Get out,' he says through gritted teeth. 'I mean it, Francesca. Get out or I won't be held responsible for what I do.'

Laurence finally lets go of my arm and, at the twinge of pain, I'm aware of how hard he was gripping it. This all feels too terrifyingly close to my run-in with Damian back in the summer. I never thought Laurence would be capable of this sort of behaviour. I trusted him. I loved him. What the hell has happened? Is it me? Is there something about me that brings the monster out in people?

Everything has escalated so quickly. I think that maybe I should have listened to Francesca yesterday when she warned me about Laurence. After all, she's been in a relationship with him for years – maybe she's seen this side of him before. But it's just so hard to equate this version of Laurence with the one I've known forever. The funny, kind, sweet guy who's been my best friend since we were kids. He's like a changed person. Could he really have been hiding a darker aspect to his personality all this time? Even as it seems preposterous, the thought terrifies me.

'What the hell have you been saying to Alice?' he growls, taking a step away from me and towards her.

'Only the truth,' she replies, her eyes filling with anguish. 'I don't know what's happened to you, Laurence. I think you need to get help.'

He shakes his head. 'Look, Fran, I know you're upset, and I don't blame you, but spouting these lies isn't helping anyone.'

'It's helping Alice,' she says, throwing me a look of solidarity over his shoulder. 'It's why I came. I was scared for you, Alice.'

I swallow.

'What are you talking about, Fran?' he snaps. 'I know things ended on a bad note between us, but I really don't think that you coming here and insinuating things about me is going to help anyone, least of all you.'

'I don't need to insinuate anything,' she replies. 'I just saw you manhandling her with my own eyes. Alice looked terrified. She still does.'

They're both staring at me now and I guess I probably do look terrified. My mouth is open and I realise I'm in shock, still unable to believe that Laurence is this person who only seconds earlier had me in a vice-like grip. Surely he just got carried away in the heat of the moment. I rub the bruises on my arm, feeling slightly nauseous.

Laurence's expression darkens further. 'Look, Francesca, I'm going to need you to leave or I'm going to have to call the police. This is the second time you've let yourself in here. It has to stop or we'll be forced to get a restraining order.'

'You're the one who needs a restraining order,' she spits. 'God, you've really got her fooled, haven't you?' She shakes her head, her face drawn, her eyes still darting between us.

'Fran,' I croak. 'Maybe it's best if you do go. This arguing isn't helping anyone.'

'I would,' she says, 'but I don't want to leave you alone with him. I'm worried what he might do. If I leave, I'll call the police anyway to report what I saw here tonight.'

'Jesus, you can't go round saying all this stuff, threatening to tell the police a bunch of lies,' Laurence cries. 'Aside from wrecking my relationship with Alice, you could ruin my reputation. My livelihood. If my clients lose their trust in me, then I may as well kiss goodbye to my career. Not to mention the fact you went through my laptop and could have seen their confidential files.'

'The only thing I saw was your search history,' she says. 'And that was enough.'

My head is spinning with all this back and forth. The betrayals, the lies, the manipulation. It's all too much. They're still throwing accusations at each other, and I don't know what's the truth and what's simply bitterness over a bad break-up. I need to get out of here, clear my head. I make a move to slip around Laurence but I'm shocked when he turns to bar my way.

'Don't leave!' he insists. 'Don't listen to her. Just stay and we'll talk it through.' He glances over his shoulder. 'Fran, do us all a favour and go! You need to get on with your life and leave us alone to get on with ours. Just get out!'

'You were the one who called *me*,' she retorts. 'And I'm not going until I'm happy that Alice is safe.' She casts a panicked look my way and beckons me to come over to where she's standing.

I try once again to get past Laurence, but he's not budging. I'm literally pushing at his chest now, and actually considering climbing over the breakfast bar to get away. This is ridiculous. I'm not exactly scared by his refusal to let me pass, but it's certainly not making me want to stay. Fran pulls at his arm, but he shrugs her off and then slams both fists down simultaneously in anger – one on the counter, one on the breakfast bar.

Now I'm scared.

I glance down and notice his hand is resting on top of the large, sharp kitchen knife that I used earlier to chop the salad, its blade sticky with tomato juice. I can't believe we were having a normal, civilised meal only minutes ago.

I catch Fran's eye and she too sees where his hand is. She gives a sharp inhale that matches my own.

'Hang on a minute,' Laurence says, as though he's just realised something important. He frowns and turns to look at Francesca, the knife now gripped firmly in his hand, pointed in her direction. 'You . . .' he says.

'Put the knife down!' I manage to cry, terrified at what he might be about to do. But before he has a chance to use the weapon, Francesca lunges for my gold pineapple lamp on the side table, lifts it, and hurls it with all her strength at Laurence's forehead. He raises his hands too late as it hits him with full force on the temple, yanking the plug from the wall.

I stagger back with a scream as he sways and then crumples, tipping on to his side and smashing into the edge of the counter before slumping to the floor in a bloody heap. At the same time, the lamp falls on to the kitchen tiles with a terrible metallic clang before the room falls briefly silent.

I can't even process what's just happened. It doesn't feel real. It's too dreadful. Too monstrous. I'm frozen in shock. Silent as the grave, while Francesca starts heaving and panting, her breaths far too loud.

Francesca and I both raise our eyes for a second to look at one another. Her face is a mask of horror and I imagine my expression mirrors hers.

'Oh my God,' I whisper, the words running into each other.

'He was going to kill me,' she cries, her breath still coming in ragged gasps. 'You saw him come at me with the knife, right?'

I nod, and then crouch gingerly over Laurence to see that the knife is still in his loosely curled fist. There's a dent in the side of his head and a cascade of bright blood soaking into his blond hair.

'I think you killed him,' I say as my whole body begins to shiver and tremble uncontrollably.

She puts two fingers to his neck and after a moment she nods.

This can't be real. I barely understand what's happened here tonight, but I think . . . I think Francesca might have just saved both our lives.

Chapter Forty-Four

Now, Seven Months Later, May

Ringwood Herald

Francesca Davies cleared of killing ex-boyfriend in Ringwood after claiming self-defence

Talia Saminaden

Laurence Kennedy, below left, died of a head wound in Ringwood, Hampshire.

A woman has been cleared of murdering her ex-boyfriend after telling a court she was acting in self-defence when she threw a brass lamp at his head after he came at her with a kitchen knife on the evening of 22 October last year.

Francesca Davies, an animal-shelter worker, 31, was visiting her ex-boyfriend Laurence Kennedy, 32, at his home in order to aid his new girlfriend,

Alice Porter, 31, who she believed was in mortal danger from Kennedy.

Kennedy, a registered psychotherapist, died instantly of his head wound, the court was told.

Porter said Davies was defending them both after Kennedy became aggressive and violent with his current girlfriend, grabbing her by the arms and refusing to let her leave.

Shortly after, he picked up a sharp kitchen knife and advanced on Davies who said she was terrified for her life.

Following a ten-day trial, Davies was cleared of murder, Hampshire Police said.

Thomas Green QC, prosecuting, said Davies threw the lamp as it was the heaviest item within reach.

Detectives are not looking for anyone else in connection with the man's death, the force added.

The four of us stare critically at the paint samples on one of the walls of what's going to become the office of my new accountancy firm – A Porter Associates.

'I think I like the dark blue, and then we could have bright orange accents,' I say, imagining how stunning it's going to look with plants and comfy chairs, clever lighting and, best of all, a decent coffee machine.

'You want to be careful it doesn't end up looking like a Mexican restaurant,' Daisy says, trampling over my interior design vision with her size-seven cork wedges.

I instantly picture the decor of our favourite restaurant, Hibiscus, and realise she might be right. 'Okay, well maybe not the orange, but another pop of colour would be good.'

'Gold, maybe,' Elizabeth suggests.

Elizabeth and Graham have finally sorted out their issues. After events with Laurence, she confronted him with her worries that Graham might still have feelings for me and he was so horrified that he told her he would never talk to me again if that would make her feel better. He also said they could move to the other end of the country if it would help. Obviously, she didn't want that situation for any of us, but it made her understand how far her husband was prepared to go to prove his love for her. He wasn't jealous of Seth, or in love with me; he was simply worried about my well-being because I'm Elizabeth's sister and he wants me to be happy, so that she's happy.

'Ooh yes,' Miriam agrees. 'A touch of gold would be perfect.' Miriam has already handed in her notice at Faraday's to join my new firm. Apparently, Paul was completely panicked by her resignation. He even offered her a pay rise, but she declined. It will just be the two of us to start with, but we're hoping to grow the business eventually.

Francesca's court case is now over and she was cleared by the jury, thank goodness. The past few months have been a strain on all of us, but it was worse for her, because she was the one who had a murder charge hanging over her head.

That terrible night, Francesca and I called the police straight-away. There was a massive investigation – CSI, interviews, lawyers, the whole nine yards. The tech officers examined Laurence's computer and discovered his search history – his research into using hypnosis to change a person's perception of someone else. Of using the power of suggestion. No wonder he didn't want to show me his computer. Of course, as far as the police were concerned, that search history didn't prove he'd used hypnosis on me. It was all circumstantial. But it was obvious to me and everyone else that that's what happened. None of that changed the fact that Laurence had threatened Francesca with a knife.

Daisy felt as shocked and betrayed as me by Laurence's actions. Our lifelong friendship had been corrupted. And while she and I loathed what he did and who he had become, we also mourned the loss of one of our best friends.

After last year's events, I decided to put all my energy into my career. I enjoy my work, I'm ambitious. It allows me to tune out the anxiety and fear that's become a constant companion. I can't quite believe I'm branching out on my own. The huge bonus of this office is that it comes with a tiny studio flat at the rear of the building that I'm going to do up and eventually live in. It needs a *lot* of work, but right now my priority is the office and my new business.

In the meantime, I'm back living at my parents' place, but this time I'm actually happy to be there. Grateful to them for supporting me. For picking up the pieces every time I've broken down over the past ten months.

I've been trying to build my relationship with my parents. Dad explained that he never wanted me to be unhappy, he just wanted me and Seth to work things out so that I would have security. I told him that I appreciate him worrying about me but I don't need a man to provide for me. That I'm capable of providing security for myself. He replied that there's more to security than a career. Companionship and love are part of that. I reassured him that I have good friends and a good family, and that's enough right now.

Surprisingly, and wonderfully, Mum has decided to go back to college to study to become a midwife, something she's always wanted to do but never had the courage to try. She said she knows that most people are retiring from work at her age, but she persuaded my father that she needs a new challenge, a focus other than the house and family. He's fully supportive.

I realise now that my whole life I've been this passive person. Yes, I work hard and it probably looks like I'm a go-getter, a successful career woman. But the reality is that I've always gone along with what other people wanted. I moulded myself to fit their ideas of what I should be. I became an accountant because my dad said it would be a good career for me. Okay, so he was right. I am good at it and I do enjoy it, but, still, it wasn't something I chose for myself. At Faraday's, I was waiting for Paul to deem me worthy of becoming a partner. Five years I worked there, for him to pass me over. I could have pushed him on the matter. Or left and set up my own practice a couple of years ago. Or gone to another firm where they appreciated me more. But I didn't. I gave *him* the power to change my life.

With each of my boyfriends, they pursued me. They told me I was the right girl for them, but I never asked myself if they were the right ones for me. Instead, I was flattered. I shaped myself to fit their lives rather than the other way around. *Too passive*. I won't make that mistake again. If and when I feel ready for another relationship, *I'll* be the hunter. The one who chooses. I'll find the person who suits *me*. Not that I can imagine getting back into another relationship anytime soon.

I'm grateful to Francesca for saving me. We've became much closer in the aftermath and during the trial. Sadly, she's moved away and now lives just outside Southampton, so still quite near, but no longer only up the road. She said that Ringwood held too many painful memories for her, which I totally understand.

I also bit the bullet and have been getting regular therapy sessions. They're helpful, but they leave me feeling exhausted and fragile. Although my therapist says this is normal. That I should think of them like a detox for the mind.

I'm not entirely free of Damian. I reported his behaviour to the police and they had words with him, but there's not a lot they can do. He shows up in Ringwood from time to time. I see him around town and I'm not sure if he's still stalking me, or if it's just a coincidence, but I'm hoping he's finally got the message that I'm not interested. That I'm no longer intimidated. I try not to let him faze me.

I'm more upset by Laurence than by Damian. I knew Damian was an arsehole. But Laurence . . . he was my best friend. The person I trusted most in the world. I thought I'd found my soulmate. I was devastated by his actions. It turned everything I knew inside out. That he would do such a thing to me. It shocks me every day.

Despite the relative calmness of my life now, there's still this needling voice in my head wondering whether, if Laurence hadn't done what he did, maybe I'd be happily married to Seth by now. It's likely that my attitude towards my ex-fiancé has been skewed by Laurence messing with my mind. I know it's pointless to play these 'what if' games. This is my reality now, and I have to tell myself it's for the best. That it all happened for a reason. But I wish I could lay that voice to rest.

To that end, I've finally agreed with my therapist that she'll incorporate some hypnosis techniques in my next few sessions to try to explore how deeply my memories have been manipulated, and if the effects are still ongoing. I'm dreading them, but also hoping that they may shed some light on what actually happened to me on my wedding day . . .

Chapter Forty-Five

Now, 10 June

As I walk down the dusty street, I catch sight of myself in the window of a café and I'm actually quite happy with my reflection. I've dyed my hair a little darker – warm chestnut was what it said on the packet – instead of my usual mid-brown colour. This new shade makes my eyes look greener. I've never been too bothered about my appearance, but I've made more of an effort today.

Now that the court case is finally over, I can breathe a sigh of relief and move on with my life. The only thing is, I'm not used to living in a city. Ringwood was familiar and comfortable. Southampton feels impersonal and busy with its complicated road system and endless sprawling suburbs. It was heavily bombed during World War Two so the mid-century architecture is quite harsh – big sixties tower blocks of grey concrete interspersed with shopping centres and a few more recent upscale areas of developed dockland. I guess it's quite cool if you're a city person. Sadly, I'm not.

Anyway, I'm here now, staying in a grotty B & B in Shirley Park. This is all part of my long-term strategy. It's been going to plan for the most part, despite taking far longer than I originally hoped.

I always knew Laurence was in love with Alice. It was so obvious, even if he wouldn't even admit it to himself. For a counsellor, he was surprisingly unaware. I needed to get back at him for that – for pretending to love me when it was her all along.

In order to ruin both their lives, I decided to try out my skills on Alice, and pin the blame on Laurence. I knew the overlaying of memories had been proven to work. But I wanted to see if I could push the boundaries. To discover if I could make someone stop loving a person, by changing their perception of them.

Never in a million years did I dream it would work as well as it did.

I quicken my pace, realising that I've been dawdling for the past ten minutes. I'd better hurry, I don't want to miss him.

I knew Alice would most likely be susceptible to the techniques as I'd already done a few covert tests and discovered that she's a 'high', which means she's part of the 10 per cent of the population who are highly hypnotisable and respond well to most suggestions. She's one of those people who get imaginatively engaged, losing herself in a good book or jumping out of her seat at scary movies. This was what gave me the idea in the first place. Realising that she would be highly hypnotisable.

I studied Psychology at uni with Laurence. After graduating, I took a hypnotherapy course, planning to use it to complement my work as a psychologist. But soon after completing the course, I had a mini breakdown. Panic attacks and anxiety, followed by a long bout of depression. I decided that psychology wasn't the right career for me. In fact, I recognised that the stress of any career wasn't what I needed, which is when I got a job at the animal shelter and my state of mind instantly improved. Animals are my happy place.

I was content working there. I was content with Laurence. Until I realised that he was in love with Alice.

But that was okay, because eventually I fell in love with someone else too.

Just before Seth met Alice, Seth met me. Our paths crossed when he and a friend visited the animal shelter where I worked. His friend came away with a two-year-old ginger tom cat. Seth came away with me.

Seth said he liked my quirkiness and thought I was the sweetest, kindest person he'd ever met. I'd never felt about anyone the way I felt about Seth Evans. He made me feel special. Safe and cherished. Like I could do anything. Be anyone. Here was this incredible, handsome doctor who loved me for me. Who made me happy on a whole other level.

But then Alice came along and ruined it all.

They met one night at a pub near his parents' holiday home, and he immediately ended things with me. Seth never understood how deep my feelings ran for him. He already knew I had a boyfriend, so he didn't think I was serious. He thought we were simply having a 'fun fling'. He didn't know that I was on the verge of breaking up with Laurence to be with him.

Seth excitedly told me that we had to stop 'fooling around' because he'd found 'the one', not for a moment thinking that my heart was breaking. How could I then confess my feelings to him, when he was so besotted with someone else? When he told me her name was Alice Porter, I almost choked. Needless to say, he wasn't very happy to discover she and I were friends.

He asked me never to mention our fling to anyone, saying that he didn't want some brief affair to tarnish what he had with Alice.

I was devastated, and that devastation, instead of fading away, has solidified over time, hardening into something dense and unyielding. Something that isn't going to disappear.

I'm certain that my friendship with Alice was the reason Seth was so reluctant to come down from London to meet her friends and family. He knew he would have to see me too, and he was scared that I would say something to betray our past. Even though I assured him I wouldn't. He needn't have worried. I would never have used our affair like that. I wanted Seth to fall in love with me, not hate me. I did as he asked and kept quiet, because when you love someone like I love Seth, you would do anything for them.

To make matters worse, once Seth started going out with Alice, Laurence morphed from this sweet, funny guy into a bitter, disinterested boyfriend. It was obvious that he was jealous of Seth. That it was eating him up inside seeing their relationship progress so quickly.

Over the past couple of years, I've tried to forget Seth, but the more I try, the more my feelings have intensified. I'm fixated on him. Some might say obsessed. But I know that I'll never feel the same way about anyone else. He's my soulmate. He just hasn't realised it yet.

I stayed in my relationship with Laurence to be close to Seth. To hear about his life first-hand from Alice. In a strange way, I imagined that her life with him was my life. I was living vicariously through her until such time as I could replace her in his affections. It was then that I understood how my previous career choice could come in handy.

I didn't know exactly how I would win him back, so I devised a step-by-step strategy to do it in stages using my skills in hypnotherapy:

First, split up Alice and Seth – check.

Next, get Laurence to break up with me – check. I needed Laurence to end things with me rather than vice versa so that Seth and I could bond over our devastating break-ups. So that we could soothe each other's broken hearts.

I practised my hypnosis skills on all kinds of people. It was actually quite fun. Obviously, there's no such thing as mind control, but there are things you can do that come quite close – little suggestions and persuasions. It helps if you already have a rapport with that person. If they trust you. In the months leading up to the wedding, I 'suggested' to Laurence that he search hypnosis websites and forums. I also found the password to his laptop. This later helped convince Alice that I'd seen Laurence's search history with my own eyes, and could back it up with the fact that I knew his password. I was initially going to alter his search history myself, but I worried he might spot the searches and wonder who had been messing with his computer.

Over a period of months I used hypnotherapy to try to convince Alice that she shouldn't go ahead with the wedding. That Seth wasn't the man she thought he was. That he would be bad for her. That he wouldn't be a good husband. I was so frustrated that she seemed to remain as in love with him as ever. I thought I'd failed. All I had managed to do was give her some low-level anxiety that she blamed on pre-wedding stress. Whenever I saw her, I would get her into a hypnotic state – at the pub, her hen weekend, even at the church, right before the wedding – and suggest she break up with Seth. But I guess she really did love him too much to let my suggestions take hold. She seemed as set on marrying him as she had ever been . . .

Until she walked down the aisle and Seth turned to look at her.

It was so poetic! So wonderful. I couldn't believe that all those snatched moments of trying to get her to realise he wasn't the man for her had manifested itself in such a jaw-dropping way. She literally didn't recognise him, or his parents for that matter. It was as though she'd erased their faces from her mind. And to make matters even more exquisite, she became nervous around him. Anxious. Scared, even. So, even if she did start to recognise him again, by that time, she would be so turned off that nothing would induce her to reconcile with the man she had loved.

Before the wedding, in a fit of anger, I suggested that Alice should delete all her photos of Seth and his family from her phone, from the cloud and from social media. I did it because I was so sick of seeing their loved-up photos online. Of everyone liking her posts and making vomit-inducing comments about how gorgeous they both were. Alice thought they were such an untouchable couple. She thought their love was better than everyone else's. I never dreamt that making her delete the photos would later help reinforce her conviction that he wasn't the 'real' Seth. It actually worked out perfectly.

Of course, she turned to Laurence for consolation. I was counting on it.

When they eventually got together – as I knew they would – I made use of the times when I returned to the flat to collect my stuff by making Laurence paranoid that Alice was going to leave him. I also made sure to bump into Alice a couple of times, acting hurt and betrayed while dropping little suggestions that Laurence was controlling and unreasonable. I'm sure he was nothing of the sort, but in her mind he was gradually moving away from being her wonderful best friend to being an unrecognisable jealous boyfriend. Easy for her to believe after her traumatic relationship with Damian.

In addition to that, I suggested that he was guilty of sabotaging her wedding. He didn't do himself any favours by refusing to let her see his laptop. But if he had, she would have seen his damning search history. I had to drive a wedge between them in order for her to believe that he was capable of hypnotising her against her will.

I wanted to punish them both for treating me so shabbily. Why should they get their happy ever after? Alice ruined my chance at happiness with Seth. And Laurence kept me as his runner-up girlfriend as he didn't have the balls to go after the one he really wanted. How did they expect me to feel? Grateful?

I never planned to kill Laurence – I'm not a monster. *No. All I wanted was to set him up as the person who sabotaged her relationship with Seth. But it all spun a little out of control.*

I ended up having to kill him to shut him up. When I went round there that night and Laurence was losing his shit, he turned to face me and I saw a look of comprehension in his eyes. Like a lightbulb coming on. It was clear from the look that Laurence realised it was me who was behind the hypnosis. I couldn't risk him telling Alice, so I picked up that hideous brass pineapple lamp and lobbed it at Laurence's head.

The third and final stage of my plan was to pursue Seth. To comfort him after his break-up. He was so sweet to me after I faked my heartbreak over Laurence. But he never acknowledged our romantic past. He withdrew into his shell and I couldn't get close. I didn't want to use hypnosis on him. I wanted our love to be pure and honest. And then I became tangled up in the investigation and court case so there wasn't the opportunity to win him back.

But now, after all this time, I'm going to try again. I guess this time around I may not have the luxury of winning him back the straightforward way. I may have to put my hypnotherapy skills to good use again. I don't think Seth will be as suggestible a subject as Alice was, but I can drop little suggestions to aid him in recovering from his heartbreak.

He started his job at Southampton Hospital last year and, 'coincidentally', I've just got a new job working in an animal shelter not too far from his new apartment. Today is the one-year anniversary of his nonwedding, so I'm sure he'll be feeling pretty low. He'll need cheering up.

My heart leaps. There's Seth now. He's on his phone, smiling, walking to his favourite coffee shop. As luck would have it, I'm headed there myself . . .

Epilogue

Now, 10 June

On the one-year anniversary of my non-wedding, I've just had my third hypnosis session with my therapist and I'm so angry I can barely breathe.

Hidden memories have begun floating to the surface. Little toxic bubbles that are bursting and popping, releasing their truths one by one by one.

I now know what happened to me.

I know what Francesca did.

I remember it all.

Right now, there's only one person I want to talk to about this. I take my phone from my bag and call a number I haven't called in almost a year. It rings twice.

'*Alice?*' he says, his voice full of surprise, and tinged with something like hope.

'Hi, Seth. It's been a while, I know. Can we talk? It's . . . quite urgent.'

'Oh. Yes, sure. I'm just about to get a coffee. Are you free now? I'm only twenty minutes from Ringwood. Do you want to join me?'

My heart begins to swell as I realise there's nothing I'd like more.

ACKNOWLEDGEMENTS

Huge thanks to Sammia Hamer, my wonderful editor. It's been a joy to work with you on *The Silent Bride*. Endless gratitude to my developmental editor, the supremely talented Hannah Bond – thanks for knowing exactly what this book needed to pull it into shape!! Thanks also to Leodora Darlington. You've been an amazing friend and mentor over the past couple of years. Thank you for believing in this book and for connecting me with the fabulous Thomas & Mercer team. Thank you to everyone else at Amazon Publishing who has helped bring this book into the world. I'm forever grateful for all your hard work and talent.

Thank you to Sadie for doing a fantastic job on the copy-edits, to Nicky Lovick for your excellent proofread, and to Tabitha Owen for your sensitivity read, allowing me to breathe a little easier!

I'm so thankful to my beta readers Julie Carey and Terry Harden for always having the time and enthusiasm to comb through my books with such care. Thanks also to my readers – the bloggers, the reviewers, the sharers, recommenders and tweeters. There are too many of you to mention, but you know who you are. None of this would have been possible without you! As always, huge gratitude to my friends and family for your constant love and support. Love you! Xxx

A LETTER FROM THE AUTHOR

I just want to say a huge thank you for reading *The Silent Bride*. I hope you enjoyed it. If you'd like to keep up to date with my latest releases, just sign up to my newsletter via my website and I'll let you know when I have a new novel coming out. Your email address will never be shared and you can unsubscribe at any time.

I love getting feedback on my books, so if you have a few moments, I'd be really grateful if you'd be kind enough to post a review online or tell your friends about it. A good review absolutely makes my day!

ABOUT THE AUTHOR

Photo © 2022 Shalini Boland

Shalini Boland is the Amazon and *USA Today* bestselling author of seventeen psychological thrillers. To date, she's sold over two million copies of her books.

Shalini lives by the sea in Dorset, England, with her husband, two children and their increasingly demanding dog, Queen Jess. Before kids, she was signed to Universal Music Publishing as a singer/songwriter, but now she spends her days writing (in between restocking the fridge and dealing with endless baskets of laundry).

She is also the author of two bestselling sci-fi and fantasy series as well as a WWII evacuee adventure with a time-travel twist.

When she's not reading, writing or stomping along the beach, you can reach her via Facebook at www.facebook.com/ShaliniBolandAuthor, on Twitter @ShaliniBoland, on Instagram @shaboland, or via her website: www.shaliniboland.co.uk.

Visit Shalini's website to sign up to her newsletter.

Follow the Author on Amazon

If you enjoyed this book, follow Shalini Boland on Amazon to be notified when the author releases a new book!

To do this, please follow these instructions:

Desktop:

1) Search for the author's name on Amazon or in the Amazon App.
2) Click on the author's name to arrive on their Amazon page.
3) Click the 'Follow' button.

Mobile and Tablet:

1) Search for the author's name on Amazon or in the Amazon App.
2) Click on one of the author's books.
3) Click on the author's name to arrive on their Amazon page.
4) Click the "Follow" button.

Kindle eReader and Kindle App:

If you enjoyed this book on a Kindle eReader or in the Kindle App, you will find the author 'Follow' button after the last page.